The Dark Mo(
Book O

One Dark Night

Anna Faversham

Copyright

©

2014

All Rights Reserved

No part of this book may be stored or reproduced in any form, by photocopying or by any electronic or mechanical means, including information storage or retrieval systems, or recording, or otherwise, without prior written permission from the author.

The places in this book are either real or imagined. Some events are loosely based on reality. The characters are fictitious. Any resemblance to real persons, living or dead, is purely coincidental.

To

Marek, Rose, Monty and Laurence

Table of Contents

Prologue	Faefersham Court, Kent, England	1
Chapter One	"Guns ablazing"	4
Chapter Two	"Say that again"	7
Chapter Three	"As cold as the arctic wind in winter"	16
Chapter Four	"Dark indeed"	22
Chapter Five	"Looked at her with disdain"	27
Chapter Six	"Even the dog knew"	35
Chapter Seven	"Devoid of finer feelings"	42
Chapter Eight	"She saw him wink"	48
Chapter Nine	"I'm not asking you to lie"	55
Chapter Ten	"Fumbleduck and dragonpoop"	61
Chapter Eleven	"In the safety of Daniel's warm jacket"	67
Chapter Twelve	"She'd been a fool"	73
Chapter Thirteen	"Betrayal cannot be tolerated"	78
Chapter Fourteen	"She began to feel like a real spy"	88
Chapter Fifteen	"Daring to steal my future"	92
Chapter Sixteen	"Thorsen's words haunted her"	99
Chapter Seventeen	"Merciless pirates"	104
Chapter Eighteen	"You must be in *big* trouble"	110
Chapter Nineteen	"I charge you to be guardians of that truth"	115
Chapter Twenty	"A pox on them that taxes us"	119
Chapter Twenty-One	"Guilty of murder"	126
Chapter Twenty-Two	"His sword displaying his intentions"	134
Chapter Twenty-Three	"He is to be gibbeted"	139
Chapter Twenty-Four	"She could struggle no more"	145
Chapter Twenty-Five	"He hated that blond-haired, slippery son"	150
Chapter Twenty-Six	"Where they'll all hate you"	157
Chapter Twenty-Seven	"Sinking sands"	167
Chapter Twenty-Eight	"That thorn in my side"	172
Chapter Twenty-Nine	"Lucy's eyes grew large with fright"	181
Chapter Thirty	"Were these two men in league?"	190
Chapter Thirty-One	"While Wintergate slept"	192

Chapter Thirty-Two	"Finally penetrated Karl's armour"	198
Chapter Thirty-Three	"The bold bringer of the rose"	201
Chapter Thirty-Four	"Who was I to point the finger"	209
Thirty-Five	"If only time would stand still"	215
Chapter Thirty-Six	"My new son"	222
Chapter Thirty-Seven	"People are not presents"	224
Chapter Thirty-Eight	"An empty seat"	232
Chapter Thirty-Nine	"You're warning me, aren't you Josh?"	237
Chapter Forty	"Lucy must never know"	246
Chapter Forty-One	"More of this very soon"	252

THE END

Twenty Questions for Book Clubs 255

One Dark Night

Prologue
Faefersham Court, Kent, England

1813

"Tuck up your skirt." Young Douglas Harper twirled his cricket bat in frustration. "Then you can run better."

In mock horror, Lucy responded, "Certainly not!"

Laughing, Master Douglas, known to her as Dougie, called out, "Bowl the way I showed you."

Lucy turned and took six paces further back. Then, as her dress only allowed short steps, she pattered towards Dougie standing ready in front of the stumps and hurled the leather ball with all her might. Thwack! The sound of the willow bat striking leather heralded another ball sent for six into the bushes by the lake. The two friends scampered after it.

"I'll wager I can climb the oak faster than you," said Dougie picking up the cricket ball.

"It's a wonder I can climb at all in this dress."

"Give me your hand, and I'll help you."

They settled onto their favourite, springy branch. "Hush," whispered Lucy, "Look."

Into their view came Sir William Harper, sauntering around his estate on the fine summer's day. He was being followed by his housekeeper as if she were a dog on a lead. Exasperated, he turned on her. "Mrs Yorton, this is not the time nor place to have this..." he hesitated, "this discussion on Lucy's future."

Undaunted, Annie Yorton drew closer. "Airs and graces. What good are they to her? You allow her to wander around the house as if..."

"And why does that trouble you?" Sir William moved closer to the lake and watched a mother duck lead her solitary duckling further away

One Dark Night

before continuing. "I find you ungrateful, Mrs Yorton. When you announced you were with child, I permitted you to marry my butler who has been devoted to you both. It is most unusual, as you know, for household servants to be allowed to marry, yet in your case…"

Annie Yorton closed in on him. "Oh yes, I know I run this household in tip-top fashion. I know why I'm here." Her eyes narrowed. "Since your wife died in childbirth," this oft-repeated phrase always elicited a reaction, "there's never been a need for you," her voice gathered pace, "or anyone else for that matter, to have cause for concern about the standards in Faefersham Court." At this point she made the mistake of pausing for breath.

"I gave you good rooms at the top of the West Wing to call your own. I've ensured Lucy has a chance in life not usually given to one of her station. She has been educated alongside my son. What more can you possibly want?"

"Master Douglas is, without a lie, a fine young man, and it is improper for Lucy to be encouraged by you…" Annie Yorton searched for words then, raising her voice, declared, "to think of herself as his equal."

Striding away towards the bushes alongside the lake, Sir William growled, "Don't insult my judgment, Mrs Yorton! Lucy has provided Master Douglas with companionship and someone to compete against in his education. Besides, Lucy is just eleven years old…"

Annie's voice became shrill as she tried to keep up with Sir William. "You should have sent him away to school, not have a governess for them both, then she could have taken her rightful place alongside me in the servants' quarters."

"I will hear no more of this. You have a privileged life yet you resent… Bah! You've said far too much, away with you."

"You forget," Annie knew how to milk a situation, "You forget I know all that goes on here." She broke away and swept across the lawn towards the side of the manor house. Sir William's eyes squinted as he watched her go.

In the high branches of the oak tree, Lucy and Douglas exchanged troubled looks. Lucy's expression changed to frightened as she reflected

One Dark Night

on the likely outcome of the overheard exchange. She was the ill-timed daughter of servants. Douglas was the heir to a large estate. "I think we are to be separated, Dougie."

One Dark Night

Chapter One
Wintergate, North East Kent – Lucy
"Guns ablazing"

Christmas 1820

Thwack! It was not the sound of leather on willow. It was the forcible impact of Annie Yorton's hand with Lucy's head.

"You misbegotten slut!" hissed Annie. "Why I have to be burdened with a useless daughter I'll never know." Annie followed this with an exaggerated sigh. "Bring in some wood and make up the fire. Then get out." With her feelings made obvious, she left the room and stomped up the stairs.

The next time she does that, I'll hit her back. Lucy had thought this before but she wasn't one for screaming, shouting, spitting and hitting. As soon as she could afford a decent dress, she'd go into Merrygate in search of a post, perhaps in one of the new hotels, somewhere she could live-in.

Having stacked the wood in the hearth, Lucy grabbed her shabby shawl and headed towards the sea. It was a cold, clear Christmas Day, and she sat hunched in her favourite place.

It had been a wonderful world – her world – lost now, maybe forever. But no one could take away her memories. Hidden from view, high on a ledge of scrubby bushes jutting from the cliffs, she could hold these memories in her mind, in her heart, where no one knew they existed. They warmed her when nothing else could. Whenever possible she would go back in time to watch the characters as if they were in a play. Ignoring the man searching for mussels at the foot of the cliffs, she drew her knees to her chin, tucked her toes under her outgrown dress, snuggled into her thin woollen shawl, and remembered.

One Dark Night

The stimulating lessons with Dougie's governess, the freedom of the gardens and, most of all, that last Summer Ball, these were memories that would live on regardless of what else happened. She recalled her loving father, in stentorian tones, announcing guests resplendent in satins and silks. Then, bidden by Sir William, he betrayed her presence in the gallery. "Sir William Harper welcomes his son, Master Douglas Harper and his young companion, Miss Lucy Yorton, both hiding behind the long-case clock." He had held his right hand high and, taking her cue from Dougie, she came out to the top of the long winding staircase. With all the grace she could muster, she overcame her embarrassment and laid her hand on the gold and white balustrade garlanded with greenery and marigolds. Her eyes, her mind, her heart took in the glorious sight below. She curtseyed as Dougie bowed low. How grand her father looked in the Harper livery. And it was so kind of Sir William to invite them to spend a few moments with the delighted guests. She had willed the whispering silks to haunt her: one day she would dress like that.

That day had not come. The next morning, pulled from her roots like a weed, her mother had dragged her to the crossroads and they had taken the coach to Wintergate with nothing but a bundle of belongings between them.

The spell was broken and she shivered. She must tuck away her memories of her father, Dougie, and all she'd held dear. The tiny workman's cottage at the end of a shabby terrace was home now. Whatever made her mother leave such a comfortable situation? It was true she'd made the cottage cosy. True too that her mother no longer had to work, not since Lucy had found work seven long years ago.

A metallic scraping noise jarred Lucy's thoughts back to the bleak scene before her. What was that mussel man doing? Lying flat, she edged herself to where she could peep over to the rocks below. He had dug far too deep; mussels didn't hide way down in the sand. He was also in the one place which was hidden from the sight of the revenue officers at Watch House. He wasn't alone either. A rough-looking seaman was filling in the hole, now as deep as a grave. She watched as, without a word, they covered the sand with huge chalk rocks and, with a

One Dark Night

flourish, flung seaweed on the top. They had buried something. Or, God forbid, *someone*?

"Give us yer hand, Tynton, and swear an oath on your son's life."

Sydney Tynton spat on his hand, held it out, and muttered something inaudible to Lucy. She did, however, catch his last few words. "You now owe me."

"You just let me know and we'll be there, guns ablazing."

Lucy withdrew as quietly as she could. She wished she'd never heard. Sydney Tynton was the disagreeable master of the farm where she worked.

The pale, winter sun was setting sending a shimmer of sparkles, like scattered diamonds, over the surface of the sea. She must hurry home, making sure the volatile farmer Tynton would never know what she had seen.

One Dark Night

Chapter Two
"Say that again"

January 1821

"You useless creature! Christmas is well over now. You tell me you can only work a half-day because it's *raining*!" Annie Yorton would win any competition for the best scoff. "Rain never hurt anyone." She stood arms akimbo in the door of her cottage. "Losing pay *does* and it has been happening all too often. You're not coming in here with empty hands. Make yourself useful and get some driftwood." She slammed the door.

Lucy peeped through the rain-lashed latticed window – a good fire burned in the grate and the hearth was stacked with logs. There was no point in arguing. Anyway the rain must ease soon and she was already wet through so she collected the big, log basket from the back door of the cottage and carried it towards the stream which had carved a useful path to the beach. The north-facing shore had fine sands and on either side of the crescent bay, white chalk cliffs rose to more than thirty feet. They gave way in the centre to a narrow strip of high sandy banks which allowed a driven donkey or pony to toil upwards to the village.

Reaching the beach, Lucy took stock. The tide was out revealing the fallen chalk rocks from the high cliff faces. The fishermen, who beached their little boats here, had to be skilled seamen to avoid the shallow waters and rocks. Lucy glanced at the Custom House, like most others, it was called Watch House. It sat high on the cliff, a cold, grey stone fortress on the east side of the bay. Sometimes she would observe the comings and goings from her sanctuary on the other side of the bay but there was very little action of consequence. Smugglers were not fools; they'd not use a bay overlooked by the revenue men. The wind was cold and the sky heavy with grey clouds. She must hurry or face a further downpour. Strewn along the tideline, driftwood told of the latest wrecked boats in the recent storm, a gift tossed up on the sands and left by the receding waves. If the weather were better, everyone would be combing the beach for wood and hoping for more than that too, though the revenue men usually got there first. Once, crates of wine floated in and beached all around the bay; most smashed against the rocks.

It only took a few minutes to collect as much as she could carry but longer to trudge back home. The cottage she lived in was called China Cottage, and each of the four cottages in the terrace had names reflecting the destinations of the ships that set sail regularly from the Thames' estuary. She stopped to leave a little of her load in old Bodger's back yard at the other end of the terrace. His was called India Cottage. Poor old Bodger, deaf and mute; he had many reasons to feel sorry for himself but he never did.

~

Before dawn the following morning, Lucy cleaned the grate, swept the hearth and laid and lit a fire. She wiped the sooty bottom of the kettle before filling it from the churn outside. Bodger, old as he was, would fill their churn from the well and bring it on his little hand cart and her mother would give him a farthing.

When the water in the kettle was warm, she added it to some milk from the pail in the cold scullery. She drank a little and dunked some stale bread in her cup. The best part about working on a farm was that she knew the milk had not been tampered with. Some people had to put up with all sorts of dubious additions by unscrupulous sellers. This milk was pure and creamy and she was allowed a small pail each Monday. With the addition of a little water, she could make it last the week in the winter. The birds heralding the advancing dawn interrupted her thoughts. Now there was only time to take her mother, still in bed, a cup of warm milk before leaving.

Lucy hastened over the crossroads, passed the gatehouse and then swiftly ran along the pathway to Jerusalem Farm. The name was "a jest" said the farmer, Sydney Tynton, then he'd follow this with the

One Dark Night

explanation that "the farm down the road be called Bethlehem but there ain't no Christ 'ere in Jerusalem 'cos that's where he was got rid of!" The only person who appreciated this attempt at jollity was farmer Tynton himself. He would guffaw, strut and spit. Then Mrs Tynton would thrash him out of the kitchen with her broom shouting "Don't you spit in 'ere." He'd raise his hand and she'd raise her broom again shouting, "Touch me and I'll make sure Daniel hears of it." It would be funny if Mr Tynton didn't always take his annoyance out on his labourers, who were becoming fewer each year.

"I s'pose you're here early hoping for a bit o' porridge." Sydney Tynton was not known for his generosity. He was known for slurring his words though.

"Come on in, Lucy. Get yourself some porridge from the pot, then you can give me a hand with the vegetables for this evening." Mrs Tynton pulled Lucy past her husband who was blocking the doorway to their farmhouse and addressed him firmly, "She'll be out to give you a hand when I've finished with her, and not before!"

Mr Tynton had to have the last word. "You make sure she is. We don't pay 'er to be coddled all day." He slammed the door behind him, tripped over nothing very much, probably his own feet, and swore profusely.

The reason for Mrs Tynton's unusually confident refusal to be intimidated stood by the farmhouse stove, legs astride, hands behind his back and keeping an amused eye on his parents. Alongside him lay a black and white, long-haired dog which regarded Lucy with interest.

Lucy had not spoken to Daniel for some years, maybe three or four and their paths had rarely crossed. But here stood Daniel, his eyes taking her in, stripping her of her pitiful clothes and betraying the merest hint of a smile. Lucy blushed. Drat. If only she'd known he was to be home.

"Hello Lucy."

The blush grew. "Hello Da… Mr Tynton."

Daniel's smile grew too. There was a controlled silence before he replied in his relaxed country burr. "It's been a while, hasn't it?"

One Dark Night

Lucy's face was still as red as a ripe apple. He'd kissed her once when she was just thirteen and he was seventeen. The look on his face told her he'd not forgotten his game of stealth as he'd wrapped his arms around her waist, spun her round and stolen a kiss. Six years had passed and she'd never been kissed since, though some had tried. She attempted to think of an answer that wouldn't give away her racing thoughts, but couldn't.

Mrs Tynton was staring at them both. "Get your porridge, Lucy, and hurry up about it." She ambled off towards the scullery.

To reach the porridge on the stove, Lucy had to pass Daniel and the dog, and neither moved. Rather than squeeze between him on her left and the kitchen table, she walked around the other side, collecting a bowl as she went. Still Daniel did not make way for her. "I would be obliged, Mr Tynton, if you would move just enough for me to reach the pot."

"Say that again and I'll move."

Lucy raised her eyes to meet his sparkling blue ones. He was jesting. "Why?"

"I like to hear you talk."

"Why?" Lucy wondered if it was wise to hold her ground now that Daniel was no longer a boy.

"It's good to see you've still a lot of fight in you, Lucy. I've been hearing a few tales." He nodded his head in the direction of the scullery. "But I can hold out longer and I'll not move until you say that again for me."

"Why?" The word had come out quicker than she'd intended. Should she play these games with someone who held her livelihood in his hands?

Daniel took hold of her frozen hand. Lucy withdrew it and immediately regretted her instinctive reaction. His eyes had not left her since she'd walked through the door and her nerve was failing. "You don't talk like the rest of us round here. I've missed your voice and, like me Ma says, you sound like you're from the gentry."

He meant it. Lucy could see that gentle look appearing in his eyes, the one she took to bed with her and to her sanctuary on the cliffs, the

One Dark Night

look which warmed her and fought to stay in her fading stock of cherished memories. Playfully, Lucy dropped him a curtsey and said, "Kind sir, I would be obliged if you would move just enough for me to reach the pot."

"Gentle lady, you shall have your wish." Daniel bowed low with a flourish of his hand and a courteous smile. He turned to the dog lying by his right foot. "Josh, this lady is a friend," he placed his right hand on his left shoulder. Josh stood, plodded slowly towards Lucy, sat down again and held up a paw. Entranced, Lucy took his paw and shook it gently. "She wishes us to move. Would you be so kind as to shift a bit for her?" He clicked his fingers and the dog followed him as he moved just enough to give access to the steaming pot on the stove, leaving him close enough to ensure she brushed against him. He pointed at the floor and Josh lay down again.

Lucy quickly filled her bowl, mindful of Mrs Tynton's admonishment, and sat at the kitchen table. Had she to eat the oatmeal porridge with Daniel's eyes on her all the time? She looked up, her eyes flicking around him rather than on him.

Daniel interpreted correctly, picked up a bowl, filled it with some porridge, and placed it beside her. "I'll get some more milk."

Lucy, now half way through her thick porridge with just a trickle of milk, stopped eating. The last time she'd had porridge with lots of creamy milk was at... she could not bear to finish the thought. She'd had sugar too.

Daniel returned with a bowl of sugar and a jug of milk. "A second helping never does me any harm," he said.

"Lucy! You finished yet?" Mrs Tynton did not sound pleased.

"No, she's not, Ma. I'll send her out to you when she has."

"Thank you, Mr Tynton," Lucy whispered.

"*Daniel*, Lucy. Call me Daniel, like you always did. And say it often – I like to hear it like *you* say it." He passed her the sugar and the milk. "Have you had porridge this good before?"

"A long time ago, Daniel."

"You don't say much about where you came from, do you?"

One Dark Night

The colour rose in Lucy's cheeks: her mother had forbidden her to speak of her time at Faefersham Court and all that happened there. She was to tell people no more than her mother was a widow. A respectable widow. Perhaps her mother was right. It was unwise to say too much to the Tynton family; they were not known to be God-fearing, and she had to work twice as hard as some of the other workers to be sure of being employed through good times and bad. "It's made a wonderful start to the day, Daniel. Thank you." Lucy stood up and began to take her bowl to the scullery.

"I'll be gone in a day or two," he paused until she turned around, "but I'll be back."

The emphasis was definitely on the latter part of the sentence and it recalled to Lucy's mind some of the things that had been said about Daniel in the last few years. She knew he could have the pick of the village girls both here and over by Bethlehem Farm where he now lived with his uncle. It was said that he was never seen with the same girl twice. She must be sure to keep this in mind.

Mrs Tynton gave Lucy a scathing look as she entered the scullery. "It won't do you no good to make eyes at my Dan. He's promised to another."

What Lucy replied, though true, bore no relation to what she felt. "It's just banter, Mrs Tynton, I meant no harm. I was surprised to see him, that's all." She hurriedly started washing the pots and pans.

Mrs Tynton was not fooled. "It's best you don't get fond of him, Lucy. I know you were friends when you first arrived in the village and I'm glad, really glad, that he brought you to work here. You're reliable and hard-working, but the good of my son, my only son, comes first. Make sure you know that and all will be well between us."

"Thank you, Mrs Tynton. I'll be careful."

"Aye, you'll need to be with him around."

Astonished, Lucy stared at Daniel's mother.

Mrs Tynton smiled. "Aye, you heard right. I'm just warning you, friendly like, our Dan's a catch and he enjoys toying with the bait, nibbling it and swimming away." She went back into the kitchen but turned as she stood in the doorway and said loudly, "And remember this well, he's promised to another."

Daniel passed his mother, gave her a hug, and said, "Thanks, Ma. That's enough of that." He continued into the scullery where he filled a bowl with water before taking it back to Josh.

Lucy, though amused by Daniel's response, nodded solemnly to Mrs Tynton: she understood. She resumed washing the pots and pans. Mrs Tynton brought in a kettle of hot water and a carving knife with notches in the handle. Mr Tynton used to jest with his wife saying there was a notch for every chicken he'd killed. She'd answer back saying she'd never seen him kill a chicken, she always had to do it, and he'd throw his head back and roar laughing. Lucy wondered if she and Mrs Tynton were the only ones who didn't like his jests, because the farm hands would often join in laughing. Probably just being polite to the master.

"Mind your hands, Lucy, you know how Mr Tynton keeps this carving knife well sharpened." She straightened her apron and said, "Right, I'm off to the barn. When you've finished here, scrubbed the table and all that, you'd best hurry on down to the bottom field. Mr Tynton's digging out the ditches again and he'll be needing all the help he can get. This rain keeps on pouring down."

Lucy groaned inwardly. Working anywhere near Mr Tynton was punishment enough but carting the sodden earth away, taking it further into the fields was hard for men, and it would be nigh on impossible for her on this soggy ground. Why was she being sent to do this? The answer, of course, was likely to be that it was as far away from Daniel as possible.

"Nellie, take Nellie," called out Daniel.

"Of course she'll take Nellie, Ned too. Not everyone round here's soft in the head, Dan."

"Yeah, Ma. I'm not so sure of him out there though. And he's got a sore head this morning – just when he's needed tonight."

Mrs Tynton marched over to her son wagging her finger and, lowering her voice, said "Mind what you say. She can hear you."

"I'm not saying anything Lucy won't already know. He's drunk half the time and gambling the rest of it."

One Dark Night

Lucy heard, and Lucy knew. But what did he mean about *tonight*? Was there some sort of gambling going on?

"Dan, don't talk like that about your father. It's not right. It isn't easy trying to make a living on ten acres."

"I know, and he's told me a hundred times that I've got it easy on uncle's forty." Daniel was not long deflected from his track. "And you've to make sure there's someone down there to do the lifting of the pails into the panniers."

"Yes, Dan," Mrs Tynton sighed in an exaggerated fashion, "Old Ben's going down." Then Lucy heard the front door shut. Just Daniel and her now.

She picked up the carving knife and held it by its wooden handle. She felt the blade – thin and sharp – it would carve through anything. She dunked it in the water and wiped it carefully. It wasn't until she had put it away safely that her thoughts returned to Daniel, though these were interrupted by a loud knock on the back door. She opened the door. A brawny man was framed by the doorway with Ben, an older, jolly farmhand, famed for his tales, hiding behind him. She backed away from the big man's leer.

"You're a lass I wouldn't mind taking a tumble with. When you gonna give in, eh?" He reached out to grab Lucy then seemed to back away. "Glad to see *you're* here, Dan. Ready for the dark?"

Lucy turned to see Daniel directly behind her. His eyes bored into the burly man's as he abruptly said, "I'll be out. Wait around the front."

Although a little startled, Lucy's curiosity overcame her and, after he'd gone through the kitchen and out of the front door, she quietly followed. The next noises she heard were a smack and a thump. She glanced out of the window. Daniel had the big man by the collar. "I've told you before: not her. Got it?"

Lucy drew away from the window and silently thanked Daniel – if only he were here all the time. She hurriedly returned to her duties and opened the door of the stove, threw another couple of logs into the fire, and put the filled kettle on the top of the stove. It was evidence, if required, that she had needed to go into the kitchen. Next she brought in the clean dishes and took them over to the cupboard by the front door.

One Dark Night

"She'll be coming in and we'll be there to welcome her." It was the voice of the brawny man. Lucy doubted he could whisper if his life depended on it.

Then Daniel said firmly, "You do your part and I'll back up my father, if necessary."

Lucy didn't catch anything more. Daniel's hand was on the latch. Lucy fled to the scullery.

Who was this "she"?

Chapter Three
"As cold as the arctic wind in winter"

Her duties at the farm finished, Lucy ran home. If she was quick enough she would be able to go to the morning service at the church. She dashed in to the cottage, leapt up the stairs and changed into her better clothes before returning to the front door to bang the mud off her boots.

"I can no longer wear this old blue spencer, mother." Lucy could never bring herself to use the familiar "ma" or "mama"; her mother was her biological mother and little else.

"If you had to eat slugs for breakfast, you wouldn't have much else in life to complain about, you ungrateful girl." Annie Yorton looked disdainfully at her nineteen-year-old daughter who was trying, with little success, to button up the little jacket she'd had since she was fourteen.

"I shall be going to the market as soon as possible and I'll buy a warm cloak."

"You'll do no such thing!" Mrs Yorton pursed her lips, narrowed her eyes and stared at Lucy. "Have you been keeping money back?"

"Not yet, but I intend to." Occasionally Mrs Tynton would give her an extra few pennies, sometimes as much as sixpence for working until a job was finished and Lucy was determined her mother would never again get her hands on this. By the summer she could have enough for a dress as well as a cloak.

"And how do you expect me to clothe myself if you are wasting all the money? Don't think I don't know you get fed at the farm whereas I have no such luxury. What am I supposed to eat?"

The word "slugs" came to mind but Lucy knew there was little point in arguing or it would end in her mother's threats to throw herself off the cliff after leaving a note with the parson to say she'd been driven to it.

The church bells stopped ringing. The service would be starting very soon and they both hurried to the nearby church. Mrs Yorton wrapped her velvet-trimmed cloak around her tightly, put on her smile, and greeted a lady alighting from a carriage.

"Good morning, Mrs Thorsen."

"Good morning," responded the lady, with little warmth in her voice.

Lucy, ignored, observed the village spinsters and widows clustering around her mother, all twittering like starlings roosting in the autumn.

"Oh, Mrs Yorton, how do you know that fine lady?"

Mrs Yorton kept her secrets well, so long as she kept her mouth shut. Lucy found it easy to deduce how her mother *knew* Mrs Thorsen, for there was her son, Lieutenant Karl Thorsen the Riding Officer, standing by the carriage, watching. He was good at watching. He took his mother's arm and guided her through the ladies towards Lucy.

"Good morning, Miss Yorton." He tipped his hat. "You are still working at the Tynton's farm, is that not so?"

Lucy had known of Lieutenant Thorsen for some while. He was certainly a man of consequence, evidenced by his dress. It was unusual for such a man to acknowledge her formally. "Good morning, Lieutenant Thorsen." Lucy decided to give him the smallest of smiles as she lowered her eyes and bobbed in acknowledgement. She liked his sandy hair with the curls around his forehead but she was not impressed in any other way. He had lately taken to spending time with his widowed mother and now he was bringing her to the church at Wintergate. Surely it would be easier to take her to the church closest to their manor house?

"I'll speak to you after the service," he said.

Clearly her avoidance of the question was noticed. He was a gentleman, he'd been a naval Lieutenant, the son of a naval Captain, direct in his speech, and as cold as the arctic wind in winter.

One Dark Night

Mrs Yorton bustled towards them. "Lucy, you're making me late. Go in at once." Her planned charm assault on the young Lieutenant failed due to his hasty entrance to the church alongside his mother.

Mrs Yorton was not the only person to resent the smart Lieutenant speaking with Lucy.

"Fancy yourself, don't you?" The cocky face of one of the village girls was thrust in front of Lucy and soon joined by another. "You need takin' down a peg or two."

The second one wanted to add a threat of her own. "Yeah, watch your back."

Lucy was used to being ridiculed but this was a step further – a threat. As she had no inclination to make friends with them, she ignored them.

Lieutenant Thorsen sat in a reserved pew at the front. Mrs Yorton and Lucy were not quite at the back. This gave her the opportunity to observe Lieutenant Thorsen. He was courteous to those arriving near him, attentive to his mother and clearly confident. Yet he had rattled her. Something didn't seem quite right. A man with his background usually did not work, certainly not hunting smugglers as a Riding Officer. She'd noticed him watching her for some weeks now. She wished he wouldn't; it made her feel so uncomfortable.

She enthusiastically sang the first hymn though her mother told her to hush because her voice spoilt the sound of the choir in the gallery.

The parson had recently returned to his home parish from Torwell Bridge and brought a young wife with him. He had shown concern for both Lucy and her mother, and was most respectful to all. He was well regarded and not at all the usual sort of parson. Jolly and kindly, he was a little deaf in one ear and short-sighted too which gave him a look of caring as he inclined his head towards his parishioners when they spoke.

Her thoughts were interrupted by the feeling of being watched. Lucy knew she had no unlawful habits or connections so why, at every opportunity, did Lieutenant Thorsen turn and stare so? He should know better.

One Dark Night

The parson, Bible in hand, commenced his sermon and Lucy refocused on the service. She could not help but smile for, before he took his place in the pulpit, he always appeared to distrust it, as if it would roll away. Or perhaps he thought it would collapse under his weight. He was very large "big and beautifully made" he would sometimes say with an endearing smile.

"The text for today is taken from the gospel of Saint Luke, chapter eleven. The disciples of Jesus have asked him to teach them to pray. Our Lord taught them a simple prayer for he knows how we always forget what we ought to remember." He paused and there was the merest hint of a chuckle from the congregation. "He began with 'Our Father'." Parson Raffles left his distrusted pulpit and stood at the front of the central aisle. Raising his voice, he said, "Father! Yes, we are to call the creator of all 'Father'. This makes us all the children of God." He paused to allow this concept to be considered. "You may have a kind and good earthly father, or he may be a rogue with little care or concern for you, or you may no longer have a father on Earth. But we all, yes all, have a Heavenly Father. A father who knows, not just more than us, but everything there is to know."

It was impossible for Lucy's mind to wander for it was as if God the Father, in the absence of her own, was speaking to her directly.

Unfettered by the pulpit, the parson wandered across the front of the church, his cassock flying out making him look immense. He also attempted illustrating his points by flinging his arms wide and high. "Many a child has lost his father in the war, or at sea, but, fear not, dear child, you have God the Father to whom you can turn. Make sure you talk to him." Then he whispered, as if to conceal his words from the earthly fathers, "It's not wise to ignore our fathers."

From where Lucy sat, she could see Lieutenant Thorsen in rapt attention until the parson bellowed, "At the end of the prayer which Jesus taught us, He returns immediately to emphasize that "If ye forgive *not* men their trespasses, neither will your Father forgive your trespasses.' Jesus makes clear that God forgives our sins as we forgive those who sin against us."

One Dark Night

The Lieutenant now appeared to be studying the stone floor. Lucy tried not to wonder what sins he needed forgiven. She must consider her own soul, not his. Then she found she could not let go of the fleeting thought that perhaps the Lieutenant was unable to forgive someone else.

As they stood for the last hymn, Lucy noticed him glance over his shoulder again. What did she know of him? He was in charge of the Riding Officers and took his duties very seriously. He had been in the Service for only a short while but had established new operational methods along this part of the coast. He had been so successful that he was much respected amongst the Preventive Services. She'd heard that, instead of lone Riding Officers attempting to patrol single-handedly, he'd set up bases at strategic points and the Riding Officers became part of the larger preventive operation. He commanded respect amongst those who attempted to follow the law. She knew little more and certainly, thus far, had had no reason to concern herself with him.

After the service, Annie Yorton animatedly talked to anyone who would listen while Lucy was expected to wait quietly by the gate.

Lieutenant Karl Thorsen whispered in her ear, "You look as though you need new clothes," and indicated with a nod that her spencer was undone.

Embarrassed both by what he said and how he said it, Lucy retorted, "I am aware of that, Lieutenant Thorsen." She gave no explanation – why should she?

"You are working all week. Don't they pay you enough?"

Oh, so he was trying to put Daniel and his family down. "They pay me quite well."

"Then why can't you purchase something that fits? That patched grey dress is too short, your ankles are on show, and it's too tight and your boots won't last much longer."

"I *mistook* you for a gentleman, Lieutenant." Lucy walked away yet added, "Our household expenses are no concern of yours."

The Lieutenant followed. "Revenue *is* my concern."

Lucy could see little connection between her lack of good clothing and his dutiful collection of rightful revenue. She took a few steps further away.

One Dark Night

"How money is obtained and how it is spent is a subject pertaining to my duties." Karl Thorsen pursued her. "It's not easy to hide things from me. It's my sworn duty to know what's going on, even that which is hidden. Your mother's clothing and yours are too dissimilar to ease my mind on matters which are in my charge."

"Good heavens, Lieutenant Thorsen, are you saying my mother is obtaining money by unlawful means?"

"I'll speak to your mother."

"No, please don't, Lieutenant." Lucy's voice showed her loss of composure. "I will be blamed for something I have said to you. See, she is watching us."

Lieutenant Thorsen turned, nodded towards Annie Yorton, then strode away towards the parson.

One Dark Night

Chapter Four
"Dark indeed"

"Oh, Mr Raffles, do come in." Mrs Yorton fluttered around the parson like a white butterfly around a cabbage. "How good of you to call. Please sit down." She patted the more comfortable of her two chairs and sat in the other. "I thought you gave a very good sermon this morning; it's reassuring to be part of such a caring parish. You've been so good to me in the troubles I've had." Having not spoken at all since she left the church, she now could not stop. "I still find it difficult to live alone with such a rebellious daughter; she could do with an *earthly* father's hand from time to time." Mrs Yorton never spoke of her supposedly dead husband except when some deep instinct told her that sympathy must be elicited and quickly. "She's been such a trial to me, so sullen and I worry about her constantly."

Parson Emmanuel Raffles was by far the most colourful character for miles around. He stood at least four inches above other men and was certainly much wider. Good cheer radiated from him, and his parishioners felt a cosy glow toward him and the God he served so well. He had a penchant for hats and regardless of what he was supposed to wear he would don a different one each time he went out. Mrs Yorton's agitation had caused her to neglect to take his hat from him when he sat down. Today's favourite, a black felt with a red band around the circular crown, rested on his knee until he twirled it on his finger revealing a package underneath. "It is Lucy I wish to see."

"Oh I do hope she has not been troublesome to you too. I've tried so hard…"

"We must not forget, Mrs Yorton, that God himself has trouble with his children." The parson raised an eyebrow as he looked her straight in

One Dark Night

the eye. "A finer daughter no one could wish for." Mrs Yorton pursed her lips as he continued. "As you so rightly pointed out, Mrs Yorton, you are both a part of a caring parish and I know you are an intelligent and accomplished lady." God would surely forgive his flattery. "We're all so busy we sometimes don't notice those closest to us as much as we should." Recognizing a dangerous turn in his remarks, Mrs Yorton attempted to interrupt but was thwarted. "You, for instance, you care about your neighbours. They speak well of you and how you will take them a hot meal if they are sick, and have passed to them garments you no longer need."

Mrs Yorton relaxed; she almost purred. "If I had more, I would give more, Mr Raffles."

"God has given you great beauty, a gift we can all appreciate." On the tip of his tongue was something about inner beauty being of more consequence but instead he said, "Where's Lucy?"

Mrs Yorton frowned. "Well..."

"I have something to give her."

"Oh I can pass it on to her."

Emmanuel Raffles leaned forward and, with a twinkle in his eye, twirled his hat again and with a voice that was used to shouting from a pulpit to the back of a very large congregation, he bellowed, "Lucy!"

Lucy tumbled down the stairs in response and through the doorway – that voice always drew forth whatever he required.

"My wife has this little gift for you." He handed her the parcel. "She says it no longer fits her but might fit you." He watched Lucy's conflicting emotions cross her face as she glanced at the parcel and then her mother. "She also said it was not to be given away." Then with great emphasis and a steely glance at Mrs Yorton, he added, "If it does not fit, please return it."

Lucy unwrapped the parcel and held up a finely embroidered spencer of plum red woollen cloth. She could barely conceal her delight but Parson Raffles forestalled any gushing gratitude by raising the palm of his hand.

One Dark Night

"We must remember," there was a pause, "Your mother is a woman of good taste and I am sure your choice of dress for church attendance must cause her some embarrassment."

"Choice?" Lucy was about to say what choice? Then she caught the twinkle in the parson's eye.

"I think you should take time to visit the market and purchase, with the money you earn each week, a decent dress, one that covers...er..."

"The parts it should cover," offered Lucy.

"Quite." The two of them shared the merest hint of a smile.

Parson Raffles pulled himself out of the chair slowly, making use of the time to look around the cottage and at Lucy and her mother with more discerning eyes than he had applied in the past. It was fortunate indeed that he had been alerted to Lucy's situation. Unusually, he patted Mrs Yorton's hand as he took his leave saying, "A dress for Lucy, yes, it's important for her to do you credit. I think you manage well, surprisingly well. However," he lowered his head towards her, "we must both be aware that she should no longer be addressed as 'Lucy', she is a young woman and I think you should encourage people to call her Miss Yorton. She is, after all, your daughter." He put his hat on and raised his hand in farewell. "Miss Yorton, I trust you will enjoy your time at the market."

Mrs Yorton watched from the door as he rolled along the road and, when she was sure he could not hear, she turned to Lucy and growled, "So you thought you'd get your way by whining to the parson, did you? Well, let me tell you, you ungrateful, slovenly child, that if you continue to tell your lies, you'll find yourself alone in this world."

Lucy held back the answer that popped unbidden into her head. Lieutenant Thorsen had put another thought there which agitated more now. The money Lucy earned could not possibly pay for the rent, the food and, most particularly, her mother's fine clothing. She had, long ago now, mentioned that she had a legacy. But from whom and how long would it last? Or was this just another of her lies? If so, from where did her money come?

~

One Dark Night

Late that afternoon, after finishing all her chores, Lucy seized a handful of her freshly baked bread, snatched up her thin, black shawl and ran to her treasured hideaway on the cliffs at the west side of the bay. She climbed down on to the ledge, careful not to disturb the ground – no one must ever find her sanctuary – and sat with her back to the overhanging cliff. Perfect privacy. She wrapped her shawl around her old gaping spencer, tied it tightly and made herself comfortable behind the scrubby bushes. She thought about the gift from the parson's wife, Emmeline. How kind, and it fitted perfectly. Was it coincidence? Had Mrs Raffles seen her need? Or had it been Karl Thorsen? She said his name aloud with some contempt but should she reconsider? Had he mentioned her predicament? He'd clearly got the measure of her mother. Lucy reasoned that it was better for her not to grasp all that her mother was, though her deceits were seeping into her thoughts more frequently of late. She was certainly not what she claimed to be.

A raucous laugh came from above. Men were tramping along the clifftop. It was the sundown patrol noting the number of beached fishing boats before darkness set in.

"So will there be sufficient men? Is twelve enough?"

Lucy had heard that the Wintergate Custom House had lately achieved a reputation for being very successful and, unlike other Custom Houses, its officers were incorruptible.

"Twelve? There'll be more than that."

The two men continued patrolling the bay and left Lucy to her thoughts. Most of the King's preventive men in Kent were drawn from the ranks of the bo'suns and petty officers in the Navy. "Thems that like givin' orders," she'd heard someone say. Customs' men were almost universally hated, particularly in this part of the county. She knew too, from working at the farm, where old soldiers frequently begged for work, that at the end of the hostilities with the French, thousands of men returned to their homes with no prospect of finding employment. The soil was good for farming, the sea was there for fishing – things could be worse. With so many men returning home all at the same time though, there simply wasn't sufficient work for all of them to be able to feed their families. Many got into debt and prison or the workhouse, or

One Dark Night

were forced outside the law and Lucy had been cautioned by the farm labourers not to ask questions, something she found difficult. She had never mentioned what she had seen on that cold Christmas Day. After all, whom could she trust and what had Mr Tynton been burying? Surely it couldn't have been of any value. No one in their right mind buries anything in the salty sea-washed sands. And you wouldn't bury a body in the sand, you'd take it out to sea and throw it overboard.

The murmur of voices that had receded now came closer as they returned.

"Thorsen was the key to capturing that lot along the coast. Planning. That's what Thorsen does so well."

"How come he's here at all? I reckon he doesn't fit in. I think there's more to it."

"Don't start thinking, Jennings. That's not what you're good at. We should make the most of his talents while we can."

Oh, this was interesting. To overhear customs' men was a rare occurrence. Karl Thorsen had quite scared her this morning and left an uncomfortable impression that would not go away. Now here was gossip giving her a reason for that feeling. *There's more to it.*

"They rarely let a dark go by," said Jennings, "Something will be happening tonight, somewhere."

Wasn't Daniel talking about *a dark*?

The men had moved away, tramping towards the Custom House, and Lucy peeked through the scrubby bushes towards the lanterns burning in the windows. "Watch House" it was called and since Lieutenant Thorsen moved in, they were well known for their watching. There was no moon tonight and gathering storm clouds prevented even the dim light of the stars.

Dark indeed.

One Dark Night

Chapter Five
"Looked at her with disdain"

Lucy arrived at the gatehouse at Jerusalem Farm the following morning looking as if she'd climbed out of the well. Her wavy, fair hair hung from her misshapen straw bonnet in dripping strands, and her shawl, over her old spencer and grey Sunday dress, could not save her from being drenched through. The gatehouse wasn't much of a house at all. The primary aim was to store hay and it was merely a three-sided stone shelter built with knowledge of the prevailing winds but it afforded fair protection for workers in thunderstorms or animals in bitter weather. Lucy knew there'd be only a half-day's pay again, for as soon as Mrs Tynton finished with her in the farmhouse, there'd be little or no work in the fields in this weather. She took off her shawl and wrung it out, shook her bonnet free from dripping rain, and attempted to tie her hair up again.

Footsteps. The sound of heavy, running footsteps coming from the direction of the old wooden farmhouse. Daniel and Josh burst into the gatehouse.

"Don't you go shaking your coat all over Lucy." Daniel steered his dog into a corner and bid him lie down on some loose straw. "Dry out on that, Josh." Josh seemed more interested in nosing into the straw bales until Daniel snapped his fingers. "No bones for you there, Josh." He dipped his head to Lucy and she gave a courteous bob to him. "Wasn't sure if you'd make it in this morning. Ma will be pleased to have a hand though."

"Thank you, Daniel. I'll be happy to help. I thought I'd wait a while and try and dry out a little."

One Dark Night

"No, come on, we'll run back together and we'll get you dried out in front of a roaring fire."

Lucy picked up her bonnet, wrapped her soggy shawl around her and peeked out. Daniel turned to Josh and whistled like a blackbird. Lucy shook her head in amazement. "Indistinguishable from a real blackbird, Daniel!"

"Gets him moving fast." He scooped up her hand and pulled her along as he ran towards the door. Josh, tail swirling, got there first, barked and the door was opened by Mrs Tynton.

"Come on in, you ragamuffins. What's the matter with you, Dan? Getting yourself soaked through again."

Daniel, still holding Lucy's hand, towed her to the stove, gently shoved Josh to one side with his foot, opened the front and put another log on. "Get us some towels, Ma, will you?"

Mrs Tynton was ahead of her son, and pointed to two warming towels by the side of the stove. "Lucy, I think you'll need to remove all your clothes and we'll dry them off."

Daniel could not hold back. "Yeah, I think you're right, Ma." He put his arm around Lucy's shoulder, removed her shawl, then took her by both shoulders and began to remove her spencer. "It'll all have to come off, Lucy, or you'll be feverish before the day is through." His words were solicitous: his back was towards his mother: his face was mischievous.

Lucy heard herself say, "I shouldn't have come." It wasn't what she had intended to say, but nothing sensible entered her mind. Her mind was on her churning stomach, her knees were feeling wobbly too, and she knew she couldn't mention those.

"I'm glad you did, and I'm sure Ma will be pleased too."

"Aye, that I am." Mrs Tynton came down the stairs that ran between the kitchen and the scullery; she was carrying a brown cotton dress. "This might fit, Lucy. Try it on and if it does, then you can wear it while your clothes dry out."

Daniel knew it was time to disappear upstairs.

One Dark Night

But not for long, for just as Lucy finished drying her hair and Mrs Tynton handed her a brush, someone hammered on the kitchen door. Mrs Tynton looked uneasy.

"Go sit yourself down in the parlour, Lucy. I've some business to attend to." Daniel nodded towards the room on the other side of the front door. "It'll give you a chance to catch your breath." Then he flung open the front door and raised the palm of his hand and said, "Round the back – scullery door."

Lucy was impressed: these men obeyed without objection. Yet she was also puzzled. Who were they? If they were farm labourers, why caution them not to speak? Where was Mr Tynton? He usually dealt with the workers. Within a few minutes, from the window of the parlour, she watched them leave. Satisfied, purposeful and making for the gatehouse.

Daniel put his head around the parlour door. "It's cold in here, Lucy. Come back to the kitchen, have some porridge and then Ma's got a job for you." He closed the door behind her and continued, "There's always a few men we can rely on to work whatever the weather. They worked through the night to get a job done."

"Barn roof!" shouted Mrs Tynton.

Lucy hadn't thought of that and she was annoyed with herself for being so suspicious. Karl Thorsen – he was the problem. He'd filled her with doubts and surely it was not good to doubt the few friends she had. Alone in the kitchen, she ate her porridge quickly, helping herself to the milk and sugar laid out for her. Daniel and his mother now seemed to be very busy indeed. Daniel was upstairs and sounded as if he was moving furniture. She even wondered how he could be upstairs yet the sounds seemed to come from just behind her. One day, if she were ever to be left alone, she'd take a look upstairs. Mrs Tynton was huffing and puffing in the scullery and finally put her head around the doorway.

"I need you to go to market for me right away, Lucy. The rain's easing."

She'd never asked her to do that before. Was this another ruse to keep her away from Daniel? "Of course, Mrs Tynton, I'll be glad to do that for you." This was true: it would allow her a chance to look at

One Dark Night

clothes, just like the parson suggested. She'd have to wait until the end of the week for her pay though.

~

Lucy was lucky. It should have taken half an hour to walk to the market at Brookington, maybe longer in this mud, but Bodger was also going there. And Bodger was driving a donkey cart. He stopped to let Lucy climb up next to him. He put an old blanket over her head and shoulders, and managed to convey with a mixture of sounds and gestures that he'd "got a job".

"So have I. I have to get a bigger kettle," said Lucy, letting Bodger read her lips.

Bodger's weather-beaten face looked surprised. He held his arms wide and then high. She was unsure if he was jesting about the size of the kettle or telling her something different. A jolly smile to him would have to cover the possibility of either.

The donkey, having felt the slap of the reins as Bodger waved his arms around, gathered speed and reached the market in good time despite the road being muddy and their having to get out and push at one point. Lucy thanked Bodger and he conveyed it had been a pleasure.

The colour and bustle of the market enthralled her. She had no money to buy anything of consequence; perhaps she could buy some material and make something? No, the bolt of linen was over two shillings a yard and cotton not much cheaper, so she contented herself with looking. She approached a stall that was selling clothes cast off by what passed for gentry in this forsaken corner of England. There was a pale pink silk gown with deeper pink ribbons around the hem and neckline and she buzzed around it like a bee to a blossom. The stallholder looked at her with disdain; he needed no expert eye to see that Lucy was not a potential customer and consequently he stared at her without any attempt to conceal his opinion. Lucy could approach no nearer; his lewd thoughts were plain to see. She hurried away towards another stall with clothes more suited to her restricted means. They were not just second hand, but third and fourth hand-me-downs. "How much is this blue dress, please?"

One Dark Night

"Too much."

Angry, yet thinking it unwise to retort, Lucy's eyes welled up with tears. Was she really so impoverished looking that she was afforded no respect at all? She could not believe she looked so poor, not now she was wearing Mrs Tynton's dress which reached all the way down to her ankles. The high-waisted dress was still acceptably fashionable in country towns so how could people be so unkind? Then she saw the two girls who'd told her she needed taking down a peg or two. They were sniggering behind one of the stalls.

Her much anticipated visit to the market was rapidly being spoilt but she fought back. She headed for the tinker's stall and bought a large kettle. She returned to the more interesting stalls and was attracted by the haberdasher's stall. Mrs Tynton had given her tuppence and told her to buy herself something to eat and not to hurry back. Strange. Very strange. Or was she overly keen to keep her away from Daniel?

Some pretty, black buttons, similar to the ones on the old spencer she was wearing, took her mind to more immediate matters; she must not waste the time here. If she bought three she could sew them on where the button holes were and link up the buttons with some ribbons. It would allow a little more room. Not an idea that would feature in the fashion magazines but perhaps a useful one to stop the spencer flapping open in the cold.

"How much are the buttons, please?"

The stallholder expertly eyed her. "Too much."

Lucy was not so easily put off this time. "I'll only need three."

"I only sell them in sixes."

"If you let me have just three, how much would that be?"

"Penny. But I only sell them in sixes."

Lucy could see that some persuading was needed. "If you allow me to buy three buttons for a penny, then I'll pay another penny for some ribbon."

The stallholder looked across to her ribbon section. "Penny won't buy much ribbon."

Heavens, thought Lucy. This woman was not much good at her job.

The two girls had followed her and smirked.

One Dark Night

"A yard," boomed the man on the next stall. "Can't you tell, woman, this young lady ain't no revenue spy. Take no notice of them girls, they're just jealous. One day this pretty lady will be able to buy your whole stall. You wanna make her a good customer now."

Lucy could feel her colour rising. It was as Daniel said. She did not speak like everyone else and strangers were wary of her.

"You shut your mouth. I'll sell to a haughty miss if I want to and not if I don't." The woman stood arms akimbo and turned to Lucy and said, "Well, miss, I'll let you have a yard of the blue and three buttons for tuppence altogether. That good enough?"

"Very good, thank you," said Lucy with a grateful smile to the man on the adjacent stall.

The woman scowled as she took the tuppence and handed Lucy the ribbon and buttons. Lucy was now not so keen to look at the clothes, yet to try for a position in fashionable Merrygate, she needed to know how much a cloak would cost. And a dress. And boots. Just then, Bodger tapped her on the shoulder and, as best as he could, offered to take her back again. She accepted thankfully: it had started to rain.

On arrival at the farm, she knocked on the door and became aware of an immediate silence followed by some kind of muttering or whispering. She tried the latch to no avail. She hoped someone would answer the door soon or Mrs Tynton's brown dress would be soaked too. The door was flung open and there stood Daniel. He waved her through.

"Don't stand there getting yourself all wet again and don't mind this lot, they'll not be here much longer."

"The lot" looked at Lucy suspiciously and she felt a blush rising. It was not helped by Daniel putting his arm around her shoulders. Was he showing off? Showing that every girl was his? For the first time, she resented his touch.

"She's been to the market for Ma. Back a bit earlier than expected, aren't you Lucy? Caught all us workmen taking time off for a bite to eat in front of the warm hearth."

The ten men seated around the kitchen table relaxed their forbidding stares and murmured one to another.

One Dark Night

Shaking off Daniel's arm, Lucy said, "I'll put this new kettle in the scullery, Da…, Mr Tynton."

Daniel's mother was in the scullery and she glared at Lucy. "You're back early. Not expecting anything to eat are you?"

"Oh no, Mrs Tynton, I'm early because old Bodger let me ride on a donkey cart he was using."

"It isn't her fault, Ma, and you don't need to worry." Daniel had followed Lucy into the scullery. The men in the kitchen clattered around as they left, shouting farewells of varying sorts and Lucy rushed to the front door to close it behind them. Now it was quiet again except for Daniel talking to his mother in the scullery.

"That may be so but since that Thorsen man arrived it pays to be careful." Mrs Tynton, having got started, continued. "He was seen talking to her yesterday, and I'll have to warn her to keep away from him if she wants to work here."

So, those girls outside the church were informing on her even to Mrs Tynton.

"Ma, she's not one of them. Not one of us either, I know. Lucy's not anybody's. Her mother may be *respectable,*" Daniel said with undisguised sarcasm, "but how can you associate this half-starved girl with them? It's quite clear she's unaware of anything except how to survive. Her mother is well dressed and oh so *genteel* but doesn't give a damn about Lucy. I've been past their cottage and heard her mother shouting 'Out! Get out and stay out.' And I've heard a lot more too." Daniel, becoming aware of the possibility of Lucy overhearing, lowered his voice. "That's why she's always here first and in all weathers."

"Things are tough enough as it is, Dan. If you're going to take risks it'd be better Lucy wasn't here getting drawn into things."

Lucy was aghast and went to the doorway. "Please Mrs Tynton, I'll go. I'll not cause any more problems."

"No, lass, I'm glad you came, that I am. Just a bit of a bad day, that's all. Things not gone as well as they should."

Daniel smiled. "I'm sorry you heard some of that, Lucy. Come, I'll see you to the door." He looked out. "Rain's stopped. Take the rest of the day off and don't worry, you won't lose any pay. Keep that dress

One Dark Night

you've got on, Ma says it doesn't fit any more. Take your other clothes, they're nearly dry now. Make sure you hurry home before the next downpour."

"Thank you, Daniel. I'm sorry to cause trouble for you and your family."

"You can cause me as much trouble as you like, so long as you work here." He paused, his blue eyes tenderly looked into hers. "Stay close."

Lucy's heart lightened. If only Daniel was at Jerusalem Farm more often. Instead, it was Mr Sydney Tynton she had to work for and it was Sydney Tynton's voice that shouted at her as she passed the gatehouse. Waving a jug of ale, he yelled, "That's your lot, girl, wandering around as if you own the place. You don't work here anymore. You understand?"

One Dark Night

Chapter Six
"Even the dog knew"

Annie Yorton's eyes never left Lucy's brown dress until she blurted, "Wangled a frock out of someone, have you?"

"No, it wasn't like that at all, mother. I got very wet and Mrs Tynton gave me this to wear while..."

Her mother couldn't wait for the explanation. "I was an orphan at your age and had to go into service to have a roof over my head. You don't seem to realize how fortunate you are."

"I am well able to assess my situation."

"Don't come those fancy phrases with me, my girl. With a new dress and a new spencer, you'll not be able to pretend you're some poor waif."

She knew it would be better to ignore her but retorted, "Mother, these clothes..." Lucy held out the bundle of her old clothes "were soaked through and I could not have worked in them. Mrs Tynton kindly..."

"Don't you answer me back." Mrs Yorton's hand caught the side of Lucy's head almost knocking her bonnet off and sending her stumbling sideways into the open door frame and into the arms of Lieutenant Karl Thorsen.

"By thunder! I'd not expected you to *throw* yourself at me, Miss Yorton. And making such a din that you neither heard me knock nor open the door."

Lucy tried to extricate herself from his hold but he held on to her gently but firmly. Was he being kind or mischievous? Lucy, still reeling, instinctively pulled a few locks of hair from her bonnet to cover where the blow had fallen. She knew from past experience that it would

One Dark Night

now be blazing red and tomorrow it would be black and then it would go blue and green and then yellow – oh the shame.

"Come in Lieutenant Thorsen. It's cold out there. Shut the door and warm yourself by the fire here. I'm afraid Lucy's such a clumsy girl."

"Thank you." The Lieutenant, wearing his Riding Officer uniform, stood still for a mere few seconds but the silence was powerful. He stared straight at Lucy. "Have you been at the farm?"

"Yes I have," Lucy said with a hint of defiance.

"Why are you home early?"

Lucy thought for a moment. "The weather is not conducive to working in the fields."

Lieutenant Thorsen did not conceal his scorn. "Not conducive! More like inconvenient."

Lucy briefly considered whether the word "inconvenient" was suitable for describing working in soggy fields in the pouring rain. Then almost tangibly she felt within her the dawning recognition of how naïve she had been. He knew that wasn't the reason she was home early. Flashing through her mind was the picture of Daniel hurrying her away from sheltering in the gatehouse. Even the dog knew something was hidden in the straw. Coupled with Mr Tynton being in there when she left, the stark realization of something being concealed dropped into her mind. The knowledge had been there all the time but had been buried like a seed potato. And now here was the recently arrived local head of customs visiting her mother.

Lucy's reluctance to respond allowed Mrs Yorton to compose a conciliatory answer in a compassionate tone. "I wish she didn't work there; I'm quite concerned about it really."

"Are you? Why?"

"Well, you know me, Lieutenant, I'm a God-fearing widow and I know what people say about that Tynton family."

"Oh? What do they say?"

"Well, far be it from me to tittle tattle but everyone knows they're not respectable folks and I've not brought Lucy up to mix with such…"

One Dark Night

With no useful evidence of wrongdoing forthcoming, merely waffle, the Lieutenant said, "So would you prefer it if Miss Yorton had a suitable situation with one of the honest parish families?"

"Why yes, of course." Then Lucy's mother hesitated. She'd fallen into a trap. Lieutenant Thorsen's eyes were hard. She began slowly, "She's not one for doing much but she should be able to find herself something." Her pace quickened, "Nothing fancy. She's been helping out in the farmhouse scullery, so a scullery maid should suit."

"I thank you both for your thoughts on my future." Lucy decided not to hide her growing anger. "I am…" Sydney Tynton's dismissal crashed into her thoughts and prevented her from sounding confident. "I shall evaluate…"

"There she goes again! Fancy words hiding her lack of action. God knows I've tried to keep her away from bad influences but…"

The Lieutenant felt free to interrupt the interrupter. "Leave it with me, Mrs Yorton. I think it would be much better for you if your daughter had work which reflected your upright character." He then turned to Lucy and said abruptly, "Report to me at Watch House tomorrow morning, sun-up." He turned to go, then stopped at the doorway and called back, "And wear that dress."

How dare Karl Thorsen tell her what to wear! What right had he to interfere in her life?

~

Her bonnet was misshapen from the rain so she was wearing her muslin cap when she knocked on the big oak door of Watch House. She had slept well and confused thoughts had been replaced by sound common sense – if he hadn't called at her house yesterday, she'd most likely be without a job today. Daniel might want her to work, Mrs Tynton too, but it was *Mr* Tynton who ran the farm, and with a fist of iron. Lucy reached up to the huge iron knocker and banged it again. Yes, Sydney Tynton was as hard as this knocker. A nasty… An eye appeared at the peephole and a voice said, "State your name and business."

"I am Miss Yorton and I am here to see Lieutenant Thorsen."

"Lieutenant Thorsen is expecting you." The door opened. "Follow me."

One Dark Night

Lucy resented this. He had no right to *expect* her. Nevertheless, it was sensible for her to consider this option. Huh. Who was she fooling? There were no options. If there were, she'd had left Jerusalem Farm long ago. So she smiled at this young man, cheerful and smart in his uniform and said, "Thank you." She'd be polite too. Unbidden, her mind flew back to life at Faefersham Court. Perhaps, if she didn't have to work close to Thorsen, *Lieutenant* Thorsen, she corrected herself, then maybe she'd find this a good place to work. She wondered what they had in mind. The boy knocked loudly.

"Come in!"

Lucy was shown into an office where Lieutenant Thorsen was sitting behind a huge desk and leaning back in his chair. Alongside him was another uniformed man, clearly of some importance. Lucy stood alone in front of them both and lowered her eyes; that's what servants did at Faefersham Court and they didn't speak unless spoken to.

"Colonel Bigmore, this is Miss Yorton, the young woman I told you about."

Lucy bobbed slowly and courteously. She didn't know this gentleman but it was obvious he was a military man, probably from somewhere along the coast.

He stood up and circled her. "You say she will be loyal to the King?"

"I am confident she will."

"So, Miss Yorton, what do *you* say?"

Lucy wanted to say something she knew she shouldn't so there was a moment before she replied, "I shall be pleased to be offered a position within the King's service and can confirm that I am a loyal subject of the King."

Colonel Bigmore looked astounded. With a puzzled expression he reeled around on his heels and demanded, "Where did you find this person?"

"She is the daughter of a widow living here in Wintergate. She has had little opportunity to mix socially having been obliged to support her mother."

"*How* has she supported her?"

One Dark Night

Lieutenant Thorsen paused. "She has been working at Jerusalem Farm."

With a voice that could call a whole battalion to order, Colonel Bigmore thundered, "Jerusalem Farm! And you have plans to take her as a servant here?"

"I do, sir. I do. She is a lamb amongst wolves and I think we can turn this to our advantage."

"She will live-in, of course," said the Colonel warily.

"I think that is essential for security purposes, sir."

Colonel Bigmore nodded. "Watch House is under your command; I hope you will not be disappointed."

Thorsen waved his hand to dismiss Lucy. Fuming, she strode out of the office and turned to close the door. As she did so, she heard a growling attempt to whisper, "Thorsen, if I were you, I'd get myself a wife to deal with these household matters."

"Whilst in the service of the King, I'd still need to make a personal judgment, Colonel."

The young man who had met her at the door was standing a few paces away and escorted her to a windowless waiting room with nothing but two high backed chairs. "Wait here. Lieutenant Thorsen will come for you." He lit a single candle before he left.

Live-in! Live-in where? Here with Thorsen? What about her mother? Her mother clearly had no idea it was to be a permanent position in Thorsen's quarters. She sat down on one of the chairs. Watch House was a round, stone building, crenellated, like a small castle and there were no windows at this level at the front. She felt as if she were in a prison cell. She was just beginning to shiver when Lieutenant Thorsen flung open the door.

"Come with me, Miss Yorton, I'll show you where you'll be working."

Lucy looked at him and resented his assumption that she would take anything offered, even if it was the truth. If only she could turn it down and announce *I already have a job at Jerusalem Farm. With Daniel.* "Lieutenant Thorsen, Mrs Tynton is expecting me at the farm." That at least might be true.

One Dark Night

"That job is in the cold and wet and amongst a pack of thieves. You'll take this job in the warm and learn quickly how to become a maid-of-all-work." Then Lucy thought she heard him mutter, "Maybe more."

Lucy didn't know which part of his speech to object to first but the attack on Daniel's reputation angered her most. "That 'pack of thieves' as you called them has been very kind to me. Yesterday they gave me this dress you ordered me to wear."

Lieutenant Thorsen took hold of her arm and pulled her round to face him. "They gave you that dress? Why? What is that Tynton man to you?"

"I am employed by the Tynton family. That is all." As soon as she said it, she could feel her colour rising. She was no longer employed. Even if she could work at the farm for a few more days, Sydney Tynton would have his way once Daniel returned to his uncle's farm.

"It's time you acquired a little more wisdom, Miss Yorton. Don't ever see that family again – and that includes Daniel Tynton."

"I *shall* see him again. If I take this job, I shall need to tell him that I can't work on the farm."

"You will take this position because it's in the warm and dry and it will probably save your life. *I* shall tell Daniel Tynton that you will not be working in the cold, wet fields again."

"Why should you care where I am working?"

He almost dragged Lucy up the stairs leading to his private quarters. "This place needs more servants. You'll find out why. I have even been *ordered...*" Lucy could not imagine anyone attempting to order Thorsen. He read her expression. "Yes, *ordered* to find a competent maid-of-all work whom I could vouch for. I have found you and I have vouched for you."

Lucy was stung. She was being treated as if she were a chattel. "Vouch for me?"

"Yes, *vouch* for you. Do you think just anyone can work for the Lieutenant in charge of Watch House and all the revenue men hereabouts? I suppose it doesn't occur to you that this village is overrun with smugglers and their spies?"

One Dark Night

Lucy was taken aback. No, she hadn't noticed smugglers and spies everywhere – should she have done? "I thought you had stopped the smuggling."

"Smuggling doesn't stop. It just changes hands or location and becomes more dangerous. I realize you have been sheltered by your endlessly busy life and your mother's lies, but you must now let me deal with your mother and, more particularly, the Tynton family. Have nothing more to do with any of the Tyntons. That is an order." They had reached the door to the kitchen. "You have to decide which way your life is going, Miss Yorton. Farmer Tynton will hang and I shall be the one to do it."

One Dark Night

Chapter Seven
"Devoid of finer feelings"

"There's something big going on. You mark my words." The little woman who had introduced herself as Martha was sitting in a rocking chair near the large stove in the centre of the outside wall. She patted her lap and a black and white cat jumped up. "Meet Scat the cat," she said with an almost toothless grin. "Scat'll make sure you never get hungry. She stocks up the larder when she thinks it's getting a bit low."

Lucy looked puzzled.

"Rats. Nice furry rats. I swear she'd plonk them on the stove if she could. Good at it, she is. Patiently waiting until the rat moves..." Martha clutched Scat and demonstrated, "Pounce!" Neither Scat nor Lucy joined in with her attempts at pleasantries. "You all right, girl?"

"I hadn't expected to be here."

"Aw, girl, you'll be a bit flutterbustered, I expect. That there Lieutenant Thorsen, well, he kind of takes you over. I know – it happened to me." Martha gestured to the little stool by the other side of the hearth. "Sit down, girl, and we'll get to know each other. Lieutenant Thorsen didn't have time to get us acquainted. He never has got time. He goes looking for it and it hides from him."

Lucy smiled, shrugged her shoulders, sighed, and sat down. "I should be at work on the farm."

"You don't want to be working on a farm in winter. The heavens are emptying their bath water on us again, see, look out the window. You're better off here, you mark my words."

Defeated. She always felt defeated. If it wasn't her mother, then it was the lack of available work, and now it was Thorsen. Things had got to change. It was her life, not everyone else's. Her mother was always saying she indulged in ideas above her station. Thorsen had made the point, which had become stranded in her mind: *You have to decide which way your life is going.* She became aware that Martha was still talking.

"I came to Wintergate with Parson Raffles. He's a good man." Martha momentarily reflected. "He'd taken me into his household in Torwell Bridge and I learned to cook there. Course I could cook before, but there I was trained up properly.

"When he came back to Wintergate," Martha leaned forward as if she had something confidential to impart, "he'd been here before you see, and I grew up here," she leaned back in her chair again and said with pride, "so I came with him as the cook. Then when Lieutenant Thorsen came to Watch House in charge of the revenue, somehow, and I still don't know how, though perhaps the parson was short of money, I was made *his* cook. He said something about my good standing as a loyal and cheerful servant. Drove me up here in his carriage and that was that. Nice carriage it was too.

"I get more pay. You will do too, you mark my words, and…" she paused for effect, "not only do I get a whole day off at Christmas and Easter, but on one day a week, that's every week, mind you, you get time off – three hours. That's time enough to go visiting your ma or, like me, have a long nap. And on Sundays we're allowed to go to church. The parson insisted on that, bless him."

Lucy had paid attention to all Martha had said but now she had other things on her mind. "Mrs Tynton will be wondering where I am." She couldn't bring herself to say Daniel's name. Had his father told him she'd been dismissed? Or maybe he'd already gone back to his uncle's farm? All she said was, "And when I don't go home tonight, my mother will be wondering too."

"All this wondering's not good for you, girl. You'll find Lieutenant Thorsen takes care of all them things. He'll be here about two o'clock for something to eat. See, I even know how to tell the time." With considerable, visible pride, Martha pointed to the clock on the mantelpiece. "Catch him then and tell him you need some messages taken."

One Dark Night

"I'm not sure I…"

"Aw, you'll be all right, girl. Best thing that ever happened to me since my man got killed in the war." She then spat out, "Clumping Frenchies. Always picking a fight." She wiped a tear from her eye and smoothed her apron with her hands. "Once you get into service there'll always be someone wanting you. You not done anything like this before?"

Lucy thought for a moment. She had experience of service as a child, she knew what servants were meant to do and she knew their various roles. She had, however, been on the receiving end of the service for, whenever she was with Dougie, the servants had had to include her too. Martha was still rocking back and forth, stroking Scat and waiting for an answer. "No, I've no experience of working like this but I have been educated to…" She hesitated, she was saying too much.

"Well, fancy you being educated. How do you mean?"

Lucy tried to find something safe to say and decided on "Educated in how to manage a household."

"Like a big manor house or something? I've been in one of them."

"Yes, Martha, that's exactly right."

"Do you think we can get this place looking like a manor house?" Martha beamed at the prospect of improving her station further.

"We could try," Lucy replied with a genuine smile, one that reached her eyes this time.

~

Early that afternoon, Lucy watched Lieutenant Thorsen tether his horse and head towards the main door on the ground floor. On Lucy's level, the private quarters, there was a good all round view of Wintergate Bay, the cliffs towards Merrygate, and much of Wintergate village. Watch House, being on a high promontory, was well placed to do justice to its name.

"He's here, Martha, and by the sounds of it he's pounding up the stairs."

"I'm all ready. You got the table looking good?"

"Indeed I have." Despite her anxieties about the man she could only think of as "Thorsen", she had decided she would accept her current

One Dark Night

situation with good grace. There being no alternative, she'd do exactly what Thorsen had said. She'd become much more than a maid-of-all-work, she'd manage the place like a proper housekeeper. It was likely to be the quickest route out of Watch House.

Martha had told her that Thorsen dismissed the previous maid the week before and she'd managed alone since then.

"I'm so tired. You cannot know how pinkled I am to have you here."

Pinkled? What a strange woman. Lucy felt needed, if nothing else.

"I've been putting the dishes on his table myself but I think you could do that for me today, Lucy. Oh, and by the way, don't be surprised if he calls you Lucy. He calls me Martha which shows just how kind he is. He'll ring a bell when he's ready."

He didn't. He burst into the kitchen. "Who laid my dining table?" Martha looked alarmed. Lucy owned up. "With the centrepiece of holly and those other red berried twigs?"

"Yes Lieutenant."

"Where did you get them?"

"When your revenue man accompanied me to get the wood he allowed me to pick them. They are growing near the wood shed." Lucy briefly wondered if she'd now got him into trouble.

"And you laid the cutlery, plates and glassware?"

"Yes, Lieutenant Thorsen."

Martha stepped in, looking uneasy but undeterred. "Lieutenant, Lucy has been *educated* and knows how a big house runs."

"Educated, by thunder! Educated," he teased. "More secrets, Lucy? And just where were you *educated*?"

Oh drat. Now she'd put herself into yet another awkward situation. "I only mentioned it to Martha so that she would not have to explain everything to me."

"Where?" Lieutenant Thorsen rarely had time to be sensitive.

"My mother has forbidden me to speak of it."

Lieutenant Thorsen looked at Lucy with his piercing blue eyes. "You arrived in Wintergate some years ago, didn't you?" Lucy confirmed this with a nod. "Do you remember much of your *education*?"

One Dark Night

Lucy resented what sounded like sarcasm. Her thoughts though turned to her time at Faefersham Court – she could never forget her life there but answered simply, "Enough to know how a household should be managed." Lucy steeled herself to remember that all he was interested in was his work and he was devoid of finer feelings.

"If you will not say, then I shall find out. But for the moment there are more urgent matters to attend to. Wherever you were, Lucy, it is not to be spoken of. Do you understand, both of you? Good!" He marched around the kitchen. "I'll not interfere with your running of my quarters, Lucy, unless I find I need to." He strode out.

Lucy allowed herself a few moments of sheer gratification. From maid-of-all-work she was now running the household – such as it was. And all this in half a day. Moments later the bell rang from the dining room and her skin prickled; he would not be an easy master and somehow she must introduce the subject of messages being taken to her mother and the Tyntons. She took a tray of dishes into the dining room and placed it on the sideboard.

"There's a leather bag with your belongings in the hallway. It includes your shell collection from under your straw mattress on the *floor*. You'll sleep on a proper *bed* here. Remove the bag to your bedroom, empty it and let me have it back immediately."

He'd searched the cottage! He had no right. Was her mother even there? "Lieutenant, may I know what my mother said?"

"Nothing. I informed her. She looked thunderous. I closed the door and rode away."

Lucy imagined the scene – she'd like to have seen that! She placed a dish in front of him on the table. Returning to a safer distance by the sideboard, she opened her mouth to ask about the Tyntons but he pre-empted her question.

"The Tyntons will be informed later." He picked up the lid of the dish Lucy had put near him and licked his lips in anticipation. "That's all, Lucy, for now anyway. Martha will show you the ropes and I'm sure you'll get along with her. Be warned, she'll let me know if you try to see any of the Tyntons, so don't be tempted."

One Dark Night

Remembering her intention to be not just a servant but a good housekeeper, Lucy asked if he would like her to serve him.

"No. I'll help myself."

Swiftly and carefully Lucy placed the remainder of the dishes within Thorsen's reach then returned to the kitchen and glanced at Martha. What had Thorsen said about her? That she was of good standing and *loyal*. She was extremely likeable but Lucy would have to remember not to divulge her thoughts if she didn't want the Lieutenant to know of them too.

"Are you all right, Lucy? Did he... was he... I mean was he bumtentious?"

"No, I wouldn't say he was that." Lucy smiled at Martha. Though not having the right words, she could convey what she meant very well. "But he has not yet told the Tyntons that I am now in his employ. Mrs Tynton gave me this dress just yesterday and I must seem very ungrateful. Surely he has no right to forbid me to see or speak to them?"

"Lieutenant Thorsen knows what he's doing, girl. He comes from a good family and he'll not do anything wrong, so you've just got to stop your worrying."

Lucy was on the brink of saying more but remembered it would not be wise. Furthermore, Martha, though unschooled, was bright enough to work out what Lucy had in mind and the look she gave Lucy forewarned her.

"If he's forbidden you to see someone, he'll have good reason. He's not a man to vex." Martha waited a moment. "Don't cross him, Lucy."

One Dark Night

Chapter Eight
"She saw him wink"

"Hello Lucy."

"Daniel!"

"Is this what you're looking for?" Daniel was sitting on the ground behind the woodshed and stroking a black and white cat.

"Scat! No wonder I couldn't find you."

The revenue man in the shelter of the doorway called out, "Who are you talking to, Miss Yorton?"

"It's all right, Mr Hendon, it's Scat. I've found her. Come Scat, come here."

Daniel held on to Scat. "Thorsen thinks he can order me to go away. I have other plans."

Into Lucy's head popped the last words he had spoken to her: "Stay close." How, oh how? Surely it was becoming impossible. "Daniel, I've been forbidden to associate with your family."

He slipped a coin into her hand. "We owe you some pay; don't give it to your mother. I'll see you next time you go to the market."

"I don't know when…"

"I do. Here, take Scat. I'll see you soon."

Lucy hurried back to Mr Hendon with Scat in her arms, chattering all the way back up the stairs to Lieutenant Thorsen's quarters. Never before had she so loved a cat. She must contain her joy or Martha would soon notice and may even work out why. She looked down at what had been her Sunday best dress, the grey one, too short and too tight. There really was no hope of Daniel liking her. The thought sobered her sufficiently to disguise her feelings and say, "Scat was hiding by the woodshed, Martha."

One Dark Night

"Mark my words, likely been watching a rat." Martha bustled around the stove stirring the porridge from time to time and preparing a pot of meagre vegetables. "Your second day here, Lucy, and the last day of January. Days are getting longer, thank the Lord."

Thorsen had called them into his sitting room the previous evening and told them that Lucy was never to go out without an escort. Thus it was that even to call the cat indoors, Lucy was watched. How in the realms of reality could she see Daniel? Only in her dreams for he was promised to another. Who? Into her head came Mrs Tynton's words, *he enjoys toying with the bait nibbling it and swimming away*. Of course. That's all he was after. Chasing her was sport to him. Much as she resented him, Thorsen was doing the right thing by keeping her away from Daniel.

Lucy sat at the little table near the window overlooking the approach to Watch House. "This will make a good desk, Martha. I'll draw up a list of my duties."

"Mine's cooking," Martha said immediately. Then she appeared to regret being so abrupt. "Other things too, of course. I know that." There was another pause before she explained her strong stance. "Took me a while to work my way up this far."

Lucy could sympathize with that. "I'll get up first, Martha, and clean the grate, lay and light the fire and put the kettle on for the Lieutenant."

"Should we be calling him 'the master'? I called Parson Raffles 'the parson' when I worked for him but this is different, i'nt it?"

She was right, of course. "You could *refer* to him as 'the master' but I think we should *address* him by his rank."

"Eh?"

Initially, Lucy was as baffled as Martha. "Ah, I see, I have not explained that very well. Let's say that we can talk *about* him as the master but when we talk *to* him we should call him 'Lieutenant'."

"So you'll be putting the kettle on for the *master*," beamed Martha, "and you'd better not forget me. Put enough in the kettle for me."

How could anyone forget Martha? She'd just poured Lucy a great bowl of porridge and dumped it on the kitchen table next to a small jug of milk and declared it to be the best porridge she'd ever made. "Thank you, Martha. Be assured I'll put that kettle on for you too." Lucy was reassured by the feeling that Martha was not trying to establish a hierarchy but rather delighted to feel the household was to be more organized.

This idea was confirmed when Martha said, "It's good to have someone like you around, Lucy. I'm real proud to have made it up to being a cook but, truth be told, and I think it always should be told, I'm not too upted on things."

"Upted?"

"Yes, upted. Knowing it all – not like some I've come across," Martha said with a frown. "That there last one..." Her mouth was full of porridge so it was a few moments before she added, "No respect. No respect at all. Talked to me like I was something Scat dragged in from the woodpile. And that ain't so." She crammed in some more porridge before continuing, "Isn't. Now that *you're* here, I'm going to say 'isn't'. The parson's wife gave up on me but I'm going to try again."

"Oh Martha, you mustn't do that because of me."

"Shall! I want to. My man was a decent, respected fisherman, got dragged to war, and now I'm a widow. But I've done all right. And now I'm the cook."

"And a very good cook too."

"Glad you like my porridge, Lucy; you finished it quick enough."

"It was excellent! Now I must finish that list of duties."

"The master says," Martha grinned, "the master says we are to have a fire in each of our bedrooms if it's cold enough for snow. There ain't too many... no." She paused before she tried again. "There isn't too many masters... that don't sound right either. Anyway, he's a good master."

Lucy looked up from her desk and smiled indulgently. She was going to like it here, even if the list of duties now ran to twenty or more. "Martha, does the master always eat dinner early in the afternoon?"

"Oh no, it's usually in the evening, and I prepare him something cold and leave it on the table for him to have if he calls in hungry earlier in the day. Like cake and bread and cheese. Yesterday was different. He doesn't tell me why."

One Dark Night

Lucy noticed how slowly and carefully Martha was speaking. She doubted it would last. She hoped not. "I presume you'll attend to the victuals, Martha?"

"Yes, I've got all the supplies coming in right. Tommy Smith brings his cart up here before he goes anywhere else. I get the pick. In fact," she stopped chopping the potatoes, "he should be here about now." She came across to Lucy's desk and peered out of the window. "What's happened to him?" At that moment there was a knock on the kitchen door. "Come in," yelled Martha proudly.

"Martha, we've had a message sent up from Tommy Smith." The young revenue man who seemed to be assigned a whole range of menial tasks, stood in the doorway to the kitchen. "The wheel's come off his cart and he can't get up to you until it's fixed."

"That's not good. I've got enough for the master... or should that be Lieutenant, Lucy?"

"Lieutenant because you're speaking to one of his men."

"Yes, enough for him and us." Martha thought hard; her furrowed brow and pursed lips made that plain to see. "I could be in trouble if he brings men in tonight." She turned to Lucy and said, "He sometimes surprises me with what he calls guests. Top revenue men, he means. How soon can he fix his wheel?"

"He said he won't be making it up here today."

"Flummerbums!"

"Would you like me to go to the market, Martha? Tell me what you need and I'll get it for you."

"I'll have to go with you, Miss."

Lucy thanked the revenue man and asked him to find a handcart and, within a short time, she was ready with her new embroidered, plum red spencer over her brown dress, and a smile on her face. What was it Daniel had said? "He'd see her at the market soon." "Now I wonder how that wheel came off the victualler's cart," she said to Martha. Martha looked cross. "And Martha, the revenue men should call you Mrs... What's your surname?"

"Fagg. Mrs Fagg."

~

51

One Dark Night

"Vegetables, Miss, you'll be wanting vegetables." The man standing behind the stall held up a turnip. "Grown on Bethlehem Farm, these are."

Lucy looked carefully at the stallholder. He was wearing very old clothes and a black hat pulled down to his eyes so that he had no eyebrows, no hair and looked very shabby. Mr Hendon, the revenue man was standing behind her with the hand cart, and watching her every move. "Bethlehem Farm?"

In a very broad country burr the stallholder said, "No finer turnips for miles around." This time Lucy was sure she saw him wink.

"I'll take four and I'll have six of the swedes and four pounds of parsnips too. Are they from Bethlehem Farm?"

"Everything on this stall is, Miss."

It didn't seem possible but could this rough looking man be Daniel? Bethlehem Farm was his uncle's farm. She turned to the revenue man and beckoned him forward. "Mr Hendon, this man will load up the cart and will you pay him too, please." Lucy could not be sure so she wandered over to buy some fish.

"All filleted, Miss. All done at Bethlehem Farm."

Astounded, Lucy scrutinized the man holding up a fillet of fish. "Bethlehem Farm?"

"Right good place, Bethlehem Farm."

"Indeed. I'll take six." Lucy looked over to the vegetable stall and saw that Mr Hendon had finished and was looking around for her. She beckoned him over. At the same time, the man behind the vegetable stall was beckoning her. This time there could be no doubt that he was Daniel. From this distance she could see that a black and white dog was lying by his feet. She strolled towards him, passing Hendon on his way to pay for the fish.

His voice was no longer disguised when he said, "Good morning, Lucy. Do you know the song of the linnet?"

What a strange way to start a conversation. "I believe I do. It's very melodious and they twitter when they are in flight."

Daniel softly whistled the song of the linnet. "When you hear a linnet, will you check and see if I'm around?"

One Dark Night

Even in those old clothes, he exuded an indefinable charm. What was it about him that made her stomach flutter, her heart pound and her face flush? Somehow she must remember that he was just enjoying playing with her. Hadn't his own mother warned her? "I thought you said you'd be returning to Bethlehem Farm?"

"All in good time, Lucy, and not before I have to."

She wanted to ask him who the girl was that his mother referred to but all she could say was, "I'm being watched all the time and I shall be in trouble if I talk to you."

"You're not talking to me, you're talking to a common trader. That revenue man is none the wiser and one of my men is keeping him busy with his fish." He pushed his hat back and a lock of white blond hair fell over his eyes but not enough to conceal the look he gave Lucy. "I'll see you again. Bethlehem Farm, though nearer to the Merrygate market, is not too far from here."

On the way back to Watch House, despite trying to be wary of Daniel and despite the cold, Lucy's heart was singing and full of goodwill for all. She asked if she might be allowed to stop at her mother's cottage.

"No more than a minute or two," he said. "We've been gone nigh on two hours already."

"I'd ask you in, Mr Hendon, but Mrs Yorton is not expecting company." She did not add *and will likely bite your head off.*

Mrs Yorton could be heard singing in a clear, sweet voice as she attended to the shrubs that grew either side of the front door. On seeing Lucy, she attempted to pick up a rose bush in a tub and said with a faint smile, "Give me a hand with this. I want it round the back."

Lucy was relieved that her mother sounded happy. Not caring, of course, but not bad tempered. "I've only a minute or two, mother. I've been to the market and I asked to call in and see how you are."

The two women struggled with the tub until Annie Yorton was satisfied with its position. "I manage. It's Lieutenant Thorsen who's found me a good boy to help with the chores. You left without a word."

"I was told not to return home and the Lieutenant said he'd explain to you."

One Dark Night

"Well, you've left me and now you've not a care in the world. Everything provided for you while I have to struggle on."

"When I get paid, mother, I will bring you something."

Annie Yorton was well practised in depriving Lucy of what was hers by right. "I should think you would! Go on, go back to your warm house and don't you worry yourself about me, I'll manage somehow." She was also accomplished in the art of sarcasm.

Lucy went through the back door and into the room at the front. A good fire was blazing in the hearth and a pot of bubbling stew hanging over the top. By the front door stood her mother's old pair of boots, muddy, wet and sandy. Perhaps she was having to collect driftwood herself now. "Have you been to the beach, mother?"

"No. What makes you say that?"

"Your boots." Lucy pointed to them. "I thought maybe…"

"Well you thought wrong."

Lucy doubted the truth of her mother's denial for there was even a telltale white ring of sea salt around the toecaps.

Chapter Nine
Daniel
"I'm not asking you to lie"

On the day Daniel decided he'd see Lucy at the market, he and Josh first visited Tommy Smith well before the dawn.

"Morning, Tommy."

Tommy Smith, still in his night clothes, looked worried. "What's up, Dan?"

"Nothing. You can go back to your wife and have a lie in."

Tommy was not yet properly awake but grasped that he'd better pay attention. "Go back to bed? Sounds good, but I've got customers to visit. Watch House this morning. I daren't be late for them. Is something wrong?"

"Well the wheel's come off your cart and you can't get it fixed until tomorrow. Understood?"

"Ah, right. Well seeing as it's you who found me that particular good customer," Tommy put his finger to his nose, "I'll be happy to oblige."

"Your wheel's round the back."

"What! You've really taken it off?"

Daniel grinned. "Of course. I'm not asking you to lie." He handed over the bolts.

"You're a strange one – not that I mean you're…"

"Aye, I know, Tommy. And don't forget, it can't be fixed until tomorrow."

"That's all right by me and, in this weather, my veg will keep until tomorrow, no problem at all, Dan." His face told a different story.

"Got a good supply?"

One Dark Night

"Yeah. That Fagg woman, you know, fisherman Fagg that was, his widow, she works up there. Told me she'd nigh on run out and would need *a lot* today."

"Yeah, there's a dozen reinforcements on their way," said Daniel laughing. Tommy Smith was a successful businessman in a small way, which was all anyone could hope for round here. "You can take a hand cart round the village but send a message to the Custom House – you can't go today, the wheel's come off." Daniel tossed him a coin. "Don't want you losing out, Tommy."

Everyone knew that reasons would never be given by Daniel and so there was nothing further to say. And Daniel knew it was better to ensure that if his cart was inspected, the wheel would be found to be definitely *off*.

~

Soon after, Daniel was in the kitchen of Jerusalem Farm having had eggs, freshly baked bread and a tankard full of Bess's creamy milk. Whenever he came home he couldn't help but compare the two farms. Here there was one cow, some chickens, a few sheep and the rest was arable land, often lying fallow longer than it should. Over at Bethlehem, four times the size, a whole herd of cows grazed the acres with a flock of sheep, and pigs and chickens – layers and broilers, also donkeys and a cart horse for heavy work. He'd bought a horse for himself too, cost a fair penny but worth it. The crops at Jerusalem didn't compare favourably either. His poor Ma. She never had more than eighty pounds a year after they'd paid the pitiful wages of the feckless lot of labourers. Still, her brother had helped them out of trouble when trouble came calling. His father would have had to put the farm up for sale if his uncle hadn't stepped in. He was the kind of big brother every woman should have.

The deal was that Jerusalem Farm was sold to his uncle so the revenue men would be unable to seize it if things went wrong for his father who, as a result of his worsening gambling and drinking, was getting very careless. In consideration for this, a sum of money changed hands, sufficient to pay his father's debts, and Daniel had promised to move to Bethlehem Farm to help uncle Fred, who'd lost a leg in the war

One Dark Night

and had no live children now. Not that anyone knew this except the close family. His father still held his head high as a landowner.

Daniel liked to run this through his mind when he came home, it gave him a feeling of security that few around here could lay claim to. Then, of course, there was the other income, the one that threatened to spoil it all. Yet how could they, and their labourers, manage without it?

"Time, Dan, time." The thumping on the door put an end to his thoughts.

Daniel, wearing the oldest clothes he could find – some of his father's – opened the door and clicked his fingers for Josh to heel. "Fiddle saddled?" Daniel grinned.

"Aye, he's tethered over there," the man pointed to a dilapidated gate to the hen house.

"Good man. And, if anyone asks where I am, you know nothing. Understand?"

"Yeah, Dan, you know I'll always keep my mouth shut. Miller's already set off 'cos he's on foot, of course."

"While I'm gone, see what you can do to fix the gate. The foxes are getting bolder."

Daniel mounted, whistled to Josh, and set off towards the Brookington market. Josh, a long-haired, silky crossbreed usually ran ahead on longer jaunts and then doubled back every now and then to check his master was still following. Daniel gave the blackbird whistle if Josh was needed and the two of them had this satisfactory understanding of what long walks were all about. But this first part of the journey was on open land and Josh had no chance of running ahead for Daniel loved nothing better than to let his horse run at full gallop.

After a short while, Daniel reined in Fiddle and took the path through Brookington Wood, which wasn't much bigger than a copse. Nevertheless, it provided, as Daniel said, "A bit of privacy, Josh, I can't be seen arriving on a fine horse in these clothes. Could betray our plans, eh?" His faithful dog looked up eagerly as Daniel dismounted and tied Fiddle to a tree well within the boundary of the wood. No one would unleash Fiddle; everyone knew who he belonged to. He clicked his fingers and walked off towards the market. "So what d'ya think, Josh?

One Dark Night

Lucy's now in Watch House. Thorsen's smart thinking or not?" It was clear to see Josh loved being a valued friend; his tail wagged all the way to the market stall.

~

An hour later and it was all over. Lucy had bought a good supply of vegetables and he'd established a way to contact her. Daniel had handed the stall back to its rightful owner and everything went according to plan. It had been unlikely Martha would have hastened to the market, there'd been a small possibility they'd send the lad on his own, but for all his smart uniform he was just a boy, so Lucy had come *with* the boy. If she was not interested then she would have found a way not to come. And didn't she look good! If anyone could make his mother's old brown dress look attractive, she could.

Daniel reached the wood, took off his father's old clothes, stowed them in the saddle bags and put on his own. "Right, we'll take the cliff path home and just keep an eye on Lucy. My eye likes doing that." Daniel chuckled. "Good thing it's only you who's got to listen to my ramblings, eh Josh?" Josh barked his approval.

A few moments later Daniel noticed Josh prick up his ears, pause, and turn to look at him. Daniel nodded and gave the sign for him to track the noise. He dismounted and followed. When Josh was sure he'd found something strange, he made a low growling sound, discernible only to those who knew what to listen for. That low growl was now coming from a clump of bushes close to the edge of the cliff. Daniel squatted then crawled along on his elbows to lie alongside the bushes. Josh was peering down his long nose towards two people on the sandy beach below. The chalk cliff wasn't very high here so it was easy to hear their voices with the onshore wind assisting. Their business together was evidently nearly concluded; the man dismissed the woman with a wave.

"Send Lucy back alone if you don't want to come yourself. I can arrange a carriage for her."

It was Annie Yorton who replied. "Never! He's treated me abominably."

One Dark Night

"He has not! He is her father and he has the legal right to Lucy and yet you refuse to bring her even to see him."

"Legal right! Well that may be true but he doesn't know what's right and what's wrong. No, I'm not going back to being a butler's wife and at Mr High and Mighty's beck and call. And you remind Mr High and Mighty that I know enough to ruin him if I choose to."

"Don't threaten, Mrs Yorton. You'll find that a very dangerous thing to do. Were you not content that your daughter was being brought up as a lady?"

"No I was not. How did that ever help me?"

"Be on your way now and make sure you use this money wisely, and take good care of Lucy because you'll be sorry if you don't. You'll be dealing with me from now on and I am not so easy to deceive as Mr Yorton."

Daniel patted Josh's head – the sign for him to crawl quietly away and together they scuttled back to the track where Daniel mounted the grass-munching Fiddle. Whoever that man was, he'd have to leave the beach at some point and return to this track so Daniel decided to hang back. A gentleman, very obviously not from these parts, appeared fifty yards ahead of him on the track and headed towards Brookington. When Daniel reached the spot where the man had joined the track he dismounted, tapped Josh on the snout gently and said, "Not yet, Josh, give it a moment and then track that man down."

Josh did. He tracked him to the Rose and Crown. A pint of ale with the barman and the gentleman's identity was no longer a mystery. Josh was happy to listen to Daniel's chatter as they turned for home. "Not dead, eh, Josh. Lucy's father is still alive. That ol' cow of a mother is a liar and a cheat, by the sound of things. I'd be certain Lucy doesn't get any benefit from that money. Wonder how much?" Daniel spurred Fiddle to a trot. Questions he'd long pondered had been answered but others had been raised. "It explains why she's not like the rest of us. From life in Faefersham Court to working in our scullery. Humbling. Yet she's never complained." Josh ran alongside and barked from time to time, just to let his master know he was listening. "But how come the ol' cow thinks she'll be able to blackmail the renowned Sir William Harper? Or is she already doing that?"

One Dark Night

Chapter Ten
Lucy
"Fumbleduck and dragonpoop"

In the week that followed, Lucy had little time to think of her own problems. She was absorbed in the comings and goings of a dozen extra revenue men. Some were members of the Preventive Waterguard and their cutter was moored in the bay. Instead of dinner for one, Martha had toiled to prepare dinner for all with assistance from Lucy. No other servants had been allowed in to Watch House and both Martha and Lucy were feeling the strain despite Lucy having arranged for some of the work to be sent out to the village. She had asked, the Lieutenant had agreed, but no food was to be prepared other than in the Watch House kitchens. It was "just a conference" Thorsen had said, probably to stop her and Martha from enjoying speculating.

"Oh fumbleduck and dragonpoop," said Martha. "The laundry man has just delivered it all back nice and clean and ironed and what do I find? Scat curled up sleeping on top of it."

Lucy lifted Scat firmly and put her on her cushion by the stove. "Dragonpoop? Martha, you surely don't believe in dragons?" Martha was so easy to tease.

"I tell you girl, there's more to this world than you and I know about." Then, lowering her voice, she whispered, "There's secrets."

Lucy might have dismissed such talk but, despite Martha mostly calling her *girl* she'd learned to admire this loveable little woman. "What sort of secrets?"

"Shush, girl. Well, before you came, I was dusting the desk, the master's I mean, and I saw things I wasn't meant to. Things no one should see."

One Dark Night

"About dragons?"

"You can scoff, girl, but I'm telling you, I saw a map and on that map I saw a dragon. 'twas far across the sea and nothing for us to worry about. But someone's seen them, else why would they show them if not to warn the sailors?"

"I think it must have been a very old map, Martha. It was indeed meant to warn sailors but they know now that America is there, not dragons."

"America? What, where the dragons be?"

"But there aren't any dragons, Martha, really there aren't."

"Oh yes there are. St George fought a dragon for England and I won't have you saying that's not true!" Martha flashed her almost toothless grin. "Besides, what am I going to threaten Scat with if not with dragonpoop?"

Lucy laughed. "Dear Martha, you are a tonic. I hope I don't lose you too." Lucy could feel her colour rising, that slip of the tongue gave away one of the deep fears from her past. Everything had been taken from her. The few belongings which Thorsen had delivered to her when she first arrived were pitiful and served to strengthen her resolve that her life must change.

Unaware of Lucy's discomfort, Martha marched to the stove to warm herself and then, arms akimbo, she said, "I'm not going nowhere. I know what it's like to lose all you've got. When my man was killed, I lost my home too. If it wasn't for Parson Raffles taking care of me, I'd be in the workhouse. I had a proper training with him. I learnt to make sure the lacy delicates were ironed last – when the iron's not so hot. Not that we have any lacy delicates here in Watch House!" She put her hand over her mouth and smothered a giggle. "I learnt... oh well, let's just say I'm lucky to be here and getting better pay, and a roof that don't leak."

"I'm glad you're here, Martha, really glad."

"You got paid all right?"

"Yes, Martha, and it's just as you said, I am paid more than I was at the farm and all my food is free."

"Free? Don't think of it like that. It's you that's not free now."

One Dark Night

Lucy's blood ran cold. Best not to question that today. "I asked the master," oh how she hated to call him that, "if we might still be allowed our time off."

Martha was quick to ask, "What did he say?"

"He said it was important that we did take a little time for ourselves."

"You know this extra pay what we get? I overheard he pays that from his *family* money. Well, sometimes it's difficult not to overhear, especially when that booming great Bigmore takes against him. That Bigmore thinks he can order the master around. But he can't. Our Lieutenant Thorsen's a navy man and Bigmore's a Dragon."

Lucy laughed. "You mean 'Dragoon', Martha."

"I do not! Dragon he is."

"You're undoubtedly right, Martha. I give in." Lucy's eyes sparkled. Martha made life in Watch House so much better than if she were still living with her mother. "So if you can manage alone, Martha, I'm going to Brookington market. I'll be sure to be back by mid afternoon."

"Young Mr Hendon will look after you. Mind you're not late."

Lucy sighed loudly and looked out of the window above her desk. Martha's words still hung in her mind: "It's you that's not free now."

~

As she drew near, the sounds and the pungent smells of the market revived and refreshed Lucy, and the money jingling in the pocket of her brown dress had almost caused her to run all the way. Thorsen had told her when he counted out the seven shillings for her week's work that this was twice what other household servants received and she easily believed him. He'd taken the opportunity though to talk about the standard of dress of both herself and Martha. At the time, she'd resented his interference. He'd said that he expected them to wear a uniform. Did he think they were his revenue men? Only the grandest of households had servants in any kind of uniform dress and then only those who came into contact with the family. Her father, in the Harper livery worn on grand occasions, flitted across her mind. With this sort of money she'd be able to visit him, take the coach perhaps? With luck she'd see Dougie too. He'd be Mister Douglas Harper now. Would he remember her? She'd have to work out if she could get there and back in one afternoon. Twenty miles there and twenty miles back. Would Hendon have to come? Her thoughts whirled; it was too far and it wasn't quite practical yet but maybe sometime soon.

Lucy stood at the edge of the market. Where to start? Then she saw the two girls who liked to torment her, and they had seen her. What did that matter? She had Hendon with her and this time she would not be intimidated by anyone.

Hendon interrupted her thoughts. "Lieutenant Thorsen said I was to remind you to look out for something that might be suitable as a uniform, Miss Yorton."

"It is unlikely I'll find something here, Mr Hendon. We'd need to employ a seamstress for a proper uniform."

"He says if you can get two dresses much the same that would fit, I'm to pay for them." He leaned forward, "I've two guineas on me." He looked uncomfortable as he said, "They're to be blue or grey."

"Blue? You think I can find two the same shade? Oh, not to worry, Mr Hendon, I can but try." The advantages of being bought a new dress, even if it were to be seen as a uniform, gathered pace in her mind. Yes, she would try very hard.

"I have orders to accompany you to each stall. In fact, Miss Yorton, I'll be *grateful* to be by your side. Despite me not being in uniform, I'm getting some hostile looks."

"Yes, we both are. Everyone suspects you're a revenue man and they've always thought I am a spy."

"I think you're right. We've been found out. Watch your pocket, Miss Yorton. We'll be targets for the pickpockets."

Lucy, having shivered most of the winter, had decided that she would buy a cloak, even if it cost everything she had. She looked at her brown dress. Yes Thorsen was right, she couldn't possibly wear the only other dress she had, that awful grey thing, it definitely did not fit. And she couldn't wear this new brown dress every day of the year. She was wearing her old spencer with the extra buttons she'd sewn on allowing her to lace up the front with the ribbon. Now that she had stopped walking briskly, she was cold. Very, very cold. She would buy a cloak first.

She headed for the stall with the oldest clothes and she asked if they had any cloaks.

"Yeah. They're at the end there. Help yourself." The woman preferred to give her time to Lucy's two tormentors making their way to the stall.

Lucy rummaged around and found a reddish brown, unlined wool cloak. It was plain except for the dirty yellow ribbon ties at the neck. They could soon be replaced, she thought. However, there was a three inch tear near the hem at the front corner. A memory surfaced of her embroidering a cushion at Faefersham Court while watching Dougie practice bowling at the cricket stumps. She could repair the tear and disguise it, even improve the cloak, with some embroidery. Hiding her growing sense of triumph, she bought the cloak and had money left over for new yellow ribbons and embroidery silks in yellow and green. Now all she needed was the time to do the sewing. She wrapped it around her; it was long, reaching her knees, and warmer than nothing.

Remembering the instruction to look for uniform dresses, she wandered from stall to stall with Hendon trailing behind. With up to a guinea for each dress, she should be able to find something practical and respectable. She did. A dark grey dress, high-waisted, and long enough to reach her ankles would serve very well over her chemise. But could she find something similar for little Martha? What about this one? It was dark grey cotton with a very faint pattern. Would that matter? It looked as though it would fit Martha, the high waist and flowing material would allow plenty of room for the cuddly Martha to bustle around the stove. If it was too long, she could take up the hem.

Hendon stepped forward, paid, bundled the two dresses together and tucked them under his arm.

"I've finished shopping, Mr Hendon. Was there anything you wanted to look at?"

"How about we treat ourselves to some hot chestnuts? I've a little money left over from the dresses and we…"

One Dark Night

"Oh that would be..." Lucy wanted to say "dishonest", but decided on the more diplomatic "unwise, Mr Hendon. The Lieutenant is bound to ask me the price."

"Then I expect you will answer the truth. But I bargained for a reduction of sixpence for buying the two dresses together. And that means I can buy some hot chestnuts and still be able to give him his rightful change."

Lucy tossed the dilemma around in her mind. Using the money for chestnuts was apparently of small consequence but there could be major undesirable developments – like not having a place to work. An image of Scat came to mind. Once Scat had got her head through a gap, the rest of her slithered through. "Mr Hendon, I worry that he'll think I'm beginning to cheat him and then he'll think I always will."

"Stay there, Miss Yorton, and I will get the chestnuts."

Thorsen could not blame her surely? Yet the fear of losing her newly found security, good pay and congenial company hovered over her. It was like a personal fog: she could never fathom which way to go.

A hand! Someone had their hand in her pocket. Quick as lightning, her own hand lashed out and her nails tore into the skin of the offender.

"Ouch! You cat," the thief screeched. "Get her, Mary, get her! Look what she's done to my hand."

Mary took aim and smashed her fist at Lucy's chin. Lucy stepped back and avoided it connecting hard enough to do any damage. She grabbed Mary's hair and pulled her sideways. The unsuccessful pickpocket bit Lucy's free arm. Hendon dashed to Lucy's rescue but was hampered by the bundle under his arm which he was determined not to drop. The two girls turned on him, thinking they could force him to relinquish the purchases. With one hand and a good kick he defended himself better than the surrounding jackals expected.

Not that Lucy saw – she'd been tugged away through the gathering crowd.

One Dark Night

Chapter Eleven
"In the safety of Daniel's warm jacket"

"What do you think of smugglers, Lucy?" Daniel stopped running but still held on to Lucy's hand as they entered the shelter of Brookington Wood. "Has anyone ever asked you?" He found a secluded position and pointed to the ground for Josh to sit.

Lucy, a little out of breath, stood for a moment before answering, admiring his brown corduroy coat, his black breeches and knee high leather black boots with a brown cuff; he dressed so much better than everyone else and here was a chance to find out more about him. He might be asking her the questions but perhaps they would give her an insight into his thoughts too. "The Bible says we should pay our taxes. Parson Raffles would agree, I'm sure. Smuggling can't be right." She withdrew her hand from his. "I know it's said that everyone's a smuggler round here but that's not really true. We all have proper jobs. I'm a housemaid, you're a farmer. I know there are some who must be smuggling. I think maybe your…"

"Oh yes, there's smuggling, Lucy. You need to know that it's all around you. No one sees it as smuggling – it's free trading. It brings in cloth, tea, gin, brandy, wine, silk and down the west coast, tobacco. Different parts of the country deal with different goods. It's not just a little local industry."

"Tobacco and brandy are not essentials for living, Daniel."

"Neither is silk. They're things that only the rich can afford. The duty on tobacco is four shillings a pound. The duty on brandy and gin is one pound for each gallon. What working man could afford even a glass of brandy? And who is getting the benefit of this wealth? Have you ever thought how the rich acquired their wealth? They should be judged by the means they used to become rich."

How could anyone disagree with that? Respect showed in her eyes as she nodded in agreement but her mind was turning over *one pound for each gallon*. Good heavens above! How could Mr Tynton afford to get drunk? No wonder so many people were making their own ale, foul though it was. Nevertheless, she still tried to defend the law. "Duty is government money. The government needs the money."

"Of course it does. But what does it spend it on? A government is supposed to be working for its people. What does it do for us?" He didn't wait for an answer. "When the war was on, you'd think we farmers could make a good living, what with Napoleon's ships blocking the trade routes and so on but some years ago the wages of farm hands started to get lower because too many men needed the work. And food prices got higher; you remember the poor harvests a few years ago? That drove prices up." Josh, still sitting by Daniel's feet, curled himself up and closed one eye; this was going to be a long wait.

"I know I found it very hard to get a job and I was grateful to your mother when she hired me in spite of your father's objections."

"Ma is a good woman and she could see the problem."

Lucy was quiet. When they'd arrived in the village, Lucy was only eleven and had been turned down for every position she'd applied for. It now occurred to her that no one had wanted a girl with soft hands, who stood tall and looked everyone in the eye.

Daniel watched as she reflected. "It wasn't so bad for our family and Ma tried to keep our farm hands fed by the little money coming in. In some years the sale price of the crops we grew was abysmal. That's a word I used a lot at the time."

Lucy blinked; outwardly she could not respond further. She'd never seen Daniel so passionate about anything before. It was clear she knew so little but she was well aware that few could rely on a regular income.

Daniel took hold of her hand again and she did not withdraw it. "The soil hereabouts is chalky which gives the crops a good flavour. Did you know that not far from here they grow the biggest and tastiest carrots in the whole of England?" He didn't wait for the inevitable "no". "We get little frost – not like further inland. Mid county there's a rich, deep loam – like a good wine with plenty of heart and body. No one in Kent should be hungry."

Lucy felt able to add something she regarded as relevant at last. "I remember the hops growing in the fields and the gardeners saying they 'growed like weeds' which always made me laugh, it was just the way they said it." She wished she'd kept quiet; she felt out of her depth yet Daniel nodded with a smile.

"Well, the price of crops slumped. Rock bottom. No one had any money to buy them so the price fell. Potatoes at not much more than a shilling a bushel, you'd be lucky to get more than that. So what's the point of growing it all? And a fisherman hereabouts doesn't make enough to keep a roof over his head. His wife has to find work too or he has to think of some other way of using his knowledge of the sea to get enough money to buy clothes, often not much better than rags, and food for his family." His eyes became harder as he continued. "There'd been no violence for some years and then, when the war with the French finished, the Preventive Waterguard took on extra boats and men and the number of Riding Officers increased. So, yes, the government has provided jobs – for some. The Riding Officers hereabouts were little more than easily bribed spies until Thorsen arrived." Daniel allowed himself a reflective, wry smile before continuing. "But other returning soldiers and sailors found they needed to do a bit of free trading to help their families. They had to be prepared to face the hangman or be sent to Van Diemen's Land. Waterloo was six years ago and it's getting worse all the time. The government, huh! They just bring in laws to suppress us. Can't have meetings now. A couple of years ago the cavalry charged, killed and wounded hundreds up north. Did you know that?"

Lucy shook her head. How could she know? Her education came to a halt years ago. "How do you know?" Daniel flashed a quick smile but did not answer. Lucy's interest was growing. At last, someone found time to explain what everyone else already knew. There was so much good in Daniel and he knew more than she had ever imagined.

One Dark Night

"There's no work even now for all the soldiers back from the war. The Buffs – fine soldiers to a man. What are they supposed to do? Starve? While the officers return to their lives of luxury on their estates? We farmers can't employ *everyone*. We can feed our own workers but most of the crops must be sold on to London and other towns, else how can we buy stock and pay the wages?"

"Should the men be looking to start their own enterprises?"

"Enterprises? It *sounds* easy, and if it were, do you think they'd risk their lives in smuggling? There's the market traders, as you've just seen, but have a think. Do you reckon they make much more than the labourers? They resort to exchanging mountains of mangel wurzels, fit only for cattle, for just a few small fish. Then some revenue man turns up and starts taking notes of who's doing what."

It was clear to Lucy that she'd not done enough thinking.

"One day, and for me that day cannot come soon enough, I intend to make this corner of England a better place for a man and his family to live. The laws of this Kingdom need looking at. Something needs to change. Taxation is choking the lifeblood out of good men. Womenfolk are worked to early deaths. I'm telling you this because you need to know that for some people *there are no choices.* And there should be!"

Oh yes, she could relate to that. "Have you spoken to Parson Raffles about this, Daniel?"

"On many occasions. He once said that God gave man free will, to choose good or evil, and I told him much the same as I have told you."

"What did he say?" Lucy's face showed her surprise.

"He said that smugglers were the enemy, not only of the law, but they were their own enemy."

"I understand the concept of being one's own worst enemy but exactly what did he mean?"

Daniel looked at her tenderly and said, "Lucy, it is very special to me that I can talk to you like this." He took a deep breath and continued. "Parson Raffles meant that smugglers were making life more difficult for *themselves*. Just think, Lucy, all that energy spent on outwitting the Customs Officers and all the energy the Customs

Officers spend on trying to clap the smugglers in jail. I must find a way to change this."

Daniel still had hold of her hand. "You are betrothed, Daniel, you should not be holding my hand."

"I am holding your hand to keep your attention. And," he turned to face her and took up her other hand, "I am *not* betrothed. Ma's got her eye on Tilda Bolton's good dowry. Ma sees one way to help the family finances: I see another."

"Are you in danger of losing the farm?"

"No. Thorsen is working on it though." He dropped her hand and kicked a few leaves towards the low lying hollow that served to rot down the dying foliage so well. "I'll have to return to Bethlehem for a while, Lucy. Thorsen has his plans and I have mine. Remember to listen out for a linnet – you never know when one might turn up."

Josh, still lying at Daniel's feet with his snout on his front paws, interrupted their discussion with a low warning growl. He peered towards the pathway above. Daniel swiftly muzzled Josh with one hand, pushed down on his rump and swept some leaves over him with his foot. "Shush. Don't utter a word. Listen." Voices could be heard and the sound of hooves. "One horse," he whispered.

Lucy's eyes widened as she saw Daniel's growing alarm when he caught what was being said. With a single movement Daniel cupped one hand over Lucy's mouth and threw the other around her waist as he pulled her to him and they rolled together into the basin of damp, fallen leaves. Partially covered in twigs and leaves, they lay motionless as the sound of men guffawing and swearing came closer.

"Don't listen," cautioned Daniel. "These men are not from round here. Part of the Hurst gang, I reckon. Drunk at this time of the day means they'll be violent and not to be reasoned with."

The voices came closer. "Tie him on," said one. "Then spread out and cover all the paths leading out of the wood, there's enough of us. I'll flay the man who lets this horse out until the job's done – you understand?" There was a low murmur before the man continued with a chortle, "Well look at this, the dirty coward, he's wet…" Daniel instantly covered Lucy's ears so that the next thing she heard was

One Dark Night

raucous laughter mixed with the sound of groaning until the voice continued loudly, "Hey you! You're goin' on a little ride. Now normally we'd wait 'til a dark, dark night but you've been snoopin' on us for too long and catchin' you back there, well, it seems like now's as good a time as any." There was some brutal slapping and sniggering before he continued. "Loosen those ties. We don't want him sittin' up all prim and proper. Now you lot clear off and, remember, no shoutin' and cheerin', this wood's too small. We don't want anyone hearin'. And if the horse comes your way, turn it round and slap him."

"What the horse or him?" The whole gang guffawed.

"Slap 'em both, if you like, but make sure the horse sticks to the paths and gets up a good gallop." And they laughed even louder.

Lucy heard shuffling noises and squabbles over sticks. Then the only sound was the voice taunting the unfortunate man on the horse who periodically groaned. Please God, don't let it be Hendon. Minutes passed. Lucy's heart raced and she hardly breathed. There was a shout. The horse received a whack. It reared and neighed. Lucy raised her head slightly and saw the man lolling from side to side as the horse galloped away erratically. Daniel gently pushed her head back down into the cover of his jacket but not before she saw the man slip under the belly of the horse. The sight of the man's head pounded by the hooves ensured she stayed in the safety of Daniel's warm jacket until he whispered, "It's over."

One Dark Night

Chapter Twelve
"She'd been a fool"

Time passed, spring flowers peeped through the growing grass, and still Lucy said nothing about what she had seen. The sound of the church bells wafted on a light breeze in a cloudless sky, calling all to the Sunday morning service, and reminding Lucy that she had seen evil and done nothing.

"Come on, Lucy. What's holding you up, girl?"

Lucy ran from her bedroom into the hallway where Martha stood waiting. She held out her dress and dropped Martha a curtsey then twirled. "Well, what do you think, Martha? Does it look presentable?"

Martha was acquiring the art of being tactful so she said, "Yes, girl, you've done yourself proud." Lucy stood still while Martha considered her from her feet upwards. "Them new boots was a good buy." Learning to speak grammatically was coming on rather more slowly than Lucy had hoped. "The yellow ribbon brightens up your brown dress real well." There was a pause while she studied Lucy's bonnet. "Well it ain't new, I mean to say, it *isn't* new but it might as well be, you've made it look much better. Those flowers and leaves in the yellow band of ribbons will make all the lads look at you. Oh, Lucy, you look like a beautiful..."

"Cow," said Lucy.

"Cow? Why no, girl, whatever makes you say that?"

Lucy giggled at Martha's astonished face. "I'm all in brown with straw and tufts of grass round my ears."

Martha laughed and resorted to her two favourite words, "Well, girl," she huffed and placed her hands on her hips, "I couldn't find the right word, I know, but you have definitely found the wrong one. You look beautiful. Quite remangled that dress, you have. But you're not thinking of going out without your spencer and cloak are you? 'tis still cold, you know, despite all them daffodils pretending otherwise."

Martha's almost toothless grins were catching and Lucy held out her arms and hugged her.

"Fluttenducks, girl! I don't remember when I was last hugged."

Lucy prevented herself from adding that neither did she, for it would have been a lie. Most nights, after blowing out the candle in her room, she remembered the murder in the woods. She tried to replace her horror and fear with the warm smell of Daniel and the tender hug he had given her before, unseen, he made sure she found Hendon to walk her home. She replayed his feel, his tenderness, and his voice as he said, "Try to forget what's happened and don't let anyone think *you* are a spy. You know I'll not be around for a while but if you need me, let Tommy Smith know when he does his vegetable rounds." And as she tucked herself under the covers, she saw his face, topped with that wonderful, white blond hair, and she smiled, always, for in her dreams, he smiled at her.

Becoming aware that Martha was watching her thoughtfully, she said, "We must go."

"Don't you think that's what I've been saying? Come on, let's get down these stairs. Young Hendon's waiting for us, by the door."

Lucy wished it wasn't necessary for Hendon to accompany her everywhere, yet he had proved his worth at the market. Not knowing what had happened to Lucy, he had searched, not found her, then used his whistle to call up reinforcements. He'd discovered her on the path from the market which bypassed the woods and he was quick to notice she was distressed. Hendon walked with her; two revenue men backtracked to see what had alarmed her. They found nothing of any consequence. Hendon therefore assumed Lucy had been frightened by the attack by the girls and Lucy said nothing to make him think otherwise. It was not until Colonel Bigmore visited a month later that the news filtered through to Martha that one of the revenue men from

One Dark Night

Canterbury was missing and had last been seen near Brookington. No one interviewed dared say exactly when this was.

As they walked to church, Lucy appreciated the fresh, salty smell of the sea, and Martha chattered all the way. She loved the lighter March days.

"We can see more properly these days. Like when you did that embroidery on that tear in your cloak. Don't it look good?"

"It's turned out acceptably well, Martha."

"The master said my grammar had improved when you first got here, but it's slipped back, ain't it? I mean, isn't it?"

"You mean *hasn't* it, Martha."

"It's all so flumming complicated. Would you keep nagging me, Lucy? The master was so pleased and I don't like to let him down. I was better when I worked for the parson because I saw him and his wife more. It made me more careful."

"You really don't need to be anxious about the way you speak. Everything you say can be clearly understood, and it is part of your charm." How fortunate Martha was to have nothing more to worry about than the way she spoke.

"Thank you, Lucy. That's made my day much better."

Lucy changed the subject from Martha's self-improvement scheme to Martha's other favourite subject. "The Lieutenant has many challenges to face." After what she'd seen in the woods that day, she'd begun to realize just how big the problem of smuggling was. "I suppose that's why he seems so aggressive sometimes."

"You know his father was killed in the war, do you?" Martha didn't wait for a reply, she was just getting up steam. "Well, he was a Captain in the navy and a hero too, by all accounts, but in the last few months of the war he was killed." Martha paused for a moment, obviously weighing up whether or not to tell Lucy any more confidences. "The master had followed his father into the navy and, in no time at all, was made up to a Lieutenant. Good man he is, as we know. Well, his father was going back to the family estate, but got killed just days before. Just days!" Martha tripped over one of the many lumps of chalk that lay scattered on the ground, muttered, but continued with increased

One Dark Night

purpose. "There's some that say the master lost his nerve at sea, but I can't see it myself, can you?" She laughed at the absurdity of it. "No there's more to it than meets the eye." She gathered her warm woollen shawl around her and in a whisper said, "I heard Colonel Bigmore say something about him, his father, I mean, being betrayed by his own side." For emphasis, she repeated, "*Own side*. I don't know no more and I daren't ask the master. Lord no, he'd explode like a ship's cannon." Martha gave a little snort and then said, "I know, I know, you're wondering why, if the master was a Lieutenant in the navy, and him being a gentleman and all that, well how come he's just a revenue man now?"

"Yes, Martha, that's exactly what I've been wondering. Why doesn't he attend to his estate? His mother is a widow. Does he have siblings?"

"Sibbells, no, I'd be sure he's honest."

"Brothers or sisters?" Lucy was now well practised in handling Martha's misunderstandings.

"It's as I said." Martha ignored the question. "There's more to it than meets the eye. He don't need this job."

Lucy decided this conversation was far too informative to interrupt with correcting Martha's grammar. A little encouragement to tell more might be useful. "So why…?"

"He's doing it out of," and here Martha took a deep breath and said with pride, "conviction."

Lucy turned to Martha with a puzzled look. "Conviction" didn't sound like one of Martha's words at all.

Martha pulled her woollen shawl tighter round her as if to reinforce confidentiality. "That's what I heard." She leaned towards Lucy. "Well, truth be told, I *overheard* it." She paused, "I can't say no more and I don't want you telling folks about it either. Whether you like him or not, he's all we've got, you and me."

"All we've got?" Lucy had hopes of more.

"Yes, Lucy, he's been a real protector to me and it's clear he's going to look after you as well."

Lucy was silent. She looked over her shoulder and there was Hendon, dutifully keeping an eye on the two of them. Was this

One Dark Night

necessary? Then a reason to guard them became clear. The two girls, the pickpocket and her friend, were lolling against the wall of Bodger's cottage. Hendon increased his pace and escorted Lucy and Martha closely until they turned the corner and were in sight of the church.

To Lucy's horror, her mother was engaged in animated conversation with Thorsen by the lych gate. Martha and Lucy both dipped courteously to the Lieutenant as they passed. The bells ceased ringing and Annie Yorton's voice was still raised. "I thank you, Lieutenant. Just a half hour, that's all." Lucy knew. Her mother needed some work doing or wanted more money from her. She hurried in to take her place in a corner near the back and was thankful Martha always sat with them despite her mother's disapproving looks.

The stone interior was brightened by the many vases of daffodils in every nook; it seemed the entire parish had brought some. Lucy noticed that each had a Bible verse propped up against the base.

"Read that one to me, Lucy, will you?"

Lucy whispered, "In all thy ways acknowledge him, and he shall direct thy paths." Martha looked a little fearful so Lucy squeezed her hand gently. "It's from the Old Testament, Proverbs."

Annie bustled in and moved Martha along so that she could sit next to her daughter. "Be quiet, Lucy."

Lucy was happy to oblige. Her thoughts were taken up with the verse. Oh God, please do direct my paths. When I am not working, and even when I am, all I can think of is Daniel. I know by heart every word he has ever said to me. Yet his father is a smuggler and I cannot get the sight of that poor man on the horse out of my head. I just don't know what to think or which path to take. She became aware that everyone else was now standing to sing the first hymn. She leapt up and tried to sing. She couldn't. Thoughts of the man's head being pounded by the galloping hooves captured her attention. Thorsen was right. He was the one who would stop such outrages. Furthermore, Daniel had never once said he even liked her. Yes, he was kind to her but the reality was she had been poorly paid and he knew this, he'd not contacted her since that awful incident in the woods and he probably had other girls who interested him more. She'd been a fool.

One Dark Night

Chapter Thirteen
"Betrayal cannot be tolerated"

"Mr Hendon, take this stool and you and I can have a chat while Lucy attends to some chores."

Lucy gave Hendon a stool to sit on just inside the front door of her mother's cottage. How her mother had prevailed upon Thorsen to allow her a little time to help with the chores was unfathomable to Lucy. It was also his mistake.

"I've a good store of logs in the back yard, Lucy, but the boy's sick, or so he says, and I need you to carry some through to the hearth."

Lucy didn't reply: her mother would not be listening.

"I have some tea, Mr Hendon, would you like a cup?"

"Tea? Why Mrs Yorton, such a luxury. How kind you are."

"So tell me, Mr Hendon. Is she..." Annie nodded curtly in Lucy's direction, "is she working hard? Not shirking like she used to?"

"There's no chance to shirk at Watch House, Mrs Yorton. Lieutenant Thorsen is strict and expects much of his servants – and there are only two. Lucy must be exhausted every night."

Lucy saw a satisfied smile settle on her mother's face. She picked up the basket she'd bought to help her mother carry just a few logs at a time and took it through to the yard. The cottages were hemmed in at the back by stone walls about four feet in height, high enough to shield the tenants' small vegetable patches from the salty north wind. Just inside the gate was the wood pile. A blackbird sang from the roof of the cottage and a linnet from the other side of the wall. The blackbird increased his efforts; the boundaries of his territory must be broadcast. The linnet was not intimidated and sang louder too. Linnet! Lucy peered over the wall. "Daniel!"

"Perhaps I should have made our secret call a seagull?"

Josh sat up, tail wagging, and clearly hoped for a pat of welcome.

"Don't stand up, Daniel, my mother's here."

"I know, don't worry. Take in some logs and then come through the gate and sit down beside me."

Lucy was quick to return yet could not disguise her annoyance at his long absence. It made a nonsense of the words he'd said to her: "stay close". Huh! "What are you doing here, Daniel?"

"You don't think Thorsen can keep me away, do you?"

"Thorsen?"

"Some time after I last saw you, he and half a dozen of his men came to see me at Bethlehem Farm. Well, *threaten* is the word."

"Threaten? What about?"

Daniel took hold of Lucy's hand and Josh nuzzled up to her. "He wanted to know what had happened to one of the revenue men who had not been seen for a while. At first he was polite and asked questions which might be expected in that sort of situation."

Lucy clutched Daniel's hand hard. "The man died? No chance of him having lived?"

"No. Turns out he has a wife and four young children. I'd have liked to help out but..." Daniel tailed off, sighed loudly, then continued. "Thorsen's parting shot was that if he found out I had anything to do with it, I'd go the same way as my father will."

Unbidden, Thorsen's words to her flashed through her mind: "Farmer Tynton will hang and I shall be the one to do it." Daniel probably didn't know Thorsen's sworn intentions so, as innocently as she could muster, she asked, "What does he mean?"

Daniel ignored the question. "He added that if he ever caught me anywhere near you, he'd arrest me for spying."

Lucy felt a shiver run through her which had nothing to do with the chilly wind from the sea. "I suppose he's within his rights to think that we might be discussing what is happening at Watch House."

"I don't need to ask *you* if anything is happening up there."

Lucy withdrew her hand from his. "Daniel, I cannot get over what happened to that poor man on the horse. Thorsen is only trying..."

One Dark Night

"I don't think that is his only purpose in forbidding us to meet. Josh knew that too, didn't you, Josh?" The dog wagged his tail. "As Thorsen mounted his horse, Josh could not help but set up one hell of a din. Thorsen's horse is uncommonly calm, known for it, beautiful black beast, so Josh had to do something more. He attempted to nip its fetlock. Very brave. The horse, Midnight its name is, reared. Thorsen was nearly thrown." Daniel's grin reflected the satisfaction he felt and he picked up Lucy's hand again. "However many times you take your hand away from me, I shall pick it up again." He winked: she blushed. "Go now, or your mother will be out looking for you. I want you to remember though, that for every day I am away," Lucy noticed he did not say *from you*, "I shall be working to fulfil my plans." He squeezed her hand and looked straight at her. His tender blue eyes kept Lucy rooted until he leant towards her: he was going to kiss her.

"I must go," she said, standing up, *before I let him.*

~

The following Sunday, the last in March, Karl Thorsen grasped Lucy by her shoulders and said, "You understand what I am saying, Lucy? We are Riding Officers and we uphold the law. You cannot be employed by me if you associate with felons or lawbreakers of any kind."

Lucy felt her stomach churn. She could not hold his stare any longer and lowered her eyes. She was not at all sure what a felon was but she just knew this included Daniel.

"Lieutenant, I have never sought Daniel out." She could say this with conviction – it was true. Besides, if she wanted to eat and have a roof over her head, she had no choice at all so it was easy to add "Neither shall I do so in the future."

"Betrayal is not to be tolerated. Lives are at stake. Yet last week your mother asked me if you might be allowed to spend a little time with her doing some chores."

Lucy returned his stare as well as she could. "I was there about half an hour, fetching wood and washing some dishes. My mother said she had not felt well that morning." With increasing confidence she reminded him that Mr Hendon had been in the cottage too.

One Dark Night

"Indeed he was. But that did not stop you having a clandestine meeting with the younger Tynton, did it?"

Lucy's stomach lurched. Was she about to lose everything? Just when she had begun to have some money to spend on herself and was in control of how much she gave her mother, this had to happen. And it wasn't even her fault. "I did not know Daniel Tynton was going to be there, Lieutenant."

"If I catch him hanging round you again, I'll ensure it's the last time." To be certain she understood, he repeated "Betrayal cannot be tolerated."

"I shall never betray your trust in me, Lieutenant." She had no choice and betrayal was not something she would contemplate anyway.

"This morning, after church, you and Martha are to return together, escorted by Hendon, is that clear?"

It was perfectly clear and it was also perfectly clear that someone had betrayed her and Daniel. "Yes, Lieutenant." Those two girls standing by Bodger's cottage – they were the most likely snitches.

"And we shall both escort you *to* church."

Martha and Lucy set off to walk to church closely followed by Hendon, and Thorsen on Midnight. Martha's usual chatter was subdued and Lucy felt as if she were a dog being taken for a walk on a rope. It was Martha who broke the silence. "Your mother's cottage has got the best name."

"Best?" queried Lucy.

"Well, there's Bodger in India, that's to remind us where the tea comes from. Then there's Van Diemen's Cottage – oh what dreadful shivers that gives me." Martha gave a good demonstration of a shiver. "Oh girl, yes, shivers. I remember when that young lad, no more than seventeen he was, got sent to the penal colony out there. His mother was sick and he'd taken a chicken, maybe two or so. Dreadful time. His mother died, you know. Expect he did too."

Hendon caught up with them and coughed before he spoke. "If he'd put his mother in the workhouse, she'd have got treatment in there. They always give them a bed and look after them. Besides, he took a whole sheep too. Far more than their needs."

One Dark Night

Lucy glanced over her shoulder. Maybe he was right. Maybe the workhouse would have been better. The sick were usually given good care. Nevertheless, sending a young man to an island off the coast of Australia was very harsh – it was the other side of the world! She looked up at Thorsen. He merely gave a slight nod of approval. No sympathy there and it allowed Hendon to add that if a young villain turned from his thieving ways and did his time, he could make an enviable life for himself, albeit it a long way from home and family.

Martha ignored the argument for penal colonies and returned to her line of thought. "And then America Cottage, and they're having problems, *skirmishes* and such."

Lucy watched Martha smile; she was evidently pleased with herself for using this particular description which was undoubtedly an overheard comment.

Martha continued. "Though I'm told it's a land full of *good* people. Pilgrims and…" She thought for a moment and clearly couldn't enlighten her listeners further so said, "And then your mother's cottage – China. What comes from China?"

Lucy considered for a moment. "We should not be short of a cup of tea, Martha, because China sends us tea too, I think." She tried to remember what she had learnt about China and envisaged herself with Dougie sitting on the lawns with their tutor. Suddenly a colourful sight popped into her head: at the end of the Summer Ball they would have fireworks. "Fireworks, Martha. They come from China. Imagine if they were carrying those, they could set some off over the ocean, what a sight, they'd be able to see for miles. With all the rockets they'd be carrying they could turn night into day." Lucy thanked Martha for being her own personal firework.

"And what do you mean by that, Lucy?" Martha was clearly unsure if it was meant as a compliment. "Do you mean I make a lot of noise?"

"Oh no, Martha. You are someone who lifts the mood. You sparkle and turn night into day." Lucy looked over her shoulder when they reached the church. Hendon was still close behind but Thorsen had stopped outside China Cottage and was absorbed by his thoughts.

Parson Raffles radiated a kindly authority as he began his sermon.

One Dark Night

"Our text for today is taken from Deuteronomy chapter seven. 'The Lord thy God, He is God, the faithful God, which keepeth covenant and mercy with them that love Him.'" He lowered his head so that he now had several chins and he began his customary wandering from the pulpit. "We are all set on this earth for a finite time." He turned to face the altar and raised his arms high. "God has given us the gift of life." He reeled round to face the congregation and boomed, "What you do with that life is your gift to Him. You can make the most of those years or you can waste them. The choice is yours."

Parson Raffles never bored his congregation. The pews were always full and lately even the aisles at the back were crammed with labourers standing. In the silence that followed, Lucy remembered how humble the parson had been when Thorsen commented on this to him. He'd laughed and said there was no other entertainment in the village.

"Do you pursue the seven virtues: charity, faith, fortitude, hope, justice, prudence and temperance?" He lowered his voice as if what he was about to say was deeply disgusting. "Or do you pursue the seven most deadly sins?" Again he paused to allow the congregation to take in the meaning of his words and, it seemed to Lucy, in order to give them some hope of recalling what the seven deadly sins were.

"Before we contemplate these virtues, I want to ask you a question. God is faithful. Are you loyal to him? Or do you betray his faithfulness to you?" He looked at his congregation with what appeared to Lucy to be deep distrust. "Betrayal. Are you in agreement with God's guidance on Sundays and then, for the rest of the week – betrayal?"

Silence reigned throughout the building. Not a soul dared move and Lucy felt condemned. The word that stood out to her was not *virtue* but *betrayal*. She was taking the protection and security of Lieutenant Thorsen but defying him all the time. The excuses she had made to herself did not hold up when confronted by the certainties of this man of God. Lucy felt a little shaky as she remembered the scene she had witnessed in the wood. Was it wrong to be too afraid to tell what she had seen? There was no doubt about it, smuggling gangs were violent and therefore evil. The ribbon of her bonnet felt too tight as Parson Raffles dramatically illustrated the need to hold on to the good. She felt

One Dark Night

she would choke and just when he paused, as he so often did, and the silence of acute expectation was almost tangible, she spluttered, coughed, and in deep embarrassment, fled from the church.

She ran past the stained glass windows through the graveyard at the back and hid behind a tall gravestone, her thoughts pounding in her head. She should have told Thorsen what she had seen in the wood. Should she tell Daniel that she must never see him again; that he must never speak to her? Daniel had told her that some people have no choices – had she not been like that just a short while ago? But now the words of Thorsen rang in her head, *You have to choose which way your life is going*. She needed time to think and her sanctuary, not visited very often now, was only a short distance away. She was about to dash away when, from behind her, Daniel tapped her on the shoulder. She had not heard him coming but here he was with his arms around her, gently wiping a tumbling tear with his thumb. He didn't pour words of sympathy, he simply comforted her.

A moment was all they were allowed before Daniel urged Lucy to run. "Quickly, hide in your place on the cliffs."

Stunned and frightened, she gathered up her skirt and fled. She clambered over the low graveyard wall and fell to the ground. Thorsen! Had he seen her and Daniel together? She must get to her sanctuary without being seen. She watched as Thorsen marched up to Daniel who was nonchalantly leaning against the gravestone. He had expertly attracted Thorsen's attention away from the fleeing Lucy enabling her to crawl to her sanctuary. She ducked down behind the long grass, peeping out like a little mouse in a hole. Had he seen her? He was now pointing towards the cliff edge.

Daniel followed Thorsen onto the cliff top and they faced each other.

"Now we're no longer on holy ground we'll finish this once and for all." Thorsen took off his coat and flung it on the grass.

Lucy could hear every word, thanks to the offshore breeze. It was at this point that she noticed Hendon watching from the lych gate.

"Are you saying I am not allowed in the church?"

Lucy could not believe what she'd heard. Had Daniel been in the church?

One Dark Night

"Don't waste my time, Tynton. When did you last go to church?"

"Why, this very morning. Parson Raffles has words of wisdom for me as well as for you." Daniel watched Thorsen's scepticism flood his face. "Life is the gift of God."

Thorsen scoffed. "The Tynton family had better make the most of the little they've got left."

Daniel looked unconcerned. He was slightly taller and had the physical advantage of a muscular frame developed by years of manual labour. Lucy's mind flitted to Daniel's last words to her: how long had he known about her sanctuary? She returned to concentrating on the developing feud. Very slowly, Daniel unbuttoned his jacket. There was only one button left and it was clear he was tormenting Thorsen.

Karl Thorsen waited no longer and landed a heavy punch upwards on Daniel's jaw. Daniel slipped out of his jacket and tossed it away. Still he showed no interest in fighting.

"You've been given many a warning. Stay away from Miss Yorton. Your intentions towards her, like every other girl you've come across, are unlikely to be honourable."

Daniel snapped, "You know nothing of my intentions and you have no right to tell me who I may associate with and who I may not."

Lucy was astonished. Daniel spoke authoritatively and with no trace of deference or fear.

Thorsen, having moved back, now moved in closer. "Miss Yorton has been told not to associate with anyone who might regard her as being able to pass information on customs' matters. In particular – you. By waylaying her at every opportunity, you are compromising her status as a servant at Watch House. Would you have her return to that scheming crow of a mother?"

"I have never asked her for information. You will never find evidence of that."

"Don't give me that bull! You think I don't know what you get up to? You think I don't know that Smith, on his vegetable rounds, is also in your pay?"

"What you think and what you can prove to be true are very different," Daniel said with confidence.

One Dark Night

"Oh I'll prove your thieving ways, Tynton. You'll go the same way as your father."

This threat did not appear to trouble Daniel. "You have my word that I will not seek to involve Miss Yorton in anything unlawful."

Thorsen spat out his response. "Your word? The word of a Tynton? The murdering, thieving, crooked scum of the land!"

"My mother is none of those." Daniel, having drawn closer to Thorsen almost imperceptibly, landed a punch which seemed more of a rebuke than a provocation.

Lucy cupped her hand over her mouth and her eyes stared in disbelief as Thorsen let rip. He tore into Daniel with such speed that Lucy could hardly bear to watch. But Daniel, though not as fast on his feet, was clearly not unused to a fight for he parried all of Thorsen's swings. Thorsen stood back for a moment as if reassessing his opponent. Lucy knew that if he could have challenged Daniel to a gentleman's fight, his sword would soon have settled the matter. Martha was always saying he was a champion swordsman; she would jump around the kitchen with the broom in demonstration of his swordsmanship and Lucy would seize the mop and they would laugh until they cried. Now here was Thorsen fighting in reality but with just his fists. He lunged at Daniel with his head lowered and landed a heavy punch that knocked him off balance. There was no mercy being shown on either side now, and Thorsen followed through with punch after punch. Daniel was not easily able to defend himself as Thorsen had boundless energy pushing every blow, but eventually he went on the offensive. He kicked out with his foot on to the side of Thorsen's knee and down went the aggressor with a momentary look of agony.

Lucy was aghast. Should she run into the church and get help?

Thorsen was up in seconds, clearly in some pain, yet throwing punches again and making up for Daniel's advantage of stature by his hurricane speed at returning Daniel's heavy blows landing on him with increasing frequency. Lucy could see the heat of determination on Thorsen's face which contrasted with Daniel's cold confidence. Then Daniel looked as though he'd decided to finish the fight with one powerful blow. He stood back then threw a straight left at Thorsen with a low, right punch following through. Lucy could not see what caused it but it was Daniel who seemed to stagger, and with a great oath born of pain, he fell clutching his left foot. Thorsen, though clearly in pain himself, stood over him triumphantly, then bent over and said something to Daniel which prompted the response, "You don't tell me what to do. Make sure you know that, Thorsen."

~

Karl Thorsen put his head around the kitchen door, then strolled over to Lucy's table near the window. "I know you were watching, Lucy. From behind a gravestone was it?" Thorsen winked.

Lucy's eyes opened wide. He *winked*. Did that mean he knew it wasn't a gravestone but would keep her secret? "I was glad to see you were not badly injured, Lieutenant." Her real concern was Daniel who had been helped away by two of the labourers from the rear of the church. Lucy had rushed back but was intercepted by Hendon who escorted her home immediately together with Martha. There was no chance whatsoever of finding out what had caused Daniel to suddenly fall.

"Have no concern for Tynton. His injury was no more than a twist of the ankle, I'm sure." He turned to look at Martha. "Something hot and tasty, Martha?"

"It won't be long, master. 'tis rabbit pie."

"A favourite of mine," said Thorsen. "God bless rabbits and the burrows they dig!" He chuckled and raised an eyebrow at Lucy.

One Dark Night

Chapter Fourteen
"She began to feel like a real spy"

It was now the first day of April and a whole week had gone by yet Lucy had heard nothing from Daniel, neither had she dared ask after him when she had been at church that morning. She sat at her desk and looked across to Martha placing jugged pigeons in a boiling pot of water. The steam billowed up the walls and she opened the window by her side and leaned out to take in the fresh sea air and the warmth of the midday sunshine.

"Come here, Jennings; drag another chair over to this table. Good light at this window; warmer too."

Lucy sat very still, she could hear every word Thorsen said. She pulled her window closed because, if Martha were to come chattering near her, Thorsen would soon realize how easy it was to be overheard. Thorsen was on the ground floor, not in his secure office but in the room used by the Riding Officers, and it seemed to Lucy that he was not being as careful as he should be, perhaps preferring the sun-warmed room to his west facing room. She peered through the window towards Wintergate and then saw that jack-of-all-work, Hendon, standing guard some twenty yards away. Of course, Thorsen was not negligent; he was as careful protecting his secrets as a squirrel hiding his nuts.

"You can open that window, if you like, Lucy; I know I'm cooking up a cloud. If you watch it for me, I could get myself twenty minutes or so. Didn't sleep well last night."

This was indeed a spot of luck. "Of course I'll watch it for you, Martha. There's plenty of logs to keep a good fog going for you, though I think you should get yourself a lid that fits better."

One Dark Night

"It'll be a good three hours for them six pigeons but I'll only need half an hour's nap and that leaves plenty of time to do the butter sauce and all the rest." Martha stood for a moment then sighed loudly. "When I'm up, you can take a rest, Lucy. Hope you don't mind me leaving you with the pigeons." Then she plodded off to her room, flapping her arms like a pigeon.

Lucy opened the window again and placed a pot of meadow flowers on the ledge so that she could not be seen by Hendon.

Initially, all she could hear were muffled mutterings. How annoying. Then, catching a few significant words, she began to follow the sense of the discussion. Thorsen was outlining a plan to Jennings and Hooper, two of the three Riding Officers who were permanently billeted at Watch House. She pushed the window open a little wider.

"We three are the only ones who know when and where the next strike is to be. We'll tell the men only hours before and insist that none of them leaves here until it is all over. This is to be the biggest clear-up operation in this part of the country."

"Much easier now we've got Mudge's maps." Jennings chuckled and continued, "Colonel Mudge – what a name. Still, by all accounts ours are better than they've got in the west country."

"You just remember, Jennings, smugglers don't need maps, and their tracks and caves aren't shown, though we can, perhaps, start to mark them on this map in pencil."

Jennings grunted in grudging agreement and Lucy's attention sharpened as she began to feel like a real spy.

"We scuppered their plans last time, didn't we? Good and proper," said Hooper with pride. "Very little got through."

"Unless we capture them red-handed, they will simply move their operations further around the coast," Thorsen spoke in a clipped, determined fashion, then rushed on with "Sydney Tynton has been to Hyrne five times in the last few weeks. He can have no farming business there." Then he reverted to his clipped speech for emphasis. "From what local sources tell me, the landing will be on the next dark and that's tomorrow." Having allowed the two men time to absorb the

One Dark Night

urgency of their plans, he said, "And it's going to be here, right in front of our noses."

"What, Wintergate Bay?"

"Yes, Jennings. Wintergate Bay."

Jennings and Hooper were silent.

"They must be planning some sort of staged diversion to lure us *all* away. The demise of that poor man caught on his way to me has meant I don't have any firm information."

Lucy froze.

"He'd heard that the Hurst gang, yes the contemptible Hurst gang, has been revived, and they were coming to see Tynton. He'd sent a message to me to say he would divulge his findings when we met up, but, of course, that didn't happen. It does add credence to this being one of the biggest landings they've made for a long time."

There was a short silence and this allowed the disturbing scene of the galloping horse to seep into Lucy's mind yet again.

"Mate of mine he was, on the 'Conquest'. We served together for some years. I'll not let his death go unavenged."

"Jennings," said Thorsen, "That's for another time. His bloodied body has been returned to his family and that's all we can do for now. But be sure," and once again he returned to the staccato fashion he used for emphasis, "not one of those who has caused the death of a King's man will live to see old age!"

Lucy suddenly remembered the pot on the stove. Carefully she crept away from her desk and filled a jug of water, topped up the boiling pot a little at a time, and put two logs on the fire, then slipped back to her place by the window.

"Ah!" said Jennings sounding pleased and a little triumphant. "It's beginning to make sense now. I've heard that Ravensgate has been mentioned several times at the 'The Bear' in the last week or so. Perhaps that's where they intend to lure us."

Thorsen responded. "Possibly. We'll just need to fake that we've fallen for their bait and then we can really catch them at it. The Tynton family will be missing a couple of members after this." The note of satisfaction in his voice could not be missed. "I haven't seen young

One Dark Night

Tynton since last Sunday but I think he's just keeping clear of me after our confrontation. He's at his own farm once again so I'm sure he'll be involved in this. He's the one with the brains, the planner."

Daniel! Was he really the man who planned these violent operations?

"No need for anyone to be afraid. We – that is you, Hooper, and Jennings, Hendon, myself and, to make it look as though we really believe it, we'll take the reserves from the village, Miller, Watkins and Rogers. The seven of us will ride out as if we're fleeing a swarm of bees."

"But what about Miller and the others? They can hardly flee from bees on their donkeys!" Jennings was not at all convinced this was a good idea.

"Leave the thinking to me, Jennings. Yesterday I made a show of equipping them with ponies. Tomorrow, once it is dark, the Dragoons will ride as far as the other side of the bay and lie in wait."

Lucy hardly dared breathe, all she could hear were some indiscernible mumblings until Thorsen spoke again.

"Only we three and Colonel Bigmore know the plan. Keep it that way. Go about your usual duties. All further preparations will be made in my office and no one, not even you two are allowed in there until early tomorrow evening." Thorsen chuckled in a self-satisfied manner. "Right then, this is to be the end of the Tynton family's smuggling racket."

What Lucy heard next goaded her into action.

One Dark Night

Chapter Fifteen
"Daring to steal my future"

Echoes of Thorsen's words resounded in Lucy's head. "They are not to be killed during the raid. I want to see them both hanged: father for murdering my father and son for constantly defying the forces of good. Indeed, more than that – for daring to steal my future. I want to see the father hanged and gibbeted and I want the son to witness that before he too is hanged."

How could she have been so naïve? It was obvious to all that Daniel's family were the leaders of the smuggling around here and Daniel was the planner. Smugglers were murderers. Smugglers were law breakers. All that she had seen and heard at Jerusalem Farm fell into place. Of course, she had known of the smuggling, but she had not realized just how much it pervaded this village. More than that: this whole county. They were cruel. She paused as all this and more raced through her mind.

Yet still she was changing out of her grey uniform dress and white frilled apron and into the brown frock Daniel's mother had given her. Still she put on her boots because Thorsen's words showed him to be cruelly vengeful and he was bent on killing Daniel. For what? Daring to steal his future? Whatever that means, it cannot be a hanging offence. When Martha came in to the kitchen just as she was lacing her boots, she took a deep breath, smiled and said, "Martha, I want to go for a long walk. I want to enjoy this sunshine while it lasts." For good measure she added, "It may rain tomorrow and I shall have missed it."

"Fluttenducks, girl, you deserve some sun. I'll take care of them pigeons and get the vegetables ready. Bring me back some herbs; I'll say the birds needed some and that will mean you don't need someone

One Dark Night

to go with you!" She said it triumphantly; perhaps she, too, sometimes longed to escape Watch House.

Lucy hugged her. "Martha, you are a joy to work with. I'll bring as many herbs as I can."

"I thought I'd do a byllasub too. Always looks good, that does."

"Syllabub, Martha, it's called a syllabub."

"Of course it is. Did I not say that?"

Lucy tucked a note she'd written into her pocket and, unable to stop herself, she asked the question that was troubling her. "Martha," Lucy hesitated, she was not sure she wanted her suspicions confirmed. "What does being hanged and *gibbeted* mean?"

"Oh! 'tis terrible, girl, terrible. They wrap them up in chains tightly and then hang them, and the bodies get left for days, months even, and the crows come and peck…oh 'tis terrible." Martha wrung her hands as she spoke. "What makes you ask such a question?"

Lucy felt every muscle in her body tense, she could hardly reply but she must say something. "I just wasn't sure, that's all, Martha."

Lucy forced herself to walk, first to the woodpile, where she kept watch on Hendon. Surely he would not be there for much longer? A sharp whistle from Watch House attracted his attention and he glanced around him, observing the whole landscape, then briskly strode to the door. Oh please God, let him go inside. He did, but she must hurry.

Not until she was out of sight and across the road that ran from Brookington to Merrygate did she stop running. Jerusalem Farm was still a mile further on, and it would be unwise to use the roads, so, despite being hampered by the mud, she set off across the field lying fallow because its hedge provided some protection from the gossips and spies.

Daniel's words were uppermost in her mind now. She remembered the awful day when that poor man had been killed by the pounding hooves of the horse. Yes, a few smugglers were violent. But prior to that, Daniel had taken such care to explain why some were forced to smuggle. He was as shocked and repelled as she was by what happened. He did not deserve to be hanged – of that she was sure and he would never be involved in murder. His actions saved lives – saved people from starvation.

As she reached the other side and stepped onto the road that passed the farm, she saw in the distance a rotund figure with a large hat. Parson Raffles. Why is he, of all people, right here in her path? As they drew closer together, he tipped his hat and Lucy felt her resolve waver. Had the parson been sent by God to stop her?

"Good day, Miss Yorton. Are you enjoying a walk in the afternoon sunshine?"

"Yes, I am looking for herbs." She had not lied but she could see he did not even consider this to be the whole story.

"You look a little flustered, Miss Yorton. Are you comfortable working at Watch House?"

How kind; he'd phrased his question in a way she could answer truthfully. "Oh yes, I have been very comfortable, thank you."

"And Lieutenant Thorsen? Is he looking after you well?"

Lucy hesitated before answering. Now she realized his words were like needle pricks. "He has been…he…" her hesitation and tone were giving away her feelings. She must be careful. "I have been fed very well and it is so much warmer working indoors than in the fields." If he had been sent by God, then perhaps she should ask for his guidance. "The Lieutenant is very serious about his duties."

"He has a very serious duty to fulfil. If a good man does nothing to hold back the tide of evil, then we might all drown."

Would the parson understand about the threat to Daniel? Tentatively she said, "He pursues his aims ruthlessly."

Parson Raffles stretched to his full height and breathed in deeply. "I have known Lieutenant Thorsen since we were both children. Karl Thorsen was always of outstandingly good character and he was destined to go to sea, like all his forebears. Viking blood, you see. Have you not wondered why he has the continental form of Charles?"

"Karl?"

"Yes. His father was Karl before him. Centuries back they all settled around Faefersham where he has…I digress." Mr Raffles returned to his theme. "Alas, a tragedy forced him to reconsider his career at sea. Yet he makes a very fine upholder of the law of the land, don't you agree?"

"The law? Well yes, I suppose he does. But I don't think the law is always right, Mr Raffles, and those who follow the law are not necessarily the kindest of people." Not only was she thinking of Karl Thorsen, she also thought of her mother – she always said she upheld the law but Lucy could not respect her mother's choices. Her decision to leave Lucy's father had meant that Lucy had been nearly destitute for the last few years. From a world of books, fine music and good company, she was now walking in a field of mud and along a road to a smuggler's farm, dressed in an old brown frock. Her mother's decisions took no account of those around her. Lucy resolved not to be swayed by the parson and his respect for the law.

Parson Raffles had paused to watch Lucy fighting her inner battle. "That's true, Miss Yorton. Laws through the ages have not always been morally right. Sometimes the law has been used for the benefit of the few and to the detriment of the many." He raised his eyebrows, lowered his chins, and continued in a ponderous manner. "There is essentially a choice to be made. To follow the law in its entirety; to select which laws you deem should be followed and which should not; or," he chuckled loudly, pulled off his hat and threw it in the air, "to follow no laws at all." He caught his hat and placed it jauntily on his head. "There is one further choice and that is to work to change the law for the better, so that it is right in the eyes of God."

Lucy stood silently. She knew so little about the law and what chance had she, as a woman, to devote her life to examining the law?

"The striking fact is," the parson turned and looked her straight in the eyes, "whatever choices we make in life, whether it be about the law, or about who we choose to marry, those choices affect our lives and the lives of those around us – forever. It is *always* more damaging to choose to disobey God's laws and, usually, the laws of the land you have to live in."

Lucy's eyes gave away her indecision. "It is not always easy to decide what is good and what is bad. It's easier for you, Mr Raffles, you are steeped in the knowledge of God's laws. How am I to know whether hanging someone is right or wrong?" Drat! She should not have said that. His acceptance of everyone, good or bad, made him a tempting confidant. "What about if someone does not deserve to be hanged?"

"Let me make it perfectly clear, we make choices in our lives and they then shape our lives for better or for worse and, once we are fully grown, we have only ourselves to blame. Take any guidance you receive with care and weigh it against the holy word of God, time-honoured patterns laid down by Him, and the direction of those who understand these things." Parson Raffles lowered his head as if humbly offering his service. "I am ready to listen to anyone and anything." He then placed his hands behind his back and rocked backwards and forwards on his feet, peering down at her.

Deep in thought, Lucy took a moment to respond. "I can see that if you do something which is certainly wrong and you know that the punishment is hanging then you should only blame yourself. But what if you consider that it is not wrong, but the law says it is?"

"Laws, for the most part, are for the common good." He took her arm, turned her around and began to walk with her back the way she had come. "If we perceive the law to be unjust, then it is wise to keep within that law but work to change it. There's no way we can change the law if we are dead!"

Into Lucy's whirling mind jumped Daniel's words to her in Brookington Wood. *I must find a way to change this.* She knew now for sure what she had to do: it was being made clear that if he were to be hanged, he could not work to change the situation of men fighting each other instead of getting on with improving the lives of those around them. She must hesitate no longer but she was now being shepherded by the parson away from the farm.

The parson stumbled over a stone and released Lucy's arm. "I believe there is something more I must say to you, Miss Yorton. It is this: I cannot make a decision for you because I do not have all the facts needed to take that responsibility."

"Mr Raffles, thank you for your words." Lucy curtsied low with an air of purpose and said, "I know what I must do."

One Dark Night

The parson responded with an understanding look in his eyes and an assenting nod. "If you have weighed the choices prayerfully and your choice is in accordance with the word of God, then you must act. And remember, whatever you decide to do, God is the governor of all things. Written in the letter to the Romans are these words, '...all things work together for good to them that love God, to them who are called according to his purpose'."

She began to run along the road towards the farm, she had so little time. Yet the time with the parson had been well spent. Although she found it difficult to weigh both sides of the argument, it was clear she had more information than the parson and her mind was made up. And the last words of the parson made it plain to her that God could overrule if she'd misunderstood because she did love God and she was trying to do what was right.

Less than an hour ago, Karl Thorsen had vowed to hang Daniel 'for stealing the future'. Whatever that meant, it was not a crime. Many a man would be captured tomorrow night for bringing in goods from the continent and making a little extra money to feed their families. She must alert Daniel to the trap and save his life and perhaps he'd be able to save the lives of others. As the parson had said, *there's no way we can change the law if we are dead!*

Lucy slowed to the quickest walk she could manage until the gatehouse of Jerusalem Farm came into view. Her courage ebbed away like the tide. Oh God, help me. How can I deliver this note? Should I walk to the door and knock? What if Daniel is not there? Voices! Whispers. Something about a "batman". Too late, she was caught as she tried to slip into the shelter of the gatehouse.

"What are you doing 'ere?" It was one of the men who'd been *fixing the barn roof.* Huh! She knew better now.

"Oh nothing. Nothing at all, I was just catching my breath for a moment."

"Away with yer, girl. You're not welcome 'ere."

For a fleeting moment, Lucy wondered if she should give them the note to pass on to Daniel. No! She could never trust these rough men and they did not trust her. Somehow she must get this note to Daniel

One Dark Night

and no one else. She lowered her eyes, turned and walked back the way she had come. In her mind's eye, she saw repeatedly the vision of Thorsen gloating over Daniel's dead body hanging from a rope. This must not be allowed to happen. With difficulty, she pushed through the hedge, hid in the ditch, then dashed to the back of the farmhouse. Thumping on the door produced no response, so she tried the latch and pushed the door open. Now where could she hide this note so that only Daniel would find it? Then she saw Josh's bowl tucked away beside the stove.

One Dark Night

Chapter Sixteen
"Thorsen's words haunted her"

The following night, a Monday, Lucy lay in bed unable to sleep. She'd been late back yesterday and her muddy boots betrayed her. Martha had been scurrying around like a lunatic as she valiantly tried to prepare the dinner on her own. Lucy had not even remembered to collect the promised herbs. Today Martha was baking trays of gingerbread, large pies, and loaves of bread. No extra supplies had been ordered in the last few days by command of the master and Martha was extremely proud of having produced a feast from "nothing but a sack of flour and flumpingducks". Lucy had wondered about the *flumpingducks* until she noticed some discarded feathers. Ducks? Long silky grey and white feathers? More like seagulls. As she was trying to make up for her lack of assistance the day before, she'd thought it better not to ask.

Too many thoughts jostled in her head so she got up and went to the window. Black darkness. What a silly thing to say. Yet it described what she saw perfectly. There was no moon, no stars either. A cloudy sky would be perfect for a landing. Inside the familiar grey stone walls of Watch House it did not seem as dark as outside. Disobeying the order to keep all windows closed at night, she opened hers a notch. She listened to the comforting sound of the waves rolling in and swishing as they sank into the sand. Then she saw a movement in the distance. She waited. Nothing further. From her window she could see across to the village but it was in complete darkness, not a single lamp burned, not even the faint flicker of a candle. She could see little of the beach. Thorsen had a commanding view of the sea from his bedroom, and the village and the shore from the connecting sitting room. Now that the window was open and she'd become used to the sound of the waves,

One Dark Night

she could distinguish other noises and then a lamp shone briefly from the window below her. This was the usual way of things; two men on lookout duty every night, able to see the beaches to the west and east of Watch House. This was Thorsen's successful way of clearing the smugglers from Wintergate Bay and beyond.

She shut the window and went back to bed. It must be near midnight and nothing had happened. Sweet relief flooded through her. Daniel had obviously found the note and called off what she had now learnt to call "a run". She snuggled into her pillow and might have fallen asleep, but Thorsen's words haunted her still. *"I want to see the father hanged and gibbeted and I want the son to witness that before he too is hanged."* She hated him. Whatever Martha thought, this man was worse than any smuggler. He was driven by revenge and, rightly or wrongly, he would see that Sydney Tynton would pay a terrible price for his father's death. If Sydney Tynton had murdered Thorsen's father then he should be brought to justice and hanged. Gibbeted? Was that really necessary? And whatever makes him hate Daniel so? She knew too little about Daniel. There was only one thing she was sure of: Thorsen was unrelentingly vengeful and she was relieved that he would not be able to capture Daniel tonight. Sleep beckoned, she shut her eyes, and felt that blessing of all blessings, the closing down of the busy mind.

Lieutenant Thorsen opened Lucy's bedroom door, listened to her breathing, and whispered, "Sleep soundly, Lucy, sleep soundly," then silently left the room.

Lucy opened her eyes. Thorsen! Did he usually do this? Her mind now banished all thought of sleep. What was that? She dashed to the window but could see nothing so she opened it slightly. If the landing *was* going ahead, it would have to be soon because the dawn would be breaking in a few hours. She listened intently but all that she heard was the sound of the swell surging on the shore, crashing and hissing as it broke and retreated. It was hypnotic but she knew now that this was not a night for sleeping. Growing louder was the thundering of a horse's hooves followed by the pounding of fists on the door. Shouts followed from the two Riding Officers conspicuously on duty and then lamps shone from the ground floor windows at the front of Watch House. She heard Thorsen shout "To Ravensgate at full gallop." She watched as Hendon, Hooper and Jennings spurred their startled horses on. Much as she hated him, Lucy could not help but respect Thorsen. Well ahead of the others, Midnight, his black stallion, could not be seen at all, except where Thorsen's pale uniform trousers appeared to be riding by themselves.

It was clear that Daniel had not received the message. The smugglers had sent the messenger to lure the Riding Officers to Ravensgate and Thorsen was playing the part of the deceived upholder of the law. If she was very quick, she could make it to her hideaway on the cliffs before the landing took place and from there she could keep watch and warn Daniel.

Wearing her brown dress with a black shawl wrapped and tied around her head so that only her eyes were visible, she ran along the cliff top until she tripped over an iron stake close to the edge of the cliff on the other side of the bay. Allowing herself no time to consider its purpose, she slowed and crouched, and even crawled when there were no bushes to hide her. She slid down into the haven of her sanctuary, unseen. But not unheard.

"Did you hear something?"

Oh no! Lucy recognized that voice. It was Colonel Bigmore's. The Dragoons must be nearby. Below her, on the shore perhaps.

"Yes, sir, I did." Lucy froze. That was a revenue man's voice.

"Right, pass the signal along and alert the others."

Relieved, Lucy realized they'd mistaken the noise for smugglers on the move. There followed a passable impersonation of an owl hooting. Then fifty yards further along, another "owl" hooted.

"Does the pastor know about the men over at the churchyard?" Bigmore enquired of the local man.

"No, well not officially. He knows we have a job to do and that some of his flock are involved in the smuggling in a small way. A glutman or two, the usual tubmen, and then the fishermen sometimes serve as spotsmen. He does his best to keep out of it. He'd definitely disapprove of the batmen."

One Dark Night

Lucy strained to hear. Had she heard right? What were they talking about? Spotsmen? What on earth...? Ah, fishermen, knowing the shores, would choose the spot to land perhaps? Batmen? Had she heard correctly?

"It's all quiet again, sir. We're lucky this ledge protects us from being seen."

But not from being heard. They were crouching in exactly the same well-hidden place where she'd seen Sydney Tynton digging. As soon as she was certain she was not being watched, she'd borrow Bodger's spade and dig up whatever he had buried. A second thought crossed her mind. If Mr Tynton were to be blamed for digging it up, that would jeopardize Daniel's life. Now what was the phrase that Chaucer wrote, *It is nought good a sleeping hound to wake.* That was it. Yes, better to let the sleeping hound lie.

"Yes, well let's just make sure we know what's what before it all begins. Thorsen's group, who *didn't* rush over to Ravensgate of course, should now be circling round ready to close in from behind as soon as the porters try bringing in the booty. Now, remember, we shan't see anything of the Waterguard until the gang are convinced this is going to be a successful run and we can catch them red-handed. We've got the new cutter, the Alert II, fastest boat built yet. Well-armed crew who'll head off anyone trying to escape by sea."

"Perhaps it was just a fox, or even a mouse, we heard, sir? It all seems quiet now."

"Concentrate, man!" Colonel Bigmore paused before he said, "You're sounding a mite nervous. Fear not, they're in for a surprise. Lieutenant Thorsen's planned this well. And, this time," Colonel Bigmore proudly said, "we've got the men and the guns to stop them one way or another." Lucy heard him smirk before he added, "You know both the Tyntons, don't you? We've discovered the old man's alias – he calls himself the 'magician'."

"Magician? Huh! Though it's true he's out-foxed us many a time in the past. He's certainly a bad lot. We've all been warned that he and his son are to be taken alive as they're to be made an example of. I suppose your men know that too?"

One Dark Night

Colonel Bigmore shifted his position noisily. "Of course. Lieutenant Thorsen's got his reasons for wanting to hang them so the crows can pick at their decaying bodies, and whether it be for revenge or justice, he's right. These gangs mete out bloody punishments: now it's their turn."

Lucy shivered and her eyes filled with tears. Daniel didn't deserve this. Aside from the gently hissing waves, all was now eerily quiet. Then she heard the unmistakable sound of donkeys plodding along the cliff top. No voices. Just the sound of hooves deadened by soft grass. Maybe the Colonel wouldn't hear them. Maybe their chatter would alert the smugglers to the trap. Her hopes were shattered by the silence from below.

She began to discern shapes crossing the sand in front of the white-topped waves. Their number grew steadily, one by one. They formed row upon row of silent, black, huddled forms squatting in the long grass at the edge of the beach. Clever. A shuffling *group* of men purposefully making towards the beach would be suspicious. This way, well, who would concern themselves with a single fisherman on a dark night?

But which one of them was Daniel?

One Dark Night

Chapter Seventeen
"Merciless pirates"

Attuned to the rhythm of the sea, Lucy gradually became aware of an additional sound, a slopping along the surface. She longed to inch forward on her elbows but the ledge only afforded total concealment if she lay flat against the cliff. Long grass hung over the concave drop of the precipice, creating a hollow just the right size for her. She took the chance. There in the bay, a little way off, was a lugger and, eyes straining, she could make out boats being rowed ashore. Only the breaking white waves betrayed their hulls. She could not hear the usual creaking of the oars, just the merest slop.

"Muffled oars," the Colonel whispered, "and that lugger's so loaded it'll get stranded if they don't unload it fast."

"Sir, there's another boat coming into the bay. It's one of theirs and loaded to the gunwhales."

Without a sound, the smugglers hiding at the edge of the sands further round the bay formed two lines leading to either side of the beached row-boats. Lucy gasped. Now she knew the meaning of the word "batmen". Each was armed with a long, stout bat and all faced *outwards*. She froze, fearful that their searching eyes would pick her out.

Coming from the shore was another group of men, also clad from head to toe in dark clothes and only discernible as they passed the white cliffs. Some led donkeys, ghost-like, to the boats where Lucy could see nods were exchanged with the oarsmen. Each had his job and no reference was made one to another. Unloading began. These men were not as she had expected from her encounters with those who'd *fixed the barn roof*. They were highly disciplined and practised. The landing was

One Dark Night

well planned. Thorsen's words exploded into her mind. "He's the one with the brains, the planner." Lucy looked for just one man. One man out of eighty or so. And they all looked the same.

An "owl" hooted. Just one "owl". There were no responses. Yet the batmen tensed like Scat waiting for movement to betray the whereabouts of the quarry. From her vantage point, she could see the customs' men gathering on the cliff top. She'd not noticed that Colonel Bigmore had slipped away from the base of the cliff but she did notice that customs' men were shinning down ropes trailing from the cliff top. Of course, that's what she'd tripped over, the stakes anchoring the ropes. They were not dressed in old, dark clothes like the smugglers, their uniform was lighter and hardly showed against the chalk cliffs.

Lucy chanced a peek in the direction of the soft scuffling above her. Dragoons! Dismounted, they crept along towards the dip in the cliffs, carved out by the stream. How many? She daren't count, she might be seen, but perhaps thirty, maybe forty. Even counting Thorsen's men, they'd be outnumbered by the smugglers.

A swooshing, followed by a crack startled Lucy. A rocket, fired from inshore, lit up the sky and the scene below etched itself in her mind. Another rocket followed.

From either side of the bay, Dragoons swooped across the sands drawing their swords as they hollered. Mounted Dragoons assembled by the stream. The batmen, alarmed by the flares, were bewildered but, threatened as they were by an onslaught of swords, they rushed at their attackers, wielding their bats. From the cliff top, a stream of rockets shot across the bay and fell into the sea beyond the two luggers and illuminated a third, fourth and fifth making their way to the shore. Was that third one flying a black flag? Something was flapping from the mast. A skull and crossbones was visible when the next rocket lit the sky. *You owe me.* Isn't that what Mr Tynton had said? This was the debt being repaid – a ship full of merciless pirates sailing towards the shore.

The Dragoons ceased their shouting and for a moment there was only the sound of sword against bat, grunting and the cries of the injured and dying. Then, taking full advantage of the continuing light, the Dragoons began calling out names. Real names, not the aliases the smugglers used.

Undeterred, and still protected by some of the batmen, the porters increased their feverish efforts to transport the cargo to the carts at the back of the beach. Heavily laden and fearful donkeys were now being pushed as well as pulled away from the row-boats. Lucy could see their labours were futile. If they were to get past the Dragoons on the sands, they'd meet the mounted force by the stream. Each rocket startled the donkeys more, and they kicked, brayed and lost some of their hastily fastened loads as they bolted, pursued by the porters. Other porters followed, desperately trying to recover the contraband and stop the barrels rolling down the beach. And all the time, the rockets lit the sky. Lucy saw chaos and incredible bravery in equal measure. Each side was battling for what they thought right.

The fighting had come closer to Lucy's hideaway and her attention was drawn by a shout of "Tynton". Leaning over the edge, she saw a batman attacking a customs' man. He raised his bat high and repeatedly clouted the man until he fell to the sand.

Lucy shuddered and whispered a prayer. "Oh please God, no, don't let that be Daniel." Surely that must be his father; Daniel would not club someone to death. He would not: of that she was sure.

"Tynton, Tynton," the customs' man still yelled.

Two mounted Dragoons raced across the sands. Too late. The batman had silenced his opponent. They were not too late to chase and seize him. Leaping onto the fleeing Tynton, one Dragoon pinned him to the ground while the other pulled off his hat and kerchief.

"The magician! We have the magician."

They might have the magician but his tricks did not cease. And now he played his ace. Not twenty yards from Lucy, someone had lit a bonfire on the cliff and the third lugger, still some way out in the bay, turned, and from its portholes guns were trained to fire over the heads of those loading the donkeys. They fired towards the cliffs where most of the hand to hand fighting was taking place. Cannon fire. Even the cliffs collapsed in places, burying both the dead and the living.

One Dark Night

Lucy could see a cutter approaching the stern of the lugger. It was The Alert II, the one they'd said was the fastest cutter in the Preventive Waterguard. Another Waterguard cutter was driving the other approaching luggers away from the shore.

A rocket lit the sky and Lucy saw Sydney Tynton stab one of his captors and escape the clutches of the other. Then he looked around him and, horror of horrors, he looked up and stared Lucy straight in the face. He raised his bat and shook it at her then fled.

Alarmed and shaking, Lucy clambered up from her ledge and ran along the top of the cliffs to one of the ropes trailing down to the beach. Unlike the agile customs' men, she inched her way down until she dared to jump the last few feet. Her thoughts were with the two badly injured men on the sand: her prayers were for Daniel. The Dragoons' blunderbusses still peppered the beach with lead balls, bangs and flashes. Her heart pounded but she crept to the fallen customs' officer. It was Hendon. She cradled him in her arms and tenderly tried to wipe the blood from his head with her handkerchief. He was probably no older than she was. Would he live?

In a voice as feeble as an old man's, he said, "There's more of them than us." He coughed weakly and said, "Tell my mother I love her and that I died bravely."

Lucy could not hold back her tear that fell onto his face. He looked up, gave a weak, crooked smile, and never spoke again. She laid his head back down on the sand, crossed his hands over his chest, and whispered, "Oh God, have mercy on him – take his soul, I pray." Blinded by tears, she tried to look for the Dragoon. Once she'd wiped her tears, she saw the brown, studded handle of Mrs Tynton's notched kitchen carving knife sticking out from the ribs of the man lying not twenty feet away, right by the cliff. Blood was still seeping from his deep wound. Mrs Tynton's words cut through Lucy's heart. *A notch for every chicken killed.* A shiver of revulsion went through Lucy; she had washed that knife so many times. She looked around, there was no sign of the other Dragoon nor Sydney Tynton.

Over the sea, lightning flashed. The silhouetted pirate ship sparked with flashing swords reflecting each bolt of lightning. Distant thunder

One Dark Night

rolled. The cannon fire stopped. The crew of the Alert II had overwhelmed their foe.

Hand to hand fighting still continued in the centre of the bay. Terrified donkeys brayed from upstream towards the village. Rockets were still firing, illuminating the smashed rowing boats. Uniformed archers were shooting arrows tipped with fire and Lucy watched as the two luggers lying close in caught alight. Efforts to douse the fires were abandoned and the few men still on board jumped into the sea and swam for the shore. They were netted and roped as they reached the beach.

Names were still being called out as each unmasked smuggler was recognized. Lucy's overriding thought was that she had not heard the name of *Daniel* Tynton. Perhaps he had escaped or maybe he was lying injured? Or worse. She must find him.

Crouching, she ran to the foot of the cliffs where she tripped over something sticking out of the sand. A knife handle. She crawled further along. Wearing black was now a disadvantage against the white cliffs. The tide had cut off any escape to the next bay, her only hope was to hide in the sandy tussocks nearer the stream but this was closer to the fighting. Her skirt caught on a knife handle and a few yards further along there was another. The "magician" certainly knew a few tricks; these knives must be spares, known only to the smugglers.

The usually peaceful little bay of Wintergate was littered with barrels and bodies and the smoky atmosphere created an eerie scene as the thunder followed the lightning until the rain came down in torrents and cleared the air. An injured smuggler moaned just to her left. She thought about crawling across to him but what could she do? It wasn't Daniel, the man was too small, no more than a child. To get to the dunes she had to crawl around two bodies. One of the supposedly dead bodies reached out, grabbed her hand, then rolled on top of her and whispered directly into her ear in a low growl.

"You scheming little slut. You're the cause of this. You've betrayed us. You'll pay for every life lost." A knife blade gleamed as vicious forked lightning lit the sky. Thunder cracked and boomed and the smuggler waited before he raised his knife and said, "Thirty pieces of silver was it?"

Lucy cried out, "No, no. I promise you, I've not betrayed you. I wouldn't."

"Shut it!" The smuggler, who Lucy now recognized from his voice as the big man she'd once seen in the doorway of the kitchen, clapped one hand over her mouth and said, "You'll die by thirty…slow… slits."

Lucy struggled to pull his hand from her mouth but he was too strong. She bit him hard. He released his hand just long enough for her to say, "I went to the farm to warn Daniel."

The man growled in her ear again. "Don't give me that! You couldn't warn him: he's at the other farm."

The folly of her actions began to horrify her. Daniel had not found the note. Mrs Tynton couldn't read so even if she had found it, it would be of no use. And now, if the farm was searched, the note would incriminate her.

Lucy felt the first prick of the knife on her leg.

"One." He growled, "And only the last will kill you."

She waited, her fear increasing with every second, realizing that each prick was to be worse. Something warm trickled over her neck. Blood. Oh God, surely my life does not end like this? The weight of the man on top crushed the breath out of her. Then she heard a familiar voice as the body was roughly shoved off her with a boot. The boot was then firmly placed on her bottom.

One Dark Night

Chapter Eighteen
"You must be in big trouble"

It was dawn on Tuesday when Karl Thorsen flung the door of the interview room wide and stood in the doorway, feet apart, one fist on his hip and the other holding a dim lamp. He stared at Lucy sitting on the floor in her undergarments with her arms around her legs. She'd used her petticoat to clean the blood and sand from her leg and her neck. She'd thrown her sand-caked, sopping wet dress over two wooden chairs, and she was shivering. Her bloodied hair hung, wet and curly, around her shoulders. She raised her eyes to the man who, boot on her bottom, had commanded Hooper to escort her back to Watch House. She thought she saw pity in his eyes: his barked words did not confirm that fleeting hope.

"What were you doing on the beach tonight?"

Steeling her nerve, she responded, "I wanted to see what was happening."

Thorsen's voice rose. "In the middle of the night?" He didn't wait for an answer. "Get out of here! Get up to your room and stay there until I come for you. Do you understand?"

She wanted to shout back at him, but a phrase of Shakespeare's, which Dougie's tutor used constantly, flashed to mind: "The better part of valour is discretion". Now was not the time to be courageous. Lucy reached out to her dress and held it against her as she stood up. "Thank you, Lieutenant Thorsen, I do."

Her repentant tone did nothing to stop Thorsen barking. "Put that dress on before you leave this room."

Lucy did as she was told and carried her petticoat over her arm. As she scuttled up the stairs, a thumping on the main door prevented

One Dark Night

Thorsen from still watching her. He opened the door and in marched bedraggled Dragoons who lined the corridor wall. Customs' men, also sandy and wet, angrily shoved cursing smugglers along the narrow gap and into the windowless interview room. The door was slammed shut and locked.

Lucy peeked over the banister and saw Hooper glance at Thorsen and shake his head. Did that mean that neither Daniel nor Sydney Tynton had been captured?

~

Lucy was asleep when Karl Thorsen thumped on the door and entered her room.

"Up! Get up immediately!"

Lucy, wearing nothing but a cotton nightshirt which Martha had given her, put her feet on the floor and covered herself with her bedclothes.

"Martha needs you in the kitchen to prepare a hearty breakfast for thirty-eight brave men."

"Yes, Lieutenant." Oh how angry she was for being so submissive, yet he had saved her from being slashed to death. Nothing in her life was simple. Every choice she made had associated problems.

Thorsen stood, legs apart, his eyes searching her from top to toe. "Are you injured?"

"It's just a scratch."

"Wash it and keep it clean." He turned and left the room, taking an inscrutable look at her before he shut the door.

Lucy's hair was still tangled and damp but shoved under her muslin cap, and in her grey dress and white, frilled apron, she knew she was passably attired if she was expected to serve the breakfast. Her boots were caked in sand, grass and blood. She would have to go barefoot.

"The Lord be praised, girl. Where have you been?"

"Martha, I am so very sorry not to have risen earlier."

"Don't come that loose sort of truth with me, girl. I know you're in trouble as deep as that sea out there, but let's just get on with this breakfast. I have eggs, milk and bread and not a lot more."

One Dark Night

Lucy glanced at the clock above the doorway. It was just gone nine. "The master says there are thirty-eight to feed."

"Yes, and he's not counting us and our brave men still out there on the sands. He wants you to take the food through to the men's quarters by half past." Martha nodded at the clock. "Then, somehow, and the Lord alone knows how, I'm expected to give that locked up rabble something too. Crumbs and water is all they'll get."

"I'll check the quarters, Martha. I'll be back immediately."

She tiptoed down the stairs, past sleeping men lying in the corridors and into the room which served as the day room for customs' men on duty. Again, there were bodies, snoring, wheezing, sleeping and generally lying where they'd dropped, exhausted. This room had a large window allowing a view over Wintergate village and the bay and was the room where Thorsen had carelessly spoken of his plans. She crept to the window. The bay showed every sign of the battle last night: two burnt luggers, barrels and debris scattered everywhere, and bodies – dead ones. It was now being guarded by Dragoons. She turned to look at the room. There were two good-sized tables, sixteen wooden chairs, and four comfortably upholstered chairs. The grate was empty but there was a stack of wood in two huge baskets alongside. She'd light a fire, which would show a willingness to be helpful.

The crackling fire disturbed those nearest and they woke the others. She was just able to push one table to the wall and this would be a place for the bread, eggs and as many plates as she could muster.

Back in the kitchen, she noticed that it was very nearly half past nine. "How can I help, Martha?"

"Flollops! You must be in *big* trouble." She held her arms wide. "You're not yourself at all."

"I've hardly slept."

"And whose fault is that?" Martha waved her wooden spoon and pointed it at Lucy.

The kitchen door burst open and Karl Thorsen strode in. "The men are stirring and will be hoping for a good breakfast, Martha." He ignored Lucy.

One Dark Night

"Lieutenant, I have boiled all the eggs and cut them in halves. If I'd scrambled them, there wouldn't have been enough plates." Martha sounded apologetic.

"We no longer need to disguise our strength," he explained, "so send to the village for supplies." He turned to raise a finger to Lucy. "You stay here."

"How many convicts are there, Lieutenant?"

"Prisoners, Martha," he corrected her. "Though I dare say you are soon to be right. Prepare only bread and water for the moment. They'll have to wait until that Tommy Smith comes, assuming he's not dead or missing."

"He's due on the morrow but perhaps I should send a message for him to get here and be quick about it?" Thorsen nodded and Martha felt encouraged to continue. "And where will you be having your breakfast, Lieutenant?"

Thorsen turned to look at Lucy who was busy breaking the bread into fist sized pieces. "Lucy will bring mine and Colonel Bigmore's into my office."

Lucy's stomach turned over.

"I have enough porridge for you both, Lieutenant, and eggs, a little cheese, and nice fresh bread too," Martha said with a proud smile.

It was only a matter of ten minutes before the whole of Watch House fell silent as everyone ate the little Martha had been able to buy before the unsuccessful landing.

"Quick, Lucy, dash up to the roof and bring me down my secret sack of flour and the butter too."

"What! The roof? I'll surely be dismissed!"

"Jennings is a right soft one and let me put a spare sack up there. It always pays to keep some by. Not a good idea to show your hand, Tommy Smith said. Good man, he brought it a day or two ago. He said it was left over from his rounds and perhaps I could stash it away up top somewhere. Stroke of luck, eh?"

Huh! Thought Lucy. That Tommy Smith knew more than he should and had turned it into a profit, but she hadn't time to think about that now. "I don't know how to get up there."

One Dark Night

"It's up that winding staircase." Martha demonstrated a spiral staircase with her hand. "I'm glad I put it up there. The master would have had me baking all night if I hadn't said the stocks were low.

"Won't there be someone on guard?"

"Not now, there won't. Not after last night. They're all sagged out and the Dragoons on the beach are on watch."

This was probably all true but surely this would be the final straw if she were caught on the roof. Nevertheless, on a promise from Martha that she would take the blame, Lucy climbed to the top of the staircase and opened the small doorway. Surely the sack of flour would be soaked through with last night's rain? But it wasn't. The flour and some butter were stored in a small cupboard built onto the side of the doorway. She took a moment to take in the view and the wonderful fresh smell of the sea. The off shore wind had cleared away the smell of the smoke and the morning looked bright and sunny. Perhaps she could grow pots of herbs up here? She took one further look towards Merrygate, and allowed herself a moment to appreciate the meadows laid out before her eyes and the flashing sea beyond. She must delay no longer; she dragged the flour out of the cupboard, taking care not to disturb the spyglass, the case of pistols and the blunderbuss. Thorsen would be so very angry if he knew.

A clattering sound behind startled her. She turned to see an arrow lying on the ground with a note attached. She ripped off the note and flung the incriminating arrow back. She peered over the parapet but there was no one to be seen. Then, as she turned away, lifted to her on the breeze, came the song of the linnet.

One Dark Night

Chapter Nineteen
"I charge you to be guardians of that truth"

The interrogation that followed later that same Tuesday had been easier than Lucy expected. Thorsen had circled her like a predatory animal, hurling questions that she could answer truthfully because he made the mistake of focusing on whether or not she had spoken to any of the smugglers and discovered from them the plans of the landing. "No," she had answered with conviction. She did not tell Thorsen that it was *he* who she'd overheard discussing the landing. Her explanation of why she left her warm bed to crawl around in a dangerous situation on a cold, wet night, was passably plausible. "I have never come across the smuggling gangs before, Lieutenant, but I heard the thumping on our door, saw you ride out and I wanted to see what really happens." Nevertheless, it was obvious to Lucy that Karl Thorsen suspected the real reason. Then he'd asked a question which reawakened her buried fear. "Do you realize what danger you have put yourself in? Did anyone, other than the man I hauled off you, recognize you?" When she'd replied that Sydney Tynton had seen her and raised his bat at her, Thorsen had wheeled round and shaken her shoulders. He'd called her a fool. He'd called her every possible name to describe an idiot. Amongst the smugglers, she was now a "wanted man".

Lucy's only consolation had been Daniel's note attached to the arrow. "Take care. Do not go out alone." He was alive!

~

"The toast is: Lieutenant Karl Thorsen."

A scraping of chairs on the wooden floor in Thorsen's private dining room drowned most of the murmurs of concord. All the men, except

One Dark Night

Thorsen, stood with glasses raised and took a sip of the port. Lucy moved silently to the door and, having finished her duty of serving the nine uniformed officers at the celebratory dinner, she thought she would slip out. Before she could do so, Thorsen snapped his fingers and caught her eye. He requested she call Martha in to the dining room too.

"Come along, Lieutenant Thorsen, regale us with how your inspired strategy led to Monday's great 'Wintergate Bay Bust'." There was a roar from the men so Colonel Bigmore raised his voice. "You've had a day and a half to concoct a good story!" He grinned broadly, sat down and thumped the table. The other officers of the customs and Dragoons joined in.

Lucy had fetched Martha and they both watched Thorsen as he considered his reply.

"China Cottage – that's what we have to thank for our successful strategy," he said. All eyes were upon him, except Lucy's, for she was remembering how the servants at Faefersham Court were trained to stand like statues. "China and the good Lord." She allowed her eyes a quick glance at Thorsen and around the men, noticing how they held him in great respect. "I was on my way to church when the conversation turned to the importation of goods from China. The ladies, naturally enough, thought of tea." A chuckle rippled around the table. "The female mind thinks of the good things in life at all times, it seems to me, and we should be grateful they do."

Martha had not had the benefit of life at Faefersham Court and her idea of *standing like a statue*, as Lucy had suggested, involved full interest in all that was being said, evidenced by her broad grin.

"They are also given to frivolity and the word 'fireworks' was introduced by Miss Yorton." Thorsen raised his arm in acknowledgement of Lucy. Lucy stood motionless, not moving even an eyelid. "From that moment, the strategy of the winning course began to form in my mind. These gangs always run the cargo ashore on the darkest nights and when we've taken torches before, the blighters seize and hurl them into the sea. What we needed was sudden, unexpected and untouchable light. That's what the rockets and, of course, the lightning provided. The information I had was that this was to be a

One Dark Night

landing by not only our local smugglers but gangs from further afield. With such numbers, it was imperative that we had sufficient rockets to keep up sustained visibility. Turning darkness into light cost me a pretty penny but it was worth it." Then he muttered something that few heard. "It's always worth it."

Thorsen mentioned the Dragoons and much else besides, but Lucy was thinking of Daniel. Where was he now? Then, as though Thorsen knew, he paused and stared at Lucy before he said, "We have many prisoners who will be taken away tomorrow, but there are two men still to be captured. But captured they will be because they are the leaders of this disreputable rabble. It can only be the Tyntons who involved the pirate boat. Without the aid of our colleagues in the Preventive Waterguard and their new cutter, and the extraordinary bravery of the crew who boarded and took captive most of the pirates, victory might have eluded us. Pirates! In these modern times, who but the Tyntons would stoop so low?" He paused, stood, and raised his glass to two officers in the Waterguard. "To the Waterguard."

The time it took to toast and congratulate allowed a moment's reflection for Lucy. What she overheard on that cold, clear Christmas Day, as she sat in her sanctuary, flooded through her mind. "Swear an oath on your son's life," the man had said to Sydney Tynton and Tynton had replied, "You now owe me." And that man, that pirate who roamed the seas, capturing the cargoes of ships, then sinking them with all on board, that lowest of the low had said, *You just let me know and we'll be there, guns ablazing.* Everything inside Lucy was in turmoil. How could she even think of siding with such violent men? The feeling of that man's blood trickling down her neck made her shiver. Standing motionless was becoming difficult.

After the toast, he continued. "I'd like to be able to say that our exploits will go down in history. We have been entrusted with a just cause and some have given their lives in its defence. We shall not name them now; we have a special time set aside to remember them." He paused and lowered his eyes. "I charge you to be the guardians of their honour and their memory."

There was another short silence.

One Dark Night

"We do not, as yet, know the full truth behind all that has happened but when we do, I charge you to be guardians of that truth."

There were nods of assent around the table.

"I should like, also, to thank those who have supported our actions." He held out his arm to indicate Lucy and Martha standing by the door. "And I should like to add that you, Yorton and Fagg, are not bound by the last charge. Instead, I charge you to be guardians of the *folklore* surrounding 'The *Great* Wintergate Bay Bust.' A little bravery added here, a little more action there: that is what I commission you to do."

The men around the table cheered and thumped the table causing a clattering of cutlery and dishes to add to the merriment. Martha grinned, grabbed the skirt of her apron, waved it as she jumped up and down and cried out, "I've already started." Then she blushed the deepest crimson Lucy had ever seen and her eyes watered.

A smile of satisfaction lit up Thorsen's face – what more could be said?

That Thorsen had killed a man to save Lucy's life would remain unsaid.

One Dark Night

Chapter Twenty
Daniel
"A pox on them that taxes us"

Very early on the Tuesday morning after the unsuccessful landing, Daniel tested his ankle. It was still painful and it wouldn't take his weight, but he'd take the chance. Since spraining it, he'd returned to Bethlehem Farm where his aunt had taken good care to bind it firmly and strap a brace to his leg. The weather was fine, his aunt had packed his saddle bag, and Daniel hauled himself on to Fiddle and whistled for Josh to follow. The news, brought to him by the roaming greengrocer, Tommy Smith, had been worse than he could have imagined. Three local men dead, six escaped injured and seventeen captured. Only three had escaped unharmed and one of those was his father. The gangs from the south of the county had fared even worse. His father should never have involved them. And a pirate boat? Pirates! In this day and age? In England! What was his father thinking? To dance with the devil is a sure route to destruction.

As he rode slowly towards his father's farm he reflected on the dire situation that so many now faced. Thorsen had, inadvertently, prevented Daniel from any involvement in most of the planning of the biggest landing in years. The daily visits from his mother, carrying information backwards and forwards had been unsustainable. His father had been adamant the landing would go ahead and he had seized the opportunity to take control.

On arrival at Jerusalem Farm, Daniel needed help to dismount and only his mother came out to greet him. "I'm that glad to see you, Dan. Aye, that I am." She hugged him, took the reins and attended to the horse. "Your father's bleating like a starving lamb."

One Dark Night

"He should be in hiding," said Daniel.

It was a good five minutes before Sydney Tynton furtively peeked into the kitchen, agitated, and raging about one thing more than any other. "I'm tellin' you Dan, she was there! There on the beach with them chickens. Turnin' over bodies. Cryin' over the dead customs' men. She's addled your brains, Dan. She's betrayed you and all of us."

His protestations that Lucy was undoubtedly innocent were too late, his father had already sent out the word that she must be found. Nobody crossed the gang and got away with it.

"Mr Tynton!" Mrs Tynton was exasperated. "Keep your noise down. You can be heard on the moon. You should stay in *the room* until Dan thinks of something better."

Daniel grasped the situation. His father was blaming Lucy rather than himself for the failure of the landing and now he was expecting his son to sort it out.

Josh was restless. He paced the kitchen floor. "Wait a while, Josh. Ma will get you something soon." Then turning to his father, he said, "Ma's right. Keep out of sight in case Thorsen's men turn up unexpectedly. I'll sit here quietly and have a think."

Sydney Tynton glared at his son. "You do that. You and me are the same blood, you get your thinkin' and plannin' from me and I've done this all for you, and set you up to keep the free trading goin' strong. A pox on them that taxes us into our graves." He turned and reluctantly stomped up the stairs, pulled up the rug at the top, opened the hatch underneath, and slid into the hidden room below, stopping only to shout to his wife to put the mat back as he replaced the hatch.

"Take no notice, Dan. You're more my blood than his. Aye and I'm that glad of that."

Daniel was well able to take no notice of their claims. He may have been born into their ways but he didn't have to follow them if he didn't want to.

Josh rested his muzzle on Daniel's knee. "Thirsty Josh? Go on then, bring your bowl over and you can have some of this milk. Don't tell ma, promise?"

One Dark Night

Josh barked and went to his bowl which was right at the back of the hearth. He barked again.

"What's the matter, Josh? Bowl too hot?" Josh barked again and Daniel stood slowly, hobbled to the stove and used his crutch to pull the bowl to the front of the hearth. As he did so, he saw a piece of folded paper underneath.

His mother reappeared, patted her apron, and sighed in an exaggerated fashion. "Your father's past his best days, Dan." Then, seeing Daniel reaching for the note, she said, "I don't know what that is, is it something you've left? I thought I'd better not move it."

Daniel looked at his mother with no hint of anger – it was not her fault she couldn't read. How had Lucy managed to get this warning note to the farm? She must have risked, if not her life, then her freedom to do so. He sat on the bottom stair and hauled himself up to the top, flicked the mat away, thumped on the floorboards and pulled the hatch open.

"You stop your thumpin', Dan. I'm tryin' to get this room made comfortable and you're shoutin' and hollerin' and givin' me away."

Daniel took no notice of his father's ire and shoved the note in front of his upturned face. "Read it! I told you. She did not betray us."

Sydney Tynton frowned. "You know I can't read too well. Anyway, it's not signed. It could be from anyone."

Daniel snatched it away from his father's face. "It says, and you can read well enough for these simple words. 'Your plans for tonight are known. Please stop the landing.'"

Sydney Tynton was not easily persuaded. "Yeah but it's what I said," and he began to shout, "it's not from her. I tell you, I saw…"

Daniel put his hand to his father's face. "Shut that great mouth of yours. As Ma says, you'll be heard on the moon." Sydney reluctantly drew breath and Daniel continued. "Who else would say 'please'?"

For a moment it looked as though his father was actually trying to think of such a person. Beaten, he fell silent.

"She did not betray us," Daniel said quietly. "Now who have you got looking for her and I'll call them off."

Sydney Tynton slumped on the floor. "A general call went round. Passed to one man who'll pass it to the next and so on."

One Dark Night

"Then I'll warn her until I can be sure that everyone knows I'll give like for like to anyone who harms her."

"Before you go, Dan, I've gotta tell you somethin'. I might not get a chance when you get back."

His father knew his time was up, the ancient priests' hole could hide him for a while but Thorsen would not give up. Daniel stayed to listen.

"Lucy's mother, that Annie Yorton, she used to work at Sir William Harper's place." When Daniel showed not even a hint of surprise, Sydney Tynton continued. "Well, he nearly lost it all some years ago when you were just a boy, and he took to organizin' the runs in the whole of north Kent." Only Daniel's eyes marked his shock. "Darn good he was too. Profits increased tenfold in no time. He had all the London and county contacts. It was easy for him to sell on the goods. Easy times for us too. I more or less just did as he said. Then he gave it up late in 1815 – when the war had ended – and your plannin', even though you were not much more than a lad yourself, kept us goin'."

Sydney Tynton watched while Daniel turned this information over in his mind. His father, known far and wide as 'the magician' was really no more than a messenger.

"It was Sir William who said that if we really must have weapons, we were to hide them 'at strategic points', then if we were stopped, we'd not have weapons on us. Apart from the batmen, of course, 'cos you can't hide those. And it was Sir William who saw to it that we had enough boats and a good return for our efforts."

"But not pirates?"

"No, Dan, that was me. Good one, eh? I had to do somethin'. When that Thorsen turned up, dead bent on killin' me, well, you know how he's stopped the good times, and I can see you've got other interests now, I thought we'd finish it with all guns blazin'."

Daniel looked with sorrowful eyes at his father trying to be cheerful in what he surely knew were his last days. But why was he confessing now? "Pa," Daniel rarely used the affectionate name, "There's nothing Sir William can do for you."

Sydney Tynton's eyes gleamed. "No one knows this. No one. The other fella who knew copped it last night. I'm tellin' you just in case I don't get to talk to you again on our own. Someone's gotta know his part in it and if you ever need money, he's got plenty. Be careful though, he's a powerful man."

Daniel's mind went back to the day he saw Annie Yorton on the beach talking to the man from Faefersham Court. Things were becoming clearer. "So what's Annie Yorton got to do with it? Does she know?"

"Nah. No one knows. What makes you think she knows?"

"I reckon she does. She's getting money from someone there."

Sydney Tynton thought for a bit. "Nah, that'll be from her husband, she ain't no widow. The butler's her husband, I expect she's gettin' it off him."

Daniel shook his head. That might be true. Or it might not. He remembered Annie making threats about Sir William. "I've work to do, Pa. Stay down there quietly and don't keep hollering for Ma."

Patience was needed as he struggled to mount Ned, the sturdy donkey. Dressed in some old clothes, few would recognize him. Josh was not happy about being left behind and gave the donkey a mean look. Fiddle, also to be left behind, shook his mane. His mother was not happy either.

"Ma, just make sure he stays in the room, and if he hears the King's men at the door, he's got to get down under." It was too cold for his father to crawl around in the void under the priest's hole all the time, but it might save him for a while longer if the house were to be searched. That hidey hole had probably saved many a priest back in the old days when they were being hunted by King Henry but could it save his father?

Ned was not a comfortable ride with the old saddle, nor was he fast. Daniel couldn't kick his painful heel into Ned's flanks. He tried, but Ned, feeling a harder kick on the one side, started turning around. Daniel had to content himself with a slap on Ned's rump and a promise that he could soon come with him to Bethlehem Farm. "I know we only have a few sheep and chickens but you've made the best guard donkey in the county, Ned. No foxes got past you with your hee-hawing and charging and making a fearsome row." He gave Ned a slap on the rump.

One Dark Night

"I'm sorry to be pushing you to get a move on, but this is your big day – show them you're as good as any horse. And horses don't guard sheep, so you'll take the prize."

Ned's pace did not improve much. "How would you and Nellie like to spend your days giving children rides on the sand?" Ned ambled on towards the sands. "Up the coast at Merrygate there's lots of visitors coming to put their feet in the sea. And someone from round here has invented a 'bathing machine'. There! What do you think of that? You could drag one down to the water's edge, the ladies then tip-toe down the steps and slip into the sea, and you'll be the hero of all. Thinking about it, those lumbering things would make a good stable for you and Nellie if we could get you up the steps. Bit of a push might do it." He thwacked Ned again. "You're not fooled by my jolly talk, are you Ned?"

Daniel imagined Lucy slipping into the sea wearing rather less than usual and his thoughts stopped him talking to his donkey who wasn't a good listener anyway. He circled around Wintergate to join the sands at the next bay along, nearer to Merrygate, where he tethered Ned to a rock. He leaned on his crutch, which had been strapped to the saddle, and took his bow and quiver which he flung around his other shoulder. Keeping close to the edge of the cliffs so that he could not easily be observed, he allowed himself a faint smile. Tommy Smith, always grateful for an extra shilling or two, had laid the ground for him to get a message to Lucy. But had Martha taken up Tommy's suggestion of storing extra flour on the roof? The most likely time for the flour to be essential would be now. Martha, not knowing there'd be a host of King's men of one sort or another and more prisoners than he'd care to think about, would be finding it difficult to manage on her normal supply from Tommy.

Daniel settled himself on the sands right up against the cliff face. Only someone lying flat on the top and leaning over would be able to see him. He waited. His hope was that he hadn't arrived too late. Surely Martha would have thought of the flour as soon as she heard of the many mouths to feed? This was not the best of plans. Suppose it was Martha who braved the narrow, stone staircase? Moments after he'd

One Dark Night

cleared those doubts from his mind, he heard the unmistakable sound of someone on the roof. He stepped back from the cliff edge and, with his crutch helping him balance, he stood on the shore rocks and looked up. There she was. With her hand shielding her eyes from the bright sun in the eastern sky, she was peering over the parapet towards Merrygate. He took the arrow from his quiver and attached his warning note. He let his crutch fall, balanced on his good leg and a rock, and took aim. Fortunately, there was hardly any breeze and the roof was large enough for there to be no chance of the arrow hitting Lucy. He picked up his crutch and hurried back to the shelter of the cliffs. The arrow was returned and landed on the nearby rocks, clever Lucy. He whistled the song of the linnet.

One Dark Night

Chapter Twenty-One
"Guilty of murder"

It was mid afternoon by the time Thorsen caught up with Daniel. Ned had plodded steadily between Wintergate and Brookington, stopping at each of the smugglers' cottages while Daniel countermanded his father's instructions regarding Lucy: she was not to be harmed. His old donkey and even older clothes had drawn no attention until he was about to return home. He was just leaving a cottage by the wooden gate when Thorsen and four of his men rode up to him.

"If you think you are unrecognizable, Tynton, you are wrong. There's always someone who lets me know."

"I hope you give them enough to buy a good dinner." Daniel was about to add "For their family" when it occurred to him who was most likely to be against him and Lucy: that Mary and her no-good friend who'd attacked Lucy at the market. Both scorned women bent on revenge.

Thorsen grinned. "I have two questions for you."

Daniel, leaning on his crutch, came through the gate. His quiver and bow were strapped to the far side of Ned who was taking the opportunity to help keep the spring grass short. If he stood where Ned was not directly in front of them, he could relax a little: he'd rather they didn't see arrows. "I'm listening."

Thorsen dismounted from glossy, black Midnight and held the reins as he looked Daniel up and down and glanced across to Ned. "Where were you late yesterday evening?"

What an easy-to-answer question. "I was at Bethlehem Farm."

"When did you leave Bethlehem Farm?"

"Early this morning, shortly after dawn."

"Why were you there?"

Daniel toyed with the idea of reminding Thorsen that he'd asked more than two questions but decided against it. "I've been there all week."

Thorsen handed Midnight's reins to one of his men and took a step towards Daniel. "You don't think I'll believe that a tumble on the grass has put you out of action for one of the biggest attempted runs for many years, do you?"

"I don't think about you at all." Not wholly true, of course, but right enough in this situation.

With lightning speed, Thorsen kicked the crutch from under Daniel's arm and pushed him over. "Just checking, Tynton."

Daniel grasped the wooden gate and hauled himself up. His aunt's splint was proving its worth and there seemed to be no harm done. If he could read Thorsen's expression correctly, then the truth had dawned on him: Daniel could not have been involved that fateful night. "Your *second* question?"

Thorsen raged, "Where is your father?"

"He's not on the farm." Daniel could not help but allow a flicker of a smile to cross his lips. He was playing with Thorsen and Thorsen knew it. He refrained from saying he's likely to be *under* the farm.

"He is wanted for crimes committed on the night of Monday the second of April and the morning of Tuesday the third of April."

"Yesterday and today?" Daniel knew he should not make light of Thorsen's pompous manner and grave accusations but the temptation had overcome him.

Thorsen was not distracted. "He is wanted for importing goods with a view to avoiding due payment. He is also wanted for murder."

Daniel was practised at hiding his reactions but felt his blood drain and his pallor showed. Seeing Thorsen's satisfaction, Daniel looked him straight in the eyes. "Murder of whom?"

Thorsen ignored Daniel's question and repeated his own. "Where is your father?"

One Dark Night

"If he's guilty of murder, as you say he is, surely you don't expect him to be sitting at home?" Daniel could see a flicker of annoyance cross Thorsen's eyes.

"You are fortunate to have such a visible alibi. We shall, of course, confirm your whereabouts over the last week. The searches of your father's farmhouse will continue – you've just missed the first. Enjoy the farm while you can," Thorsen smirked, "it will be confiscated before too long."

That the farm no longer belonged to his father was obviously still unknown to Thorsen and he decided to save the news that his father's debts had brought about the sale of the farm to his uncle. Then, to his surprise, Thorsen shouted to him as he mounted his horse.

"Miss Yorton did not betray you. The only person who could have started that rumour is your father, so I know he's not far away. Call off your gang."

"What do you think I've been doing? Visiting all and sundry in the hope of a cup of tea?"

Thorsen did not look as pleased as Daniel expected. No doubt he wanted *his* orders to be seen to be those which saved Lucy.

~

Daniel's route home took him past the parsonage. Mrs Raffles was in the garden at the side tending some climbing roses.

"Well goodness me! Is that you Mr Tynton?" She had a nervous tic, and winked.

"Tynton the younger, yes, Mrs Raffles." Daniel removed his hat and his blond hair confirmed he was indeed the young and handsome son of the farmer on the outskirts of the village.

"Come along inside and take a little tea with Mr Raffles. I've been baking all morning and if I don't call for help, my dear husband will have eaten the whole batch." Though she teased, her smile showed her love of her husband, a man who had rescued her from lonely spinsterhood and the condescension of the wealthy side of her family.

Daniel brought Ned to a halt. If ever there was a time to spend a while with the parson, it was now. As a child, it had been Parson Raffles who had taught Daniel to read and write before he'd been offered a living on the other side of the county. It was time to rekindle a closer association. "I'll be pleased to help, Mrs Raffles, I'm in need of some nourishment." And much more, he might have added.

The parson's many hats hung in the hallway and Daniel smiled. Each hat had its own peg. There were velvet caps, rough woollen country caps, small brimmed brown and straw hats and many wide brimmed clerical ones, all with a different coloured band. No doubt the row of hats served a purpose and Daniel wondered if it helped his parishioners to see the human frailties of this Godly man. Between the hats and Mrs Raffles's warm hospitality, the worst sinner would find the parson approachable.

Mr Raffles greeted Daniel with concern. "Your ankle, it's still painful? Here, let me take your crutch, and you sit near the table. With a plate of gingerbread, and maybe some of Mrs Raffles' herbal tea, we can converse like kings." Turning to Mrs Raffles, he whispered, "Some of your tea for reducing the swelling, my dear. Take your time. We'll start on the gingerbread, but do bring in the seed cake later with, perhaps a little of our best tea?" Rubbing his hands together in anticipation, he checked with Daniel, who nodded with a friendly smile to Mrs Raffles as she hurried out.

In the company of the parson, who still seemed to Daniel like a kindly schoolmaster, he sat straight and spoke formally. "You are too kind, Mr Raffles, and you have assessed my situation correctly. I need, not only a little refreshment but also your wise counsel."

The parson pulled his chair closer to the table and peered through his spectacles. "My ears are yours, though one of them won't hear much."

Daniel smiled weakly and wasted no time. "First, I must ask you if you would assist in spreading the word that Miss Lucy Yorton betrayed neither the revenue men nor the smugglers."

"I am aware, and I will ensure that all whom I meet will be made aware." He slapped the palm of his hand on the table. "Lieutenant Thorsen says he will not allow her to leave Watch House until it is safe to do so. For once, you may find yourselves in agreement with each other."

Daniel looked surprised. "He makes an unexpected ally."

One Dark Night

The parson smiled as if he had achieved the first move in a winning game of chess. "You've been at Bethlehem Farm for the last week or so, is that right?"

"Yes."

"Most of the smugglers were either taken prisoner, killed or have fled back to where they came from. I do not think you need to concern yourself…"

"But I do." The urgency of the situation pushed formal manners aside and Daniel's voice became louder. "And I shall feel more comfortable once I know an innocent young woman is not brutally murdered by some thug bent on revenge. Nor should she be punished by the law. I have evidence to prove her intentions were honourable. She wanted to stop a massacre."

"Your concern is admirable." Raffles raised his eyebrows. "I also know her actions were driven by good intentions and despite my cautionary words to her on the road to your farm, I believe she tried to ensure that lives were not lost."

Mrs Raffles entered with a tray of cake, two china cups and saucers, a jug of milk and a pot of China tea. "I've brought this in first, my dear, because the herbal tea will be better for a longer infusion."

"Just as you say, my love, you know best." Raffles turned to Daniel and said, "I hope you will forgive our little familiarities, they come so naturally now."

The interruption was timely; it was Daniel's move now and in a more sombre mood he said, "My father is sought for murder." He allowed time for the parson to absorb the severity of the situation. He undoubtedly knew most of the goings-on in the village so there was little point in hiding anything now. "From a boy, my father always warned me against murder: 'It carries the death sentence,' he said before every run."

"As I understand it," said the parson, "Your father has been the local leader of this section of the North Kent Gang for some long time?"

Daniel nodded.

One Dark Night

Raffles continued. "The North Kent Gang, over the past years has been violent, defending its territory and *killing* when threatened by other gangs or revenue men?"

Again Daniel nodded. It was, regrettably, true, but not the whole truth. "I do not recall any real violence during our operations, not in my time. Certainly I never injured anyone nor saw anything more than the occasional fist fight." He refrained from saying that his careful planning had sought to make violence unnecessary. "I know that further along the north coast there have been violent incidents." The thought of the man killed by the horse's pounding hooves pushed its way to the front of his mind. "The man found dead in Brookington Wood was killed by members of the Hurst gang."

"Have you their names?"

"Unfortunately, I don't."

The parson leaned back in his chair and peered over his spectacles. He paused longer to pour some tea for them both and offered Daniel the plate of cake. This had the effect of leaving the words hanging in the air for inspection. Satisfied they were true, he sipped his tea then nodded slowly, pursing his lips before saying. "It is not for me to pass judgment on any of the good Lord's creation. No, that would not be what God has asked of me. He has, however, given me the task of reminding people of their obligations to one another and to their creator as set out for us in the Bible." Raffles pushed his spectacles in closer to his eyes and leaned forwards. "Thou shalt *not* kill. Your father has violated the laws of man and of *God*."

This parson was a good man, he would not pass judgment, but he would not compromise on the words of the Ten Commandments, and Daniel respected this. Yet still he held on to a faint hope that a mistake had been made. "But is there anyone who witnessed my father killing a man?"

"Yes. Miss Yorton."

The minute of silence that followed felt like the ten it takes for a man to dance on the hangman's rope.

One Dark Night

Parson Raffles was indeed a good man: he broke the silence. "Hendon was found with his arms crossed on his chest. Who else that night, but Miss Yorton, would have done that?"

Daniel took a deep breath, breathed out slowly but stayed silent. Emmeline, the parson's wife, entered and placed a cup of steaming herbal tea in front of him. If she had not urged him to drink it, he might not have noticed.

The parson, also barely noticing, continued. "Furthermore, it seems your father *saw* Miss Yorton watching and therefore he's been quick to pass it around that she's to be silenced."

Daniel thought back to what his father had told him. He had said that Lucy betrayed them. He did not mention that she had seen him *kill* a man. No wonder he wanted her silenced. His hand went to his mouth and his elbow propped him up on the table. There was no way round this. Even if not captured, how could his father ever be a part of his future? And if he were to be captured, it would be Lucy who would be called upon to testify to his guilt.

"Your father was seen to kill the young customs' man, Hendon, not only by Miss Yorton but by two Dragoons."

Now Daniel spoke. "Not just Miss Yorton then?"

"No. Two Dragoons saw him raise his bat to Miss Yorton who was watching from above. They then chased him, but your father killed one of them."

"He killed *two* men?"

"I'm afraid that is true. And the other Dragoon failed to capture your father alone but can bear witness to his killing two men – Hendon and a fellow Dragoon."

"How could he have killed the boy Hendon? His poor mother; he was her only child."

"We cannot change the past, Daniel. Your father chose to live outside the laws of man and ultimately this led to his choice to live outside the laws of God. The laws of man will deal with him with no undeserved favour. If he does not repent, I do not wish to determine how his soul will fare. Jesus, who knows our trials and troubles, will do that. My calling is to remind you that you cannot change the past but you *can* change your future and the future of others."

One Dark Night

Chapter Twenty-Two
"His sword displaying his intentions"

Daniel's progress home was slow and allowed plenty of time to think. "Now I know you had a hard time of it last night, Ned. All those fireworks and guns are not good for a donkey's courage, are they? But if you could just move a little faster, I'd be grateful." There was no getting away from the fact that his father was a murderer and would hang. Sooner or later, he would be caught. "Then Ma won't be able to manage without him and the extra income from the free trading. She'll put pressure on me to marry Tilda and her thousand pounds so we can buy back our farm. No, Ned, you need to move a bit faster. We mustn't let Ma do any thinking." And what must Lucy feel about a man with a murderer for a father? Thorsen was protecting her, feeding her, clothing her; his intentions were becoming even clearer. He slapped Ned on his rump and his pace quickened. But not enough.

It was impossible not to hear what was happening at the farmhouse even from the other side of the gatehouse. Thundering hooves, shouts, thumping, and Josh barking. Josh ran to explain matters to his approaching master, circling Ned and yapping. "Stop your noise, Josh, d'y'hear. I don't want Ned kicking you and sending me flying." He flung his quiver and bow into the gatehouse which had clearly already been searched.

"Tynton!" Thorsen stormed up to him as he gingerly dismounted. "If you don't want me to have this door broken down, get it opened. Now!"

He hobbled to the stout door at the front of the farm. "Ma, you'll have to open up. There's thirty men trying to get in." He reflected on the irony of the situation, one little lady versus thirty armed men, and she was holding out. Mrs Tynton drew back the bolts and, defiantly

One Dark Night

stared up at her son. "Let me in, Ma, then let these..." he sighed, "let these men go about their duty." He hobbled to the comfortable chair near the hearth, snapping his fingers for Josh to follow him. The faithful dog obeyed reluctantly; letting clear enemies in to his territory went against all he had been trained to do.

Thorsen stood, legs apart, one hand on his hip and the other on the hilt of his sheathed sword, and in a controlled, firm voice said, "Where is your father?"

"I cannot answer that question with any degree of assurance. You know that I have only just returned after leaving this morning."

"You've not taken all this time just to return home. Have you returned earlier?"

"I have not."

"Met up with your father, perhaps? Found him a hiding place?"

"Lieutenant Thorsen," Daniel said with a note of revulsion in his voice, "I have been at the parsonage with Mr and Mrs Raffles and I am sure they will confirm this if you take the trouble to ask them."

Thorsen turned his back and spoke to Mrs Tynton whose knuckles had turned white as she clutched the back of the kitchen chair. "It will be to your advantage if you tell me where your husband is."

Mrs Tynton, eyes staring at Daniel, opened her mouth and shut it again.

Daniel attempted a conciliatory tone to draw the fire from his mother. "Lieutenant, wouldn't you say it is most likely that my father has fled?"

Thorsen, still with his back to him, continued to question Mrs Tynton. "Look at me, Mrs Tynton. Your son cannot help you now. The farm has been watched since the early hours of this morning. There has been no sign of him leaving. Did he return home last night?"

"I...I was asleep last night."

Good, his mother was following his advice not to tell outright lies. Lies that could stick to her, ruin her, lead her to the gallows.

Exasperated, Thorsen turned to the five customs' men still standing in the doorway. "Search the house again and this time I want every nook and cranny looked into and every cupboard pulled apart." He

One Dark Night

called out to those of his men waiting outside. "One of you guard the back door, one the front, the rest of you pull the barn apart. If we still can't find him, we'll search the ditches and the rest of this area until we do."

Josh, having growled since being called to heel, could contain his anger no longer and rushed at Thorsen. Immediately, Thorsen drew his sword. Josh circled behind and seized Thorsen's booted leg. Thorsen raised his sword to swipe behind but Daniel had called Josh off in the nick of time.

"If that happens again, Tynton, your dog will die."

He struggled to his feet and suggested Josh be shut in the parlour. "You don't want to be seen as a savage, do you?"

Thorsen all but burst. "You're treading a very fine line, Tynton. Your father will be hanged and gibbeted and, if I get my way, you will be too and the world will be better off without you both."

He decided this was not the time to thank Thorsen for the irrefutable alibi he had provided. Mrs Tynton sobbed and he hobbled over to comfort her whilst wondering if a visit to Sir William Harper would prove useful. After all, he'd been as much involved as his father.

Thorsen, meanwhile, sheathed his sword and surveyed the room from corner to corner. Daniel watched as his eyes swept slowly across the walls, then up to the ceiling, then down to the floor, then back to the wall against the stairs. Nobody spoke as Thorsen took the measure of the room. Then his eyes focused on Daniel. The secret room was on the verge of being detected and his father had only moments before his life would be hell on earth.

As calm as ditch water, he said, "Where is there for him to hide? It makes more sense that he would have fled."

Lieutenant Karl Thorsen marched towards the stairs. Daniel followed slowly. He got to the top of the stairs just as Thorsen reached the end of the corridor and peered into a bedroom before reappearing, triumphantly gloating. Men who had been searching the rooms now stood in the doorways. Then Daniel saw that the farmhouse dust had been blown away from around the edges of the mat that concealed the hatch to the old priest's hole. When she had hurriedly thrown the mat on the floorboards, his mother had not allowed for sunshine to highlight what she had thought was of no account: the dust blown away from the area around the mat. Only a practised eye would have seen it, but Thorsen's eyes were just that.

Thorsen slowly walked towards the old rag mat, stabbed it with his sword and pulled it towards him. His sword then pointed at the tiny fingerhold, so close to the wainscot that it might easily be overlooked. Jennings, known more for action than thought, leapt forward, pulled up the hatch and dragged it away.

"Fetch a lamp," Thorsen said, "and rope." Thorsen lowered the lamp into the dark hole and, kneeling, peered down. The only sound was the eerie creaking of the old wooden farmhouse contracting as it cooled in the early evening air. "Jennings, get yourself down there and tell me what you see." Jennings patted his pistol, then obeyed. "I want him alive," barked Thorsen.

"No sign of him now. He's been here though. Blankets, cushions, jug of ale, crumbs, a mug and bowl."

Daniel had held his breath long enough. He breathed out quietly.

"Is the bowl warm?" said Thorsen.

Daniel, still outwardly calm, now entertained thoughts of shoving Thorsen down there and nailing it shut.

"Aye, it is." Jennings sounded surprised. "There's some sort of broth in it."

Thorsen lowered himself into the priest's hole and Daniel knew that someone who could work out that the farmhouse kitchen did not extend underneath the stairs and neither did any other *visible* room, would also see the escape hatch to down under the farmhouse. When Thorsen called for three more men and three lamps to be lowered, Daniel knew that he had.

He turned and went down the stairs; he noticed that he no longer felt pain in his leg. He went out into the scullery, drank some water and stood outside the back door. Pulling out the scullery chair, he sat, unwound his bandages and took out the splint. He would miss the old rogue, so would his mother. There was a lot of noise from the top of the stairs, but not the satisfied sound of success. He looked over his

One Dark Night

shoulder to his mother whose eyes were conveying hope. He had got away! His father had escaped from down under the house and somehow evaded the revenue men stationed around the house. Daniel looked Thorsen in the eye yet knew it was still too soon to taunt him.

A shout came from the men in the barn and Thorsen ran the fifty yards to be the first to clap hands on "the magician".

Yet Daniel walked the other way. If he'd gone anywhere, it would be to the new ditch he'd been digging; it was deeper than most. If he could just have a few words with his father and tell him to get into the Hurst gang's territory, he'd be safer there. Too late.

There came a loud whistle followed by a shout. "Got him. Get over here quick." Just one mounted Dragoon and his sword. Would his father take him on?

Daniel hurried as best as he could. His father was knee deep in mud and covered in twigs. Without seeking permission, he said, "I'll haul you out, Pa." The Dragoon dismounted, stood away from them both splashing around in the mud but with his sword displaying his intentions.

"Listen, Dan, I've had it but you take care of Ma. The farm's safe in the hands of her brother and," Sydney Tynton clutched his son's arm as Daniel began to haul him from the ditch, "there's more, no one knows but me and that damned pirate. He got me to hide a bit of extra loot from the others. He was the captain, y'see, but he was scared they were plannin' a mutiny. He'd put 'em in their place, one way or another, but he thought it *prudent*," his father was clearly quoting, "*to put a bit by, just in case.*"

Daniel had hauled his father out and his father had not yet got to the point. Just before nigh on a dozen men reached them, Sydney Tynton leaned over and said, "You'll have to dig for it, deep…"

The old fool had left it too late. Thorsen seized him, regardless of spoiling his almost pristine uniform, and shoved Daniel aside. The look in his eye when he stared at Daniel said *you're next*. As his father was marched away between two burly men, Sydney Tynton bellowed over his shoulder, "And remember, only when there's an 'r' in the month."

One Dark Night

Chapter Twenty-Three
Lucy
"He is to be gibbeted"

June 1821

Summer is the best season of all, Lucy thought, as she watched the gulls swooping over the sea. The strong smell of seaweed told her the tide was out even before she leant over the parapet. She'd ask permission to collect the type that made good fertilizer. The Lieutenant had said he'd not be back until late this afternoon so approval was almost sure to be granted. Even if Jennings insisted on accompanying her, a walk along the shore on a sunny day would lift her spirits.

Since her first visit to the roof on that terrible day after the unsuccessful run, she had turned the flat rooftop of Watch House into a sunny, walled garden. There were pots of every variety of herb that Martha had ever yearned for, and a tub of flowers in each corner. There was also a barrel of compost next to the cupboard where Martha had secretly stored the flour. The seaweed, once soaked in rainwater to rid it of salt, accelerated the decomposition of the kitchen waste, producing rich brown earth at the bottom. She was sure parson Raffles could use this for his sermon. Perhaps say something like *from what seems useless, fit only to be thrown away, God makes...* Hmm. Perhaps not. Lucy was glad she was not required to compose sermons.

She sat on the bench, brushed down the nearly new, fashionable pink dress from the market and, pushing a borrowed book aside she reflected on her life, now so different from six months ago.

Then, she had worked in muddy fields for a family of law-breakers: now she enjoyed organizing a household for an upholder of the law.

One Dark Night

Then, she had worked six-and-a-half long days a week: now she had time to sit in the sun.

Then, she had slept on a straw palliasse on the floor: now she slept on a bed with warm, woollen blankets.

Then, she was spurned by all for her ill-fitting, torn clothes: now she had a cloak, and not only the brown dress but also this pink one, and two spencers, her thin black shawl, two pairs of boots and a pair of leather slippers for indoors. She also had a beautiful new bonnet with pink ribbons.

Then, her mother had shown in every way possible that she resented her even being born: now she had made herself useful and was respected. When Thorsen accompanied Martha and her to church, albeit from the great height of Midnight, the village folk would acknowledge them *all* and give a passable smile.

There was no comparison. Except that then she had not needed to be permanently accompanied by a revenue man. She could not even argue that they had more important duties. The Lieutenant had made this bay safe from *dark and dangerous* deeds. She smiled at her thoughts. Well, there had been some terrible, dark and dangerous deeds! When she thought of that night on the beach, it made her shiver. And now, occasionally, she thought of Thorsen as *Lieutenant.* He had not only rid the neighbourhood of villains, he had made her life very comfortable, but she knew what was missing. He had put a stop to Daniel being able to see her except when he went to church and sat in a pew in front of her. She longed for Sundays just to have him pass her by and throw her a glance. For nearly three long months she had not spoken to him once. She'd heard a linnet whistle on several occasions but perhaps it was just a linnet whistling because she saw nothing.

Interrupting her thoughts, an arrow arched over the crenellated rooftop and clattered to the ground. It was attached to cotton twine which hung over the parapet. Wrapped around the arrow was a note.

Pull up the twine, it is tied to string. Pull up the string and it will be attached to a rope with a loop. Loop this over the wall on the sea side but not near a window.

One Dark Night

Lucy peered down but could see no one, but there was a very happy linnet whistling. She followed the instructions. The crenellations made it so easy to loop the rope around something that would hold the weight of a man climbing up. Whoever designed castles ought to have realized that but she was glad they hadn't.

Then suddenly she was face to face with Daniel. The law-breaker. If Thorsen were to know he was here, she could lose everything.

Daniel grinned as he climbed over the low parapet and slid to the flat rooftop. "Better not to sit on the bench, Lucy." He patted the ground for her to sit on his right. Then, seeing her face as she looked at her dress, he took off his white shirt and flung it down. "You look beautiful," he said.

Unbidden, his mother's words dropped into her mind. "Our Dan's a catch and he enjoys toying with the bait, taking it and swimming away." She had no time for further thought because he leapt up, scooped her into his bare arms and gently placed her on the shirt. She had never seen him in just his breeches before. The feel of his smooth, bare, sun-browned skin made her every nerve taut – if only she could one day relax into his arms, assured that he was not the violent, rebellious destroyer the Lieutenant made him out to be.

"Have you heard the news?" He could see from her face that she hadn't. "The trials in Middleston are over – rushed through," he snapped. "I watched as eighteen men were identified as having brutally murdered or attempted to murder King's men." His right hand formed a fist as he said, "All are sentenced to hang. My father is amongst them and he is to be *gibbeted*."

Now it was Martha's words banging around in her head. "They wrap them up in chains tightly and hang them... left for days, months even, and the crows come and peck..." And here she was, sitting with the murderer's son.

The worst news was over and, no longer angry, Daniel said, "Some are hoping for a reprieve." He shook his head slowly. "My mother is inconsolable. Thorsen has gone to see a lawyer today in Merrygate to try to take our home." Daniel picked up Lucy's hand and placed it on his knee and held it there. "I'm so very sorry to bring you this news for

One Dark Night

I think Thorsen is hoping you won't find out just how vengeful he is." He patted her hand. "But I want you to know. However terrible, I think you should know what that man is driven by."

Lucy wanted to say so much and so far she hadn't said a word. She took her hand away from Daniel. The Lieutenant's vengeance was understandable. Perhaps Daniel did not know that his father had murdered the Lieutenant's father. She was almost surprised to hear herself whisper, "I'm so glad you had the accident with your foot, Daniel."

"So am I. I have much to thank the rabbits for. God bless them for digging their burrows!"

Lucy had heard Thorsen use almost the same words and wondered if God chuckled at such things.

"Thorsen was hopping like a mad frog, absolutely furious with himself for being the one to keep me out of trouble on that night." Daniel allowed himself a wide smile and a little laugh and changed the subject. "How is your mother, Lucy?"

Lucy was still numb with the news of hangings and gibbeting so it was a moment before she replied. "She is her usual self. I see her at church each Sunday."

Daniel reached for her hand again. "Yes, church attendance has increased since our parson returned. Even I am attending! Fine fellow, isn't he?"

Lucy noticed that he did not mention that he saw her each week yet barely acknowledged her. "Mr Raffles? Yes, he is and I'm glad you think so too." She left her hand in his as he drew it up to his lips and kissed it gently. Her stomach churned and it felt as if everything in her had drained to her feet. Her head felt light and she managed no words at all. She was touched so rarely by anyone. The feel of warm lips on the back of her hand would be a memory to cherish.

Daniel continued to hold her hand gently by his side. "Why is she so miserable? Has she always been like that?"

With her mother as the subject matter, Lucy found she could answer. "Yes, for as long as I can remember she hasn't a good word to say

One Dark Night

about anybody, especially me. Last Sunday, after the service, she called my father an '*old* man'."

"Well she's the one who married him – not you!"

Daniel was on her side and it was good to be with him again. "I don't understand why she left him." Oh foolish girl, she was supposed to say he was dead.

"He's still alive. Do you know that, Lucy?"

Reluctantly she nodded. "How do *you* know that, Daniel? Does everyone know?" A wave of shame came over her and she stared at her hand – still in Daniel's.

"Please don't concern yourself with others' thoughts. I'm probably the only one who knows. Even Thorsen with all his spies has no knowledge of this." He squeezed her hand gently. "I'll make sure you see your father one day, if the good Lord allows. Your mother has behaved badly and she not only blames you, she makes you pay for it."

"Why do you say that?"

"She's jealous of you. Everyone dotes on you and not on her. Including your father I suspect."

Daniel's perceptiveness embarrassed her. She had nothing to offer anyone except a past full of lies. "But I don't see how my mother can be jealous of me. Until six months ago I had nothing at all." Oh no, that sounded like criticism of the time she worked at his farm. Daniel appeared not to notice and she silently thanked him for the understanding showing in his eyes.

"She's making you pay for the mistakes she's made. She hates that you are a happy person and she isn't." Daniel reached over with his left hand and turned her face towards him. With his thumb he wiped away a tear. "Whatever she does to you, keeping you in rags, half starving you and so on, you are still delightful: she isn't. However hard she tries, you cannot be brought down."

The truth was hard to deny but so was the fact that it was Lieutenant Thorsen who had rescued her. "Daniel, I still love my mother. I know it's hard to understand. One day I hope she will love me."

"She is the one person in the world who can't."

One Dark Night

What did this mean? That she was wasting her time hoping for her mother's love? Or was he saying he loved her?

"You are like the sun, Lucy, spreading warmth and light."

She studied his wind-blown, white blond hair, his blue, sparkling eyes, and said, "And you are like the moon, cool, and often not seen for many a long time."

He answered with the merest hint of a smile. "I must go." He knelt, took a knife from his pocket and cut off one of her curls trailing from her mob cap.

She should have objected, she knew that, but whenever he came near, the thrill overwhelmed her. Her mind was saying one thing – how dare he – the rest of her was locked in a frisson.

"Now I have something of you with me always." Daniel turned his face away from her as he whispered, "For you may never want to see me again; not now the truth is known."

One Dark Night

Chapter Twenty-Four
Daniel
"She could struggle no more"

Daniel entered Annie Yorton's cottage in his usual manner. He dropped from the hatch in the ceiling at the top of the stairs and silently made his way to where Annie habitually sat in her bedroom. Her back was towards him as she faced the window to make use of the light on her sewing; a lighted candelabrum assisted. He watched her enjoying the September evening with a fire laid ready to warm her when the autumn chill came. Whereas the room that Lucy had slept in was almost bare, this one was well furnished. To the left of the door an imposing single four-poster with green velvet curtains stood with a large oak chest at the foot. A matching chest of drawers was on the far wall next to the window with fine china displayed on shelves either side of the fireplace. A large, pale green, oriental rug covered the central part of the floor. And there she sat, expensive beeswax candles flickering alongside her, humming away, just as if she were actually happy.

He took a step onto the rug, then another. In a flash he placed his hand over her mouth and the other hand at her throat. "Don't move, Yorton. Don't say a word." He relaxed his grip on her throat and slowly removed his hand from over her mouth. Annie Yorton attempted to shout but found she was swiftly silenced. "Agree to stay quiet and I will not harm you."

Annie raised her hand slowly to show assent and Daniel released her and moved the candelabrum out of reach, extinguishing the candles as he did so. He pulled the chair around to face him.

Annie was not easily intimidated. "What do you want?"
"The truth."

One Dark Night

"Truth?" Annie said raising her voice.

"I want the truth and I want it quickly and quietly. I want you to tell me what you have been receiving each month on the beach and why."

"Receiving? No more than my due, I can tell you."

"Yorton, I shan't be satisfied with your protestations. If you do not tell me, I'll turn this place over from top to bottom until I find the answers and if I must gag and tie you up to do so, I will."

Annie's sewing slid to the floor and she drew in a deep breath. "I have been granted a little money each month in recognition of my former position as housekeeper at Faefersham Court."

"Yorton, as the son of Sydney Tynton. I know more than you think."

"I know who you are!" Annie spat out contemptuously. "I have nothing more to tell you."

Daniel fingered the kerchief around his neck. He took from his belt a length of slender rope and let one end fall to the floor. "I asked for the truth and I meant the whole truth. Not this shilly-shallying you're giving me. How much have you been receiving?"

"A few guineas, nothing more."

The sound of a horse cantering towards the cottage alarmed Daniel. Annie Yorton grinned and closed her eyes imperiously. With one stride and a flick of the rope, Daniel lashed her to the chair and the kerchief was tightened around her mouth. She struggled as he tied the rope until she could struggle no more.

The rider knocked on the door. Annie wriggled and was about to stamp her feet on the floor when Daniel caught hold of them and tipped her chair back, making Annie very unstable.

He knocked again, then called out. "Mrs Yorton!" He tried the latch but Annie had pulled the bolt across.

The voice of the woman who lived in the next cottage could be heard. "If there's no candles lit, it means she's out."

"I am obliged to you. And would you know when she will be in?"

"You're not from round these parts are you?"

The man responded in the slight accent that had given him away. "Why no ma'am, not for many a year now."

One Dark Night

A door slammed. *Ma'am* had no dealings with foreigners. Spies, the lot of them.

Daniel waited for the sound of retreating hooves and glanced out of the window to watch a well-dressed man on horseback trotting away towards the Brookington road. "Such a disappointment for him to find you away from home and, as you are out, you will not be able to see me search your cottage. I shall find the money that's been keeping you in so much comfort."

The search was over in moments. He knew where half the village hid their valuables: behind a loose brick in their fireplaces. "Now I want some answers." He tipped the pouch of coins he'd found into her lap. "Twenty or more guineas, I'd say." He picked one up and turned it around. "Ah, old King George's head. Dead now." Daniel loosened the kerchief and let it fall around her neck.

"They're my lifetime savings."

"Nonsense. How much have you been receiving each month and why?"

"I've told you why."

"You've told me lies."

"What makes you think I'm not telling the truth?"

"You've told nothing but lies since you arrived in Wintergate, have you?"

"How dare you!" Annie Yorton struggled in a futile attempt to raise her arms at him. "You... you... farm boy with a murdering father! You come here accusing me of lying..."

"Aye, I do." Daniel walked towards the hearth again and reached into the left of the hole where the brick had been and pulled out another pouch. "You see, Yorton, the evidence is against you. Or is this Lucy's?"

"It most certainly is not. If it wasn't for that unkempt, useless creature, I would be a Lady."

"Shut your lying mouth. You've made Lucy work to keep you and you've taken what has been rightfully hers." A Lady? Did she think she could have been Lady Harper? He fingered the velvet curtains around the bed and the silk counterpane. "Silk. Paid the tax, did you?"

One Dark Night

"That girl has been a millstone around my neck since the day she was born! When I was ten, I had no parents at all and I was put in service. She's not had to do…" The words, which had been coming fast and filled with venom, suddenly failed her. "anything..." she finally said, her voice trailing off.

"What lies! She's had much worse. He tipped the contents of the second pouch into her lap. "Lucy's not responsible for your misfortunes. She's been the means of giving you a lazy, comfortable life. In your lap now," he ran his hand through the coins, "are more than forty guineas. And there's still more, isn't there?"

Annie Yorton did not answer. She bit her lip so hard and furrowed her brow so much that, despite her usual beauty, Daniel was reminded of a gargoyle on an old church.

"You're wasting your time, and mine, lying to me. I've seen you on the beach collecting money from someone at Faefersham Court. It used to be the butler, didn't it? Your husband, the butler, is alive and well. So why are you saying you're a widow?"

There was only a rebellious silence from Annie.

"He couldn't afford the sort of money you've been taking, could he? I calculate it's about six guineas a month." He picked up the coins from her lap, put them in the pouches and tied them to his belt.

"That's my money!"

"Given to you for the benefit of Lucy. Do you remember being told to 'take good care of Lucy because you'll be sorry if you don't'?"

"You've been spying on me! How dare you?"

"Lucy is no longer living with you yet you are still collecting money each month. I'll come to the point. You are a blackmailer, Yorton."

"Blackmail?" Annie made an excellent attempt at sounding horrified.

"You could hardly be blackmailing your husband. I'd say you're blackmailing Sir William Harper."

"If the money is blackmail money, why would I be told to look after Lucy?" She gave him a triumphant look.

Daniel knew he did not yet know all the right questions to ask. If her hold over Sir William was knowledge of his part in the free trading,

One Dark Night

then Yorton was right to ask why the money was for Lucy. It would be easy to squeeze the truth out of her if he used the old ways. Instead, he wandered across to the oak chest and opened the lid. There was more in it than when he had last looked. He crossed to the chest of drawers – it was empty. She had packed the trunk: she had plans to leave. "Going somewhere, Yorton?"

"I'm entitled to do what I want to do."

"Without a thought for your daughter?" Daniel removed two more pouches from the trunk then levered up the loose floorboard he'd found when he'd last visited.

"Why should I stay here to rot alone? Lucy's left me and she's well looked after."

"Lucy's left you! You couldn't wait for her to go. You bloodsucking crone." Daniel towered over her. "What was the deal with Faefersham Court? She'd be supported until she married? And now that she's of marriageable age she's in *service* where followers are discouraged so you go on receiving the money?" Daniel walked around behind her and pulled her hard back against the chair, then quietly said, "I'll make sure you receive not a penny more."

"Huh! You can't do that! And put that money back. It's not yours."

Daniel had by now tied twelve pouches to either side of his belt which now tended to pull his breeches down rather than keep them up.

"I don't know where you thought you were going, Yorton. But I have other plans for you."

Daniel gagged her, checked the rope, pulled himself up into the loft and crawled along under the rafters of the four cottages to Bodger's cottage where he lowered himself through the hatch at the top of the stairs.

~

Wintergate had seen the last of Annie Yorton for some long time and Bodger, the deaf mute, was six guineas better off.

One Dark Night

Chapter Twenty-Five
Karl
"He hated that blond-haired, slippery son"

Karl Thorsen rose early, setting out on his regular patrol before the morning mist had fully formed along the coastal road. He'd done what he'd set out to do. The man responsible for the treacherous, brutal murder of his father had been sentenced to hang. A weight had fallen from his shoulders. There was no chance of a reprieve for Sydney Tynton. He needed only to wait a short while and it would all be over.

Preoccupied with his thoughts, he trusted Midnight to know his routine and relaxed the reins. Many miles of the coast were now practically clear of the North Kent Gang. There had been no signs of illegal activities since the bust at the beginning of April. Almost six months and there had been little news of smuggling anywhere on this part of the coast. Of course, the younger Tynton still eluded him, slippery as an eel; perhaps he was paying the biggest price of all, the loss of those he loved. Yet surely even he could not love a father like that. Same blood though; it was likely he'd revert to a similar pathway eventually. Karl allowed himself a smile: Daniel Tynton's fate was sealed in his blood. And now he'd be able to return to running his estate. It had been costly, both in time and energy, to oversee matters at home and to avenge his father's death. First though, he should call on Hendon's mother and see if she was coping.

He grasped the reins and spurred Midnight on towards Merrygate where Hendon's mother had a small cottage. As he approached, he saw her spinning yarn in front of the doorway.

"Good morning, Mrs Hendon." Karl dismounted and tethered Midnight to the gatepost.

One Dark Night

Mrs Hendon ceased spinning and stood up. "Good morning, Lieutenant Thorsen."

"I see you are making the most of the light. I know your son was proud of you and now I can see why."

"I have been fortunate enough to purchase a loom and I wish my boy could see what I've made. Would you like to see some of the shawls, Lieutenant?"

Midnight stamped his hooves and tossed his head. "Don't be so impatient, Midnight. I have important trade to transact." Karl smiled warmly at the widow who'd lost her only child in the service of the King.

Her cheeks coloured at this unusual source of attention. "I should be honoured if you would like one enough to purchase it."

Karl laughed gently. "Mrs Hendon, I can tell you are going to be highly successful. Show me your finest wares."

"I only have pink and green yarns so far, but if you were to require other colours, I'd be pleased to take an order."

Karl chuckled. She'd obviously had a good teacher. "A pink shawl will do fine." Perhaps he should take another for Martha – he had plans to relocate her to his estate. "And a green."

It was as he was cantering away with two bundles strapped to the saddle that it occurred to him that, having paid twice as much as necessary, few others could afford to do so. She was unlikely to be selling much to the Merrygate shops with their wealthy, sophisticated London clientele, so there must be someone else supporting this enterprise.

He decided to head to the sands. He leaned forward and rubbed his spirited horse's neck and guided the black stallion to the long sandy Merrygate beach. It was still too early for many people to be on the sands and with a toss of his head and a whinny, Midnight knew he was in for a treat. "Let's thunder along the sands, Midnight. I need to live up to my name. Thor, the god of Thunder, can't have a prancing, dancing horse."

Galloping exuberantly across the sands left Midnight in a sweat and Karl's sandy-coloured hair ruffled. Once they reached Wintergate Bay,

One Dark Night

he dismounted and brushed Midnight to rid him of the worst of the salt spray and sand he'd kicked up. He combed his own hair too. "There! What a handsome pair we make. Let's call upon that scheming mother of Lucy's and find out who that visitor was." Those two village girls need only a few pennies and they'd sell their souls. He shivered at the thought yet also felt a little pity – there'd be fewer young men for them to hunt down as husbands.

Before leaving the beach, he glanced up at Watch House. He must get the timing right. If he returned to his estate too early, what could he do about Lucy? He thought back to the time when he had first approached her, outside the church. Her mother, always well dressed, accounted for her extensive wardrobe with comments on her prowess as a seamstress. The reason she gave for the contrast in Lucy's appearance was that she was rebellious and lazy. Karl's observations had given him doubts for the truth of her tales. If anything, she seemed jealous of her daughter. He'd introduced himself to Lucy and watched the interaction between the good Mrs Yorton and the unkempt daughter. He'd always thought of her as a child, possibly a little retarded, yet when he spoke to her she was spirited and intelligent. A charming, vivacious young lady, albeit dressed in a child's rags, and resenting, maybe embarrassed by his attention. She was undeniably naïve. He was glad he'd spoken to the parson's wife. It was she who'd suggested that both Lucy and Mrs Yorton would benefit by living apart. Tactfully put.

Reaching China Cottage, Karl dismounted, loosely tethered Midnight, and knocked on the door. It was time to confront the woman. Her standard of living did not match her known income. Now that Lucy had been prevented from handing over her wages, Mrs Yorton should have been casting around for ways to pay the rent, feed and clothe herself. There had been little discernible difference in her way of life since Lucy left. For all her protestations of being holier than the Archbishop of Canterbury, the story and the characters did not fit together. He'd suspected she played a small part in the smuggling, but that had stopped now. There was an element here that he'd not yet grasped. Fortunately, he now had more time to investigate how she managed to live so much better than most. He knocked again. The stranger who'd visited her last night might well be the answer.

It was not yet eight in the morning so it was unlikely she'd be out. He lifted the latch. The door was bolted. He went around to the back and hammered on the door. This door was not bolted and it took only a minute to realize there was nothing of any value left in the cottage. He pulled out the bricks by the two fireplaces. Only brick dust. Every possible hiding place was examined but nothing of any consequence was found.

He examined the ground by the back gate. Two sets of wheel ruts clearly showed. One set looked like nothing more than a donkey or pony cart heading towards Brookington. The other set of tracks was deeper, those of a heavier, larger cart and the shoes were those of a weighty shire horse. They also ran around to the front of the cottage and appeared to veer off in the other direction.

Bodger often acted as a carter. He'd call on him. He lifted the latch, no point in knocking, and went in. No one there. He did get an answer from Van Diemen's Cottage, next to Bodger's, and with the bribe of a crown he learnt a little but not anything he couldn't deduce for himself. Bodger had taken a pony cart out just after sunset last night. She denied any knowledge of another cart, and was not even tempted by a sovereign. That might mean Tynton was involved. Time to visit the parson.

"Good morning, Mr Raffles. Forgive me for calling so early."

"I have had much practice at forgiveness." The parson chortled and waved Karl through. "A little breakfast, perhaps?"

Karl politely refused. "I have something I want to show you urgently. I should be most grateful if you would follow me immediately to Mrs Yorton's cottage."

"All is well, I hope? It is not often I am called out by the forces of law and good order."

Karl was never slow in his movements whereas the parson was never fast. Before the parson had even crossed the road, Karl had turned the corner and awaited him by the front door. He pushed the now unbolted door open and ushered the parson through.

One Dark Night

"Ah, I see she has gone," said the parson rubbing most of his chins.

"Are you saying you knew she was going?"

"Well," he now scratched his head, "she had mentioned plans to return nearer to Faefersham. Understandable, wouldn't you agree?"

Karl was not convinced that Annie Yorton had packed up and left after sunset of her own accord. "Perhaps. But why leave without telling anyone and why under the cover of darkness?" The parson looked mystified. He clearly was not involved. "Apparently a well-dressed man on horseback called at the cottage earlier yesterday evening but did not gain entry. I wonder if he was a threat in some way and she decided to leave before the morning."

"Oh poor Lucy. Her mother has failed her once again." The parson drew in such a large breath that he looked even bigger than usual. "Until we can ascertain for certain who this visitor was, I wonder if we should just tell Lucy that her mother has left Wintergate – just a little quicker than I'd expected."

"The wheel tracks of one of the carts were going towards Brookington, so Faefersham is a possibility," said Karl.

After passing decisions back and forth several times, both felt comfortable that neither would say anything other than Mrs Yorton had decided to leave.

"Before you go back to your breakfast, Mr Raffles, I have a question for you."

"Is it a long question?" Raffles said, patting his stomach.

Karl ignored the implied "hurry up" and pursed his lips. A spark of anger flashed across his eyes. "Did you know that Jerusalem Farm has not been owned by the Tyntons for some years now?"

The parson looked astonished. "Goodness me, no. Who owns it then?"

"Mrs Tynton's brother."

"Oh… clever. He's never been involved in smuggling has he? Makes too good a living on his farm to bother."

"He's lent his donkeys out on dark nights." Karl gave Raffles a knowing look.

"You can hardly charge him with that."

"I would if I could prove it."

"Come now! You're sounding bitter and that's not good for your soul."

"Daniel Tynton has been deputising for his father for some years now yet I don't think I have anything I can charge him with. Not one person will give witness to that. I've offered as much as fifty guineas and nothing!"

"For the sake of your own soul, I think you should allow yourself to let the matter rest. You have brought to justice the man who did your family a great wrong. You are damaging your own life in persecuting Daniel and his mother."

Karl nodded unconvincingly and thanked the parson. He could not bring himself to say how much he hated that blond-haired, slippery son of a murdering blackguard.

~

"Left Wintergate? Where has she gone?" asked Lucy with a puzzled look.

"Gone. Just gone." He shrugged his shoulders. "She's obviously decided to leave for some reason. The parson said she'd been talking about leaving and so it's obviously a planned departure." He looked at her and said as if it were commonplace, "You'll be well rid of her."

"I don't understand why she hasn't told me she was planning to go, and *where*."

"I called on her this morning and the cottage is empty. I imagine one of the carters has loaded her belongings and taken them to some place that's taken her fancy." He called for Martha to make a strong brew of tea. "We are both in need of refreshment."

Lucy began, "My fear is that she has decided living is not worthwhile anymore and…" She could not finish.

"No. If she'd killed herself, she would not have taken her belongings." But if only the smaller cart went towards the crossroads to Faefersham or to Dover, where was the heavier cart going? Perhaps she had sold the heavier furniture. His thoughts returned to Lucy. "You need not fear that. And she was no mother to you. You are, in effect, an orphan now."

One Dark Night

Martha, filled kettle in hand, spun round, spilling water from the spout. "Lieutenant! Your heart's got itself gibbeted. Lucy's mother is not dead. She's just moved somewhere."

Karl looked shocked but he did not reprimand her. He had hoped to put the case for Lucy being better off in his care rather than with her mother. In a conciliatory manner, he said, "Put the kettle on the stove, Martha. And maybe you should make Lucy some hot, creamy milk with a nip of brandy." He pulled out his hip flask and placed it on the table, then drew out a chair for Lucy, sat opposite her and stared at this distressed little bundle. This poor girl had been so hurt by those around her who should have loved her most. He tried to find the right words to apologize for breaking the news so bluntly. He was more used to issuing orders to men on his estate or customs' men. Suddenly he found himself down on his haunches in front of her and holding the hand that wasn't wiping a stray tear. "Lucy, you don't need your mother. I will always look after you. Always."

One Dark Night

Chapter Twenty-Six
Daniel
"Where they'll all hate you"

Wednesday 12th September

On his way to the parson's, Daniel called in at Bodger's cottage by the back door. The fewer people who saw, the better. Josh stayed by the rickety gate where Fiddle was tethered.

"Morning, Bodger." Despite the futility of awaiting a reply from a deaf mute, He always paid him the courtesy of a little time to nod and grin. "All go well?" He always looked at him straight, so that he had a chance to read his lips. Sometimes he misread people but Daniel had learned to enunciate clearly because it was important Bodger didn't get his instructions wrong.

Bodger's chest got worse as the autumn days arrived so his attempt to laugh resulted in a coughing fit.

Daniel sat down while Bodger spluttered and heaved. He drew from his jacket pocket two small buns. "Freshly baked this morning and we can't have a bun without some tea. Put the kettle on."

Bodger, now recovered, waved both hands to indicate he had no tea.

"Yes you do. Here it is." Daniel produced a little packet of tea. "I'm not the son of the magician for nothing, you know."

Bodger looked forlorn and shook his head. He let out a long sigh as he raked through the red hot embers in the tiny grate, popped on a small log, and hung the kettle low over them.

"Sit down and eat your bun, Bodger. I called in on Ma and she'd just finished what she calls her 'Wednesday baking'. She's a bit low on spices these days but they're still right tasty." Daniel took a bite. "She's not looking forward to winter on the farm."

One Dark Night

Bodger showed his care by his face full of concern and hands held wide.

"Don't you worry, my good friend. There's not much we can do about my father, but the farm hasn't belonged to him for years. It was bought by my uncle. Thorsen can't take it off him and he's as mad as a March hare."

Bodger did his best to imitate a boxing hare and Daniel roared with laughter. It showed Bodger understood something of what he'd been saying.

"So! Did you have any problems with Annie Yorton?"

Bodger shook his head and grinned.

"She didn't seem too keen to be bundled onto the pony cart like that. We were kind, though, weren't we Bodger?"

Bodger demonstrated shoving the bound and gagged Annie into the back of the cart and then covering her with a blanket.

"Did you load her trunk onto the boat?" Following another nod from Bodger, Daniel rose to get the kettle and make a small pot of tea with the little water Bodger had allowed, all the time telling him how he'd contacted a friend and used his strong cart and horse to move Annie Yorton's furniture. He hadn't wanted to use his uncle's; it wouldn't be fair to involve him. The builder, on the other hand, had been a free-trader and was only too happy to help.

"Now it's time for me to go and for you to get yourself off to the market and buy some warm clothes, bedding and some good food."

Despite having driven all the way to Dover on the Monday night, and not arriving back until the Tuesday night, on this Wednesday morning Bodger looked eager – a good sign.

"Let's hope she speaks French, eh Bodger?"

Bodger found this the funniest remark of all and held his chest as if that could stop the oncoming coughing fit.

Daniel stood up, thumped the seated Bodger on his back, and to no one in particular said, "Now she'll be able to see what it's like being dragged away and dumped somewhere where they'll all hate you 'cos you're different. That's what she did to Lucy. Let's hope she likes

One Dark Night

France. It'll be a while before she sees England and she'll never again treat Lucy as if she were her slave."

~

A short time after, Daniel led Fiddle, with Josh padding by his side, to the parsonage.

"Ah... Mr Tynton. Come on in. The weather's not too good this morning. A chill in the air. Do you want to bring Josh inside? Mrs Raffles will not mind, I can assure you."

"Good morning, Mr Raffles." Then pointing Josh to a cosy spot by a wall, he said, "Josh will be fine there. He's a bit fidgety today, and I'd like a little of your time if I may please?"

The parson led the way and showed Daniel a comfortable chair on one side of the hearth and took up residence in a large chair on the other. Once he was sat down, it was not so easy to get up. "Am I required to listen or to answer questions?"

"Probably both, Mr Raffles."

"How is your soul?"

The parson had asked Daniel this question regularly and he had rarely known what to say. At least it brought to his attention the fact that he had one – something his father denied – and he was now sure of his answer. "My hope is that it will improve, Mr Raffles."

Parson Raffles peered through his spectacles as if to check the veracity of the response. He seemed satisfied, smiled broadly yet said, "You must do more than hope."

"Please call me Daniel. It's the teaching you gave me at your school, when you knew me as Daniel, that has guided my thoughts and, lately, my life."

"Ah, my school." The parson paused while he reflected fondly. "Had I not taken up the living in Torwell Bridge, it would still be a part of our parish today."

Daniel would have had much to say on the importance of schooling for all, even girls could do with a little learning, look at Lucy, but he had other matters on his mind. "Yes, it was greatly missed, as were you. The whole parish is glad of your return."

One Dark Night

"And I am pleased to be amongst you once again. But Daniel, what can I do for you?" Daniel was quiet. "Your soul will, you hope, improve?"

"It's not as black as a dark night." Involuntarily he thought of his father. "But heavy as a tub of brandy."

"Is there something you wish to confess? Many people feel the need to see me privately on such matters."

Daniel shook his head. "Not exactly that, Mr Raffles. It is more a question of wishing to discuss something with you."

"You find yourself at the crossroads perhaps?"

Mrs Raffles bustled in with a tray of cheese and plain, freshly baked rolls, and two mugs of ale. "Now had you not come to Torwell Bridge, you would not have found me, Mr Raffles." She had an unfortunate nervous tic which looked like a wink and Daniel found he was being winked at. "So you were a scholar at my good husband's school?"

"My dear, you are not to listen at the door," said the parson with a frown.

"The door is not closed and this is my way of reminding you that it should be, my love."

Daniel smiled at the parson's wife. How well they suited each other. "Indeed, I was, Mrs Raffles." He drank a little of the invigorating ale. "It is there that I learned to love books." Perhaps he should have said that in the singular for he had only one book: a book of poems.

"My dear Mrs Raffles, we are both most grateful for your thoughtfulness." The parson gestured towards the tray, "but perhaps we are keeping you from your duties?"

Mrs Raffles winked. "Of course, my love. I do indeed have much to do."

She winked again at Daniel who reflected on how unfortunate it must be to have a wife who inadvertently winked at other men, especially if you were a parson. He leapt up to hold the door open wide for her to leave, thanked her, then closed the door. Were those minutes wasted? He decided they weren't, then launched into his reason for coming. "I suppose I am at the crossroads, as you said. Though I have already chosen which way to go."

One Dark Night

"The choices we make direct our lives and, ultimately, they are our offering to God and determine our own eternity."

Daniel reflected for a moment. *Emmanuel* Raffles – didn't his very name mean *God is with us*? If only he could spend more time with this profound thinker. "I remember you also saying that smugglers were making life more difficult for *themselves* by dint of using all their energies to outwit the revenue men."

Parson Raffles nodded slowly. "This is true."

"If the local people could be encouraged to put as much energy into the production of goods as they have put into their night activities with those on the continent then this part of the county could thrive. I gave Mrs Hendon a small loan to start a weaving business. We have wool aplenty in this county and yet it was being used as currency for brandy, perfumes, and other inessential luxuries when the people need feeding, clothing and decent housing. Mrs Hendon tells me she has begun to take orders from Merrygate stores to keep her busy throughout the winter months. She'll be able to afford to pay a man to repair the roof before the worst of the winter weather arrives. And she says she will repay the loan by springtime."

"You are a man of enterprise."

"Spurred on by your words, Mr Raffles."

"Not my words alone, Daniel. I make use of the word of God."

Their conversation was interrupted again by a knock on the front door and Mrs Raffles could be heard bustling along the hallway. Daniel felt it prudent to wait before continuing.

Parson Raffles cupped his ear and peered over his spectacles. His brow furrowed and Daniel began to pay attention to the conversation happening on the doorstep. Daniel stood when he heard Mrs Raffles suggest the stranger come in.

"Mr Raffles, Mr Tynton, forgive my interruption. A gentleman here, Mr Douglas Harper, I believe you said your name was?" The finely dressed man followed the parson's wife into the room and nodded. "He is looking for Mrs Annie Yorton and Miss Lucy Yorton."

One Dark Night

Daniel and the stranger bowed in greeting. The parson half-stood and might have made it to a full bow had Mr Harper not held his hand high and said he had not come to disturb their discussion.

"You may be concerned as to why I seek them."

The parson's eyebrows arched, yet he looked at the floor. As for Daniel, still standing, his face showed no emotion whatsoever, the look of a successful poker player holding the most wanted card in the game.

Mr Harper proceeded with caution. "I was acquainted with them both some years ago. I have just returned from America and I should like to renew my acquaintance."

Mrs Raffles, sensing the uncomfortable atmosphere, and being disposed to remedy such situations, offered her usual relief with an expectant, sunny smile. "A little refreshment gentlemen?"

"Most thoughtful of you, but I must decline. I have little time to accomplish my intentions," Mr Harper said with an affable nod of acknowledgement, and Mrs Raffles left the room disappointed.

Daniel read the parson's thoughts correctly. He had seen enough to draw the conclusion that Mr Harper was unlikely to be a threat to either Annie or Lucy yet it was always wise to be cautious. He allowed the parson to pass on the news.

"I'm afraid you are too late to renew your acquaintance with *Mrs* Yorton. She left the neighbourhood just a few days ago."

Daniel's thoughts hovered around "and not a moment too soon", but he said nothing and his face remained inscrutable. He tried not to stare too hard as his thoughts moved on to Lucy: just what were this man's intentions towards her? His face seemed familiar, yet he said he'd been in America and that was verifiable by his accent.

"Do you know where I could find her," asked the stranger.

"She left sooner than expected and I do not know where she went," said the parson.

"You make no mention of *Miss* Yorton. Is she still here?"

The parson was skilled in the art of protecting his parishioners' secrets. "May I pass on your greetings? Perhaps she may then like to arrange a meeting."

One Dark Night

"You are most kind." Mr Harper drew a card from his inside pocket, requested the use of the quill in the inkwell on the nearby desk, and wrote a message. Wafting it around to dry the ink, he said, "I should be most grateful if you would pass this on to her."

"It will be my pleasure to do so," said the parson.

"I shall be staying in Merrygate tonight, at the Grand Hotel, if I should be needed.

This time the parson, determined to stand, succeeded, and led the personable young gentleman to the door.

On re-entering the room, he said, "I do sometimes miss my living at Torwell Bridge. There we had two maids and a housekeeper to attend to visitors' needs, whereas here we have only the daily maid-of-all work." Parson Raffles sat down, leant forward and, as if it were confidential, whispered, "Son of the baronet, Sir William Harper, I suspect."

Daniel sat and replied simply, "One day he'll be Sir Douglas, then." Parson Raffles gave him a knowing look over the top of his spectacles. Daniel's thoughts raced: so this was the son of the *real* magician. Daniel's father had used the name, but it was Sir William who had that magic touch. This Douglas Harper was indeed gentry. He was elegantly dressed in a dark coat trimmed with velvet, buff trousers, and tall, highly polished boots. But what were his intentions towards Lucy and why did he look familiar?

"Now Daniel, let us hope we have no further interruptions, however interesting."

Daniel returned hastily to his reason for coming. "For some time I have been planning a different future for myself and for others."

"You are saying that you will use your planning skills for a better purpose?"

Daniel nodded. "The workhouse is now full to overflowing. I have been fathoming ways to help people escape its clutches. We have too few journeymen and too many unskilled labourers. I have recently sought more bricklayers and carpenters, but good men are hard to find."

"The very words my wife used when I finally plucked up courage to ask her to marry me." Raffles chuckled just enough to make his stomach wobble.

One Dark Night

Daniel took another swig of his ale and took a couple of the proffered biscuits and some cheese. Raffles was a genial host, making time for eating and drinking as well as being an interested listener. But time should be used well, sometimes it runs out unexpectedly so, hastily, Daniel continued. "We have few industries in this part of Kent. But just a few miles away, something important has been happening. Something which I think can help the poor, the skilled, the unskilled and even the wealthy."

Parson Raffles adjusted his spectacles. "You must tell me more, Daniel."

"I know I can count on your confidentiality. To know that my father is about to be hanged and... worse, has kicked me into action. I have drawn up plans and I should like your wise counsel before I proceed further."

"Wise counsel. Ah yes, I do so love to be flattered. Perhaps I can give an opinion instead?"

~

Later that afternoon, Parson Raffles walked purposefully to Watch House. He wanted to be sure the note was delivered to Miss Yorton directly. To no avail. The young man at the door offered to pass the note on. Parson Raffles looked at it carefully. He had wrapped it and sealed it. He could refuse and try to redeliver it another day. He could ask the young man to request Miss Yorton to visit him, but that might alert the Lieutenant, or he could allow the lad who stood before him to deliver it on her return. He chose the latter.

~

"What's the significance of an 'r' in the month, Lucy?" Daniel helped Lucy down on to the long grass on the ledge she still thought of as her "sanctuary" and spread his brown corduroy jacket out for her to sit on. He had been puzzling over this cryptic clue his father had left him and not found the answer. He'd even mentioned it cautiously to the parson just this very morning; he'd talked about seasons of the year. Daniel had wondered if it was to do with digging out the ditches for the winter months. His father had said he'd had to *dig deep*. What was this *bit put*

One Dark Night

away by the pirate and where was it? Now that it was September, he'd overseen the digging out of the ditches ready for the wet winter months, but nothing had been found.

"Oh that's simple. Mussels should not be collected in May, June, July and August because that is when they breed. And the fishermen say…"

"…that collecting them in the cold, winter months – with an 'r' in them – you're less likely to sicken and die," added Daniel with a distinct note of satisfaction. "Well, I'm a little closer to solving the mystery but the mussel beds spread for miles."

Lucy's eyes grew larger as she remembered that last Christmas day. So much had happened. Even though the pirate and Mr Tynton were no longer able to harm Daniel, always being watched had made it impossible to dig the sands herself and her latest decision was she would wait until she could borrow a spade and be sure of being unobserved. If this became impossible she needed to be sure she could trust either Daniel or Thorsen before she would say anything. The usual thoughts she had on this dilemma flashed through her mind: it was unlikely to be a body, but it could be treasure. Would that treasure be hers if she were to do the digging herself? Daniel had now introduced another thought: he knew more about this and he wasn't telling her, just using her knowledge.

"What's wrong, Lucy? Is it Thorsen?"

"No. No, but he's probably riding up to Watch House this very minute. It is fortunate he cannot see us from there."

"What is it then?"

"I must go. I shouldn't really be here with you." She leapt up and scrambled up the side of the ledge.

Josh, who'd been lying quietly by Daniel's side, was concerned but Daniel let her go. If he were seen with her now, she could still be in trouble with Thorsen. Something he had said, or something she had seen, had brought a frightening thought to her mind. What could it be? He looked over the edge that was out of sight of those in Watch House. She had stared down from this side of the ledge. Great white lumps of chalk jutting up through the receding sea, all covered in anchored seaweed hiding the mussels. Except for one large, white chalk rock with almost no weed attached.

~

If he rode there immediately, he would have time to find a local inn for the night, send a message, and present himself the following morning.

To his great relief, he had recently invested in new riding attire. Dark slim breeches tucked into new leather boots, and a short riding jacket gave him the look of a country landowner if not a man of fashion. This was exactly the look required for this task though the outfit had been bought for travelling to and from the trials of his father, the other smugglers and the pirate captain and his crew. Daniel contained his feelings: the regret for his father's life wasted on brandy and gambling yet his love for the man who'd once had the respect of his hard-working mother. In just a few days' time, that man would be no more. He must now ride to confront Sir William Harper. Then, perhaps, his future would begin.

One Dark Night

Chapter Twenty-Seven
Karl
"Sinking sands"

Karl Thorsen returned to Watch House early that same Wednesday afternoon. He was weary from his ride back from his estate and uneasy because he had glimpsed Lucy walking alone along the cliffs. As the door was opened for him he noticed a letter on a silver tray and took it with him to his office. He read the contents of the letter twice before he was sure of his next move. He sent a messenger with an invitation to dine to be delivered to Mr Douglas Harper.

Then he strode into the kitchen of Watch House, causing Martha to leap up and drop Scat from her lap. "We have a guest to dine tonight, Martha. He is an important visitor from America and I should like you to produce a fine menu."

"Well stuff and duckles!" She was unable to say anything further other than by the look on her face. Horror.

"You have six hours to prepare."

"It's not that, Lieutenant. Well… that as well, but what shall I do for an American?"

"Some sort of food," the Lieutenant suggested with a grin.

Martha, eyes popping, said, "Do they eat the same as us? I wouldn't want to disfundle him."

"I'm sure you won't." Lucy came into the kitchen. His eyes followed her every move. "Lamb, do lamb."

"We could start with the fish caught fresh this morning, Lieutenant." Lucy said. "And what would you say to a berry tart, Martha?"

"I ain't never spoken to a tart."

One Dark Night

The atmosphere created by the brusque Lieutenant collapsed, smothered by Lucy's giggles and his own laughter. As he was clearly unconcerned by his lapse of authority, Martha joined in.

"I'll leave it in your capable hands, Martha." He turned to Lucy and explained that he would like her to wait on his guest in a most unobtrusive manner. "It is my intention to discuss business with him over dinner. The boy will wait on us to start and I'll call for you later."

~

Karl was rather pleased that he had accidentally intercepted the message from Mr Douglas Harper to Lucy. No doubt the boy – he must stop calling him that – had intended to give it to Lucy when she returned. She shouldn't have been out. Now that the last course was being cleared away, he could engage Mr Harper over the port in something other than polite conversation, though the tales of life in America had proved most interesting. But what Karl really wanted to know was why the heir to a baronetcy was sending messages to his housekeeper. The boy, Fletcher, trained by Lucy, had served at table well. Karl had seated his guest facing away from the door and he had given instructions that Fletcher should leave to help Martha in the kitchen and Lucy was to come and stand near the door unobtrusively awaiting any instruction. Karl had a plan. It was important for Lucy to know who he really was. The man inside the armour.

"Mr Harper, our estates are close, had you not been in America for the last five years, and I not engaged in battle with the local gangs, we should undoubtedly have become acquainted with one another sooner."

"Most kind of you to remedy the situation, Lieutenant."

Karl noted Lucy's slight turn of her head. He noticed something else as well, something that made it unnecessary for him to pursue the reason for Mr Harper's quest. That was one matter dealt with. There were others. He must not allow the conversation to lag. "It is my pleasure." The decanter of port had been passed to him by his guest and he poured a little into his glass and put it back within the reach of this interesting man. He must ensure that the subject of Faefersham Court or the name Harper was not mentioned for that would surely cause a reaction from Lucy. "I am spending more time on my estate now and I

One Dark Night

intend to leave patrolling the coasts to those who need the minimal income more than I."

Mr Harper leaned forward and said, "Yes, that would seem a sensible path. Tell me, why did you become a Riding Officer?"

Exactly the question Karl needed. "I became a Riding Officer to apprehend Sydney Tynton, because he had murdered my father. A man who was not content just to smuggle the odd case of brandy, he liaised with wreckers working out of Daly Bay." He glanced across to Lucy. Was she listening? Yes, there was a slight furrowing of her brow. "Do you know of the treacherous sands, the Goodwins?"

"Indeed I do. Sinking sands. Infamous."

Karl hurried on, he must not give Mr Harper any opportunity to mention where he came from. "My father was a naval Captain, and he chased the Tynton boat one summer's night in order to prevent them luring another ship onto the sands. My father was shot by Sydney Tynton. He fell overboard and was picked up by Tynton who sailed back to the Goodwins and left him there alone to sink and die as the tide rose. It was too dark for my father's ship to find him and they thought he was in the sea still. The truth only came to light when one of Tynton's crew turned King's evidence. There was, of course, little proof that it was Sydney Tynton, just the testimony of the man who tried to save his own skin by giving evidence. However, Tynton's identity was partially confirmed by my father's crew. Sydney Tynton, as ever, had an irrefutable alibi and was not convicted.

"I saw that as a Riding Officer I would be able to infiltrate their circles – not directly, of course, but by mixing with local people. Within six months I found the proof I needed. The magistrate who vouched for him is as crooked as any of them. No man who kills should evade justice. There must always be some kind of retribution to ensure they think of their eternal souls.

"So you see," he continued, "I was on a mission to destroy the gangs that had killed my father and, in particular, to seek out Sydney Tynton and bring him to justice. This I have done. He was undeniably seen killing revenue men – men I knew." He hadn't mentioned that slippery eel, Tynton's son. More thought was needed for that one. Unable to

One Dark Night

resist another glance across to Lucy, he noticed her discomfiture. He would make her stand there a little longer for there was still much to be discussed.

"As I see it, Lieutenant, no sooner is one gang cleared than another takes its place. There is, I believe, a better answer." Mr Harper leaned back in his chair and stretched out his legs. "America has taught me many things. A slogan summarizes a primary grievance of the British colonists and it was one of the major causes of the Revolution. It was 'No taxation without representation.' Too much taxation is the key to many ills. The word 'smuggling' seems a small price to pay when ranked alongside the word 'revolution'. We do not want revolts leading to revolution here."

There was a short silence before, hesitantly, Karl said, "Yes, the word 'taxation' is something I have been considering for a while now. If the high taxes were to be removed from most of the smuggled goods, it would not be worth the while of these men to smuggle. They could turn their hands to more productive work."

"My thoughts exactly, Lieutenant. We need this discussed at the highest levels. If my father were not so frail, I might seek to go into Parliament myself, but the demands of a large estate inevitably fall upon an only son. Have you thought about standing for election to Parliament yourself, Lieutenant? When I received your invitation, I made some enquiries about you. It appears you are highly regarded as a man unafraid to tackle difficult tasks. I also hear you are incorruptible. Parliament could do with a man like you. Perhaps we could meet again and discuss this further?"

Lucy was clearly taking an interest in all that was being said and the conversation was taking a risky turn. He dismissed Lucy, refraining from using her name. Then he raised his glass and said to Mr Harper. "I shall continue the fight. Taxes shall be my weapon. You are an inspirational man, Mr Harper." And influential too.

~

Karl lay awake that night pondering the likeness between Lucy and Mr Douglas Harper, though the latter had a head of thick, dark hair and Lucy had fair hair. Could they be related? Had they ever met? His slight

One Dark Night

American accent would have made it more difficult for Lucy to recognize him and he had never once turned to look at her and she had not known his name. It was clear that Mr Harper had not known where his letter would be delivered or he would have taken the opportunity to enquire after her.

He would speak to her in the morning and explain how Mr Harper had come to be visiting him. Opening the unaddressed letter was a fortunate mistake. He would explain that he had been protecting her from possible consequences of meeting with a stranger.

One Dark Night

Chapter Twenty-Eight
Daniel
"That thorn in my side"

The following morning, a bright and sunny Thursday, Daniel dismounted from Fiddle, ascended a flight of steps under a Doric portico, straightened his attire, and pulled the bell. One of the double doors opened promptly. "I am Mr Daniel Tynton. Sir William Harper is expecting me." He gestured towards his tethered horse but already a groom was standing alongside waiting to lead him to the stables. He noted the efficiency and the effect it had on him, others too, no doubt.

The butler showed him into the impressive library to await the arrival of Sir William. Whilst waiting, he ran his finger admiringly along the spines of the many books. It must have taken generations to build such a collection. One day he'd have more than just a book of poems to pass on to his children. His plans had been taking shape in his mind for some years but the spur to action had been the brutal murder of the revenue man killed by the hooves of the horse. It had been the turning point in his life – to be holding Lucy, but only to protect her from that awful sight and perhaps her own death because of what she had witnessed, was agony. Had she not been there he could have intervened. Then things got worse. There was the night his father was too drunk to lead the landing of goods from France; the fight with Thorsen; the night of the ambush when his father had involved pirates, and the terrible loss of life; worst of all, his father would shortly be hanged. *This rot had to stop.*

So much now hung on this interview with the man who had been the real magic behind the supply and demand for overtaxed goods. Parson

One Dark Night

Raffles was one of the very few truly good men around here entitled to ask anyone, including Sir William, how his soul fared.

His blazing thoughts were interrupted gently by the unobtrusive entrance of a slim, elegant, grey-haired man. He was immaculately dressed in a double-breasted, blue tailcoat over a buff waistcoat. Daniel had not imagined him like this. He had pictured him being big and bluff. This man had a quiet charm, befitting a gentleman not a smuggler. A footman closed the door behind him.

"Mr Tynton, I am Sir William Harper." He bowed, as if he were greeting a person of importance reflecting more on his exquisite manners than on Daniel's status. "May I offer you some refreshment?"

Daniel bowed in greeting and declined politely; Sir William's hospitality must not be allowed to inhibit his reason for coming.

Sir William indicated to Daniel to sit in a leather high-backed chair facing the window. Again, Daniel declined. The interview might be short if this calm, controlled man refused to listen.

"Delicate matters – private, you said." Sir William looked quizzically at the handsome young man standing so erect with one hand resting behind his back, like a soldier or someone with a concealed knife. "I shall sit here, opposite, and you are welcome to sit and relax at any time."

Daniel allowed himself a trace of a smile – this was not a time for relaxing. He immediately came to the point of his visit. "A young man has been asking the whereabouts of Mrs Annie Yorton and her daughter, Miss Lucy Yorton." He paused. His host was silhouetted against the morning light so Daniel changed his position to get a better look at his face. It showed neither a flicker of surprise nor interest. If he had got this wrong, he could be in serious trouble. "The gentleman introduced himself as 'Mr Douglas Harper'."

"You recognized his name, and I recognize yours, Mr Daniel Tynton. I think this will be a discussion of some length. Please sit down."

Like a wise old owl, Sir William wished to hide in the shadows. Daniel must find a way to draw him into the light. He sat in the comfortable chair opposite. "I fear your son's search for Mrs Yorton will prove unfruitful." Sir William perched his elbows on the arms of his chair and lightly drummed his fingers. Some sort of communication at last. Daniel hurried on. "This may be beneficial for you." But there was nothing, nothing at all to indicate that Sir William was ready to accept or admit to any revelations Daniel might put forward. "Sir William, my father told me of your connection with the North Kent Gang." Just the drumming fingers implying disinterest. "I believe Mrs Yorton has been blackmailing you."

"You are wrong." Sir William stopped drumming and raised just one finger towards Daniel. "If this is all you have to say, then your journey has been wasted."

Daniel thought not: he had barely begun. "Mrs Yorton has been receiving money from your butler. The amount is too much for him to be paying for a daughter's upkeep."

"My butler, Yorton, died a short while ago."

"But the money continued to be paid."

"Your point is, Mr Tynton?"

"A considerable sum of money has been paid by someone in this household to Mrs Annie Yorton on a regular basis. At first I thought it was Miss Yorton's father paying for her upkeep. Annie Yorton kept it secret because she had told the neighbourhood that she was a widow with a small legacy."

"What does it matter to you?"

Daniel ignored the question; he would answer that later. "If you are not being blackmailed, and the money is not being paid by your butler, then it leads me to believe that it is you who is paying for her upkeep, and your son, who looks so like Miss Yorton, is a half-brother to her."

"And you are hoping to profit from what you think you know?"

"First, I must tell you that Annie Yorton now lives too far away to collect further payments." He decided not to explain further for he remembered his father's words: *Be careful, Sir William is a powerful man*. That power bought him this supreme confidence. Were there flunkies listening at the door, waiting to drag Daniel away? The very thought brought a smile to his lips. "No, Sir William. I am hoping that *your daughter* will profit from this knowledge. If you are not willing to

One Dark Night

acknowledge her, then perhaps you might resume the payments to *her directly* until she is able to marry?"

"*Until?*"

"Yes. The money you have sent has been diverted from Miss Yorton's needs to Mrs Annie Yorton's desires. Lucy, for that is how I have always known her, worked on my parents' farm as a kitchen maid and farm hand, in all weathers, almost from the first month she arrived in Wintergate." Now Sir William showed some of the steel he must surely possess. His eyes hardened, his fists clenched. Daniel continued. "She owes her current position, as a housekeeper in name only – she's almost a prisoner and maid-of-all work – to Lieutenant Karl Thorsen."

"Thorsen? That thorn in my side?"

This was more like it! His reaction told Daniel he was not so far away from having a frank conversation instead of this cat and mouse game currently playing out.

"My concern is that she doesn't know her true parentage. Your son, asking questions in the village, is recognizably related to her, despite his dark hair. I would not like Lucy to find out the truth in this manner."

Sir William stood up, paced the room, excused himself, and shut the door on Daniel. Within a minute, a servant appeared with brandy glasses and decanter on a silver tray. Within five minutes, the sound of a horse galloping away from Faefersham Court could be heard. Sir William returned and sat quietly in his chair.

"Brandy?"

"I think I will, Sir William, thank you."

Sir William poured some brandy for them both then sat swirling his around the glass. "To be brief, you are saying that money sent from Faefersham Court has not been benefiting Miss Yorton?" Daniel nodded. "Furthermore, you are saying that Annie Yorton has been living comfortably while her daughter has, and still is, living in straitened circumstances?" Daniel nodded. "You would like her to receive this money so that she may become independent until she marries?"

"That is all correct."

One Dark Night

"I see no reason why that cannot be arranged. Tell me, why will my son's search for Mrs Yorton prove unfruitful?"

"She has left Wintergate."

"Why? Why would she do that if she was receiving sufficient money to live comfortably?"

"She was not given the choice."

Sir William raised his eyebrows. "I see."

Daniel wondered if this magician could imagine how Annie had been spirited away to France in the middle of the night. He would give this clever, yet frail man a reason. "She had denied Lucy the chance of making choices. Now the choice of where she lives has been denied to her." Had he said too much? Did Sir William still have strong feelings for Annie Yorton?

Deep in thought, Sir William put the tips of his fingers together, held them to his lips and clapped them silently. "So her cottage is empty?"

"Yes, I don't think the landlord will even know he's lost a tenant yet."

"He need never know. Will you do something for me?"

Surprised, Daniel tilted his head in acceptance. He was beginning to like this man. *Trusting* him was still a long way off. "If it will benefit Lucy, then I will be happy to oblige."

"You say she is almost a prisoner. What, precisely, do you mean?"

"Lieutenant Karl Thorsen has forbidden her to leave Watch House without being accompanied by one of his men." Daniel stared hard at the man in the shadows. Was that a look of shock? If she was his daughter, he should be made aware of her precarious situation. "There have been death threats issued by some of the local men because they think she betrayed them and their interests."

"Smuggling, you mean."

"I do. She did not betray anyone. Thorsen seems to have an interest in Lucy, perhaps of the romantic kind." Daniel had to pause. The words almost choked him. "Lucy has only recently been able to take short walks alone when Thorsen has not been around. She has been forbidden to meet with me."

"You are on the wrong side of the law? Or...?"

One Dark Night

"I am the son of Sydney Tynton. I have grown up in the belief that free-trading benefits the poor. I now believe there are better ways to help them."

Sir William raised his head, clearly still thinking. "I want you to persuade Lucy, let us both call her that for it is how I too think of her, yes, persuade her to leave Watch House and move back into the cottage."

Daniel's thoughts raced. He'd have to take the stored furniture back. For the moment, he would not mention that he had the money taken from her mother apart from the pouch he'd packed in her trunk and that given to Bodger.

Sir William watched Daniel's expression change from inscrutable to examining this new course of action. "You will do that for me?" Daniel nodded. "She will receive sufficient money to live independently in comfort."

"She is your daughter, isn't she?"

"And you are the man who wishes to marry her." It was not a question. Both men were quiet. Sir William studied Daniel and Daniel studied Sir William. "Let us agree that we both have her best interests at heart."

Daniel said, "Would I be wrong to say that Annie Yorton refused to allow Lucy to visit Faefersham Court?"

"You are correct, Mr Tynton." Sir William took a deep breath. "What I am about to say to you will confirm what you, as Sydney Tynton's son, already know. But before I do, I must have your solemn word that it will go no further. Not to Lucy, nor my son, nor anyone else. Such knowledge is harmful and can do no good."

This man was doing Daniel the honour of expecting him to behave as a gentleman with the further expectation that his word was his bond. "You have my word, Sir William." He would not insult Sir William by adding to that all the usual workmen's promises made upon the lives of their families, none of which meant much.

Sir William was satisfied. "When my wife died in childbirth, I formed an attachment to my housekeeper, Annie Yorton. A most regrettable mistake. When she told me she was with child, she seemed to think it was her right to be married to me. Of course, that was completely out of the question. She was a fine housekeeper and an attractive woman, but nothing more. My butler, Yorton, had always been under her spell and I allowed them to marry. Annie Yorton was in a position to know much of my business life. I had interests in America, which my son and advisers took care of. I had, as your father told you, been able to help the local people and their efforts to bring a little cheer into their lives. Your father would arrange for my men to collect the merchandise and I would send it on to various county connections and to London. Money was exchanged, of course. Annie Yorton snooped. The power of this knowledge enabled her to refuse visits to or from Lucy."

"You feel your intentions were good insofar as the free trading was concerned?" Daniel was not concealing his surprise.

"Not entirely. When I inherited Faefersham Court it came with outrageous debts. My father gambled."

Daniel could not help but interrupt with "We have that in common, if little else, Sir William."

The man seated in the shadows inclined his head, then continued. "There was only one way to save the estate from falling into the hands of a near neighbour – a cheat and a drunkard. I resolved to pay those debts and to pay them fast. The quickest way to raise such a sum of money was to act as the middleman between those who had the money to buy silks, scents, and all manner of luxuries from Paris and beyond, and the men who brought these goods to our shores."

Daniel could see that they had both resorted to nefarious ways in order to live and let others live but a hint of surprise crept in to his thoughts. This man was suddenly not holding back.

Sir William took a sip of brandy before continuing. "It did not take me long to come to the conclusion that it was better for the money to be in my hands than in the hands of the Government where most of it benefited only a few. I feel I was right, of course, but breaking the law always has a price, and I have paid dearly. Annie Yorton ensured that I have paid with the loss of a much loved daughter."

One Dark Night

Now Daniel could not hold back. "Your innocent daughter has paid a much higher price. She has been half-starved and ill-clothed in the bitter cold. She has had…"

Sir William held up the palm of his hand. "Mr Tynton, you need say no more. You have made me aware of my failings and, in the time that is left to me, perhaps I can mend matters. I think you know Lucy quite well?"

"I know her well enough to realize that I should like her to be my wife." He looked at the man in the chair opposite. A fallible man. As was he. "I know that I should like to present to her a life, not only of comfort, but of challenge. A worthwhile life which she will find fulfilling. One of interest which enables her to help others, for she has much to give, despite having had little given to her."

Sir William shifted in his chair; the sun had traversed the sky sufficiently to shine through another window, bringing Sir William's face out of the shadows. "I have sent a rider to recall my son before he discovers that Lucy is his half-sister. When I have spoken to him, perhaps we can offer Lucy a home here in Faefersham Court – until she marries."

Good, thought Daniel, his mission was accomplished.

~

In the course of the afternoon, Daniel learned much. He heard of the regular letters Sir William had received from Annie describing Lucy's recreations, interspersed with demands for new dresses and bonnets for their daughter's social life. He said he had had no reason to believe Lucy was not well cared for.

Daniel asked him when he had renounced his interest with the smuggling and Sir William responded that it was when they became violent. "I started to hear of the grounding of ships on the sandbanks with gangs of the smugglers boarding and slaughtering the sailors. Mostly they were the gangs from further south, but I had my suspicions that one or two of ours were not above silencing those thought necessary."

Sir William also explained that whilst he had been happy to organize the distribution of food and a selection of luxuries to the population in general at the expense of the bureaucratic rich, he could not acquiesce to violence, greed and wanton drunkenness. He finished by saying, "And it is one thing to trade with the French, it is quite another to be in league when we were at war with them. I heard of our navy's legitimate prize ships being lured onto treacherous sands then ransacked when most of their sailors took to the row boats. I could not continue to be involved in such treachery. Do you know that's how that self-righteous Thorsen's father died?"

Daniel hadn't known this. He would have been seventeen years old at the most. Yet it made sense. It was just after the war finished that his father assumed more control of the operation; obviously that must have been when Sir William withdrew. And a confounded muddle he made of it too. So much so, that he had stepped in to save the situation.

It occurred to him while Sir William was telling of his struggle to save his estate that it was not judicious of him to lay bare so many secrets. What could be his purpose? Or was there a clue in what he'd said? Something about *in the time left to him.* Duly, he accepted Sir William's offer to stay overnight at Faefersham Court and meet the heir to the baronetcy.

In the meantime, he revealed the extent of his own plans. If Sir William was dying, it was important to secure his goodwill sooner rather than later. To hear the real magician say he was impressed was extremely satisfying.

One Dark Night

Chapter Twenty-Nine
Lucy
"Lucy's eyes grew large with fright"

While Daniel visited Sir William, that same Thursday after breakfast, Lucy sat at her desk enjoying the warmth of the September sunshine. She was attending to the household accounts when Martha bustled into the kitchen.

"The master wants to see you," she said. "In his private sitting room." She gave Lucy her best conspiratorial look. "He's all dressed up." Then a worried look crossed her face. "If it's about me and m' speech, you will stand up for me, won't you Lucy? I know I don't use the right words but I am trying. Now we've got that boy to do odd jobs for us, I have to make sure he knows I'm to be reckoned with. I haven't called you 'girl' once today, have I?"

Lucy stood up immediately and hugged Martha who reciprocated with a very tight squeeze. Whatever the master was about to do, they would see it through together. Lucy brushed her grey dress down and straightened her apron and cap. "After that wonderful dinner you produced last night and in such a short time, it's more likely he'll be wanting to chain you to this house forever."

"Go on with you, girl. But I am getting succumplished, aren't I?"

Lucy grinned and nodded. Even her made-up words were getting nearer the proper ones. "You are indeed an accomplished cook, Martha. And don't you ever change. I love you just as you are." How true it was. Martha was a joy to be near; it was impossible not to smile, even laugh when she was around. And, despite all that had happened, Lucy hadn't smiled or laughed so much in many, many years.

One Dark Night

"Thank you, Lucy. You always make me feel..." she searched for words.

Lucy threw some to her as she left the kitchen. "Loved and needed, Martha."

She knocked on the sitting room door and waited to be admitted. What could he want with her?

Thorsen opened the door himself and waved Lucy inside. "Ah, Lucy, come in, sit down. I have matters to discuss with you, so please make yourself comfortable." He pointed to a cosy chair by the hearth.

If this was going to be a long discussion, she wished she had the nerve to ask to make notes. Thorsen had a habit of rattling off instructions by the dozen.

"Lucy, I wish to apprise you of my plans."

Lucy was not quite sure what he meant exactly but deduced that she was indeed in for a long sitting.

"You will be aware, one way or another," Thorsen stopped pacing the room and spun around to take a long look at her before continuing, "that I became a Riding Officer to combat the tyranny of the smuggling gangs. I felt compelled to seek out those who turned to abhorrent violence and, in particular, ensure that Sydney Tynton paid the due price for the cruel murder of my father."

Lucy, having heard the terrible details during dinner the previous night, tried to convey her sympathy with an understanding expression. No words of hers could soothe his anger.

"That man is to be hanged. The gang which he and his son led, has too few members now to be any concern of mine. Riding Officers will return to their previous methods of watching and reporting from within their own villages and Watch House will mostly be used for administrative purposes and for the Coastal Blockade. Boats patrolling the seas and bays will be the way forward. I shall return to my estate at Whitchester."

Lucy's eyes grew large with fright. Of course she knew that her current comfortable life could not go on for ever, but here was Karl Thorsen telling her it was over *now*. She stared at the floor to conceal

One Dark Night

her concern. An uncomfortable feeling crept over her as she noticed the silence in the room. She looked up. Thorsen was staring at her.

"I know you have had little opportunity to lead a normal life, not at all conducive to making the acquaintance of suitable marriage partners." He hesitated and watched Lucy closely. "I am aware that Daniel Tynton has been dallying with you and I trust you understand that you are likely to be one of many."

Lucy did not respond. Sometimes she'd thought Daniel was simply playing with her feelings, yet at other times she was sure there was more to it than that. But, to hear Thorsen saying what everyone else was surely thinking, came as a stab to her heart.

"I shall be asking Martha to come with me to Whitchester. More servants will be needed once I am in permanent residence."

Fear strangled Lucy's voice. He undoubtedly already had a competent, experienced housekeeper. He was about to tell her she would not be needed. She had worked hard but not hard enough to make him forget that she was always disobeying him. Oh God, help me, please help me. She did not even have her mother to return to. And Daniel – Thorsen was right – Daniel had never once indicated that he wanted to spend his future with her. If anything, he had taken a lock of her hair because it was something to remember her by, a mere trophy.

"I shall not be asking you to come as a servant."

There! He had said it. Confirmed all her fears.

"I have a confession to make. Yesterday parson Raffles delivered unaddressed correspondence and I found it on the letter tray when I came in. I opened it and discovered the message was for you."

"Me?" Lucy had never received a letter before.

"Yes. I immediately contacted the sender and invited him here for dinner. I wanted to be sure of the intentions of the gentleman who had written to you." Thorsen stopped pacing the room and sat in the chair opposite Lucy. "The name of the gentleman seeking to make contact with you is Mr Douglas Harper who is the heir to Sir William Harper and…"

"Faefersham Court!"

"Then you do know him?"

One Dark Night

"Yes and I cannot think why I did not recognize him. I..." She had been about to say that she had lived at Faefersham Court. Her mother's injunction never to speak of it still restricted her. How very stupid. Her mother had gone, left her, she had no authority over her now and talking about her time at Faefersham Court could no longer harm her.

"You did not recognize him because he had his back to you, he has been in America for some years and he spoke with a slight American accent." There was no empathy in his voice; he simply stated the facts. "How long is it since you saw him?"

Lucy could not think of the exact date. "We left in 1813, some time in the summer."

"You left?"

"My mother was the housekeeper and my father was the butler. Sir William was very kind and allowed me to spend most of my time as a companion to Dougie, Mr Harper, I mean."

"Do not concern yourself, I shall arrange for you to meet again. It does, of course, explain many things such as why your mother treated you so badly, even hated you." Oblivious to Lucy's feelings, he continued, "And why you are so very different from all the young women in this lawless little corner of Kent." Thorsen drummed his fingers on the arm of the chair – he appeared to be making plans even as he spoke. "There is another matter, most important, which I wish to discuss."

As Thorsen seemed reluctant to do this discussing, Lucy had a moment to collect her thoughts. Did she have to wait for him to make arrangements for her to meet Dougie? Could she not just take the mail coach to Faefersham and walk to Faefersham Court? Thanks to Thorsen, she had saved sufficient money to do that and she would be reasonably presentable.

Meanwhile, the Lieutenant seemed tongue-tied then blurted, "I should like you to become my wife."

Stunned, Lucy felt her blood drain. Every other thought fled from her mind and if she could have fled too, she would have done so.

"I have come to respect and admire you; essential if I am to marry you. I can offer a substantial home with many servants to attend to our

One Dark Night

needs." Thorsen allowed himself a smile. "I know the convention: you will need to think about my offer. I shall take you to see Whitchester Manor within the next few days. In the meantime, you should prepare yourself for this visit by purchasing a *new* dress."

Lucy thought she saw a way to delay such a futile visit. "Lieutenant, there is nowhere I could purchase something new. A dress would need to be made and that would take some weeks and my purse does not allow for this."

"Nonsense! Merrygate is highly fashionable with the bon ton; people of quality are spending vast sums of money when on their vacations."

Lucy had never been to Merrygate. She had seen the hoys ferrying visitors to and from London but how could she have gone dressed as she was? "I…"

Thorsen's demeanour softened as he saw her distress. "Let me fill your purse so you can buy the best available from Brookington, and a pelisse to travel in – not the old brown cloak. A reticule as well. I'm sure you will be able to spend these guineas wisely." He stood up, walked to his bureau, and returned with ten guineas. He picked up Lucy's hand and gently placed them in her palm. "Faefersham Court will have provided you with sufficient ideas for what you need." He closed her hand around the golden guineas. "I should like to speak to Martha now. Send her in." He shifted his shoulders a little as if he were rearranging them before adding, "Please."

Lucy was just about to escape when he called her back. "Here's a shawl for you, Lucy. It is to thank you for all you have done." He thought for a moment, then added, "I have a green one to give to Martha."

~

The following day was a fine and sunny Friday. Martha had been overjoyed to receive the shawl and was still bouncing around the kitchen and Scat was keeping his distance. There was no doubt about it, Thorsen's timing was impeccable. His offer for her to go with him to Whitchester was more than she had ever dreamed possible.

One Dark Night

"I'm allowed to take Scat! Think of that! The master is so kind. I think he's secretly fond of the dear little thing."

"He's a good ratter."

"He already has a cat, 'a very old, fat cat' he said."

Lucy nodded. "So he might have needed to get a new one soon?"

"Lucy! The master knows I am fond of Scat; he doesn't have those 'hiding motives' you talk about."

She knew she needed time to think, so she drew the conversation to a close. "I am jesting, Martha." It would be wrong to upset her at a joyous time like this.

If she accepted his offer, she would have somewhere very comfortable to live and would not have to work at all. If she refused Thorsen's offer, she would have no work and nowhere to live. As Thorsen had inadvertently pointed out, Merrygate might offer opportunities. She could surely prove she could serve fine folk. She would have to live-in. She had saved some money, but it amounted to too little to give her any other choice. To be his wife or not to be his wife? That was the question. She thought it almost as bad a choice as the man contemplating life or death in Shakespeare's play. Aloud, she startled Martha by quoting, "To be, or not to be: that is the question." It was at this point that she knew she had to make a little time to think through the consequences of the decision she *must* make. Why hadn't Daniel come to her rescue? Was Thorsen right about him?

The only place to go was to her sanctuary. She crossed the stream, which ran clear and sparkling as if it carried diamonds to the sea. Daniel's words popped into her head. "It's Kent's chalk that keeps our streams so clear. It stops the water weeds." If only it had been knowledgeable, interesting and exceptionally handsome Daniel who had asked her to marry him. She hurried along the cliff edge and scrambled down onto the ledge and tucked herself under the overhang where she knew she could not be seen. Thorsen had no idea how abhorrent his proposition was. She could not call it a proposal of marriage; it was more like a business contract. Would that be so bad? Most of the upper classes had to tolerate such arrangements. She thought back to the balls at Faefersham Court and how the young ladies

One Dark Night

had paraded in front of the *young bucks* as her father had called them, with their mothers desperate to attract the richest for their daughters. Now that she understood Thorsen better, and what had driven him so hard in these last years, perhaps she could endure his brusque manner. And if Daniel really cared about her, he would have told her so. He only showed her sufficient interest to keep her amenable and willing to respond to his persuasions.

There was little, if any choice. Why couldn't Thorsen have suggested she go to Whitchester as a maid, a fine lady's maid or a humble kitchen one? She would then have said yes immediately. And what had happened to his promise to reunite her with Dougie? Not that a meeting with him held much hope of a future. Perhaps she could become a maid at Faefersham Court? No, that was unlikely to be a viable option. Her mother had left suddenly, and it would be awkward to become a servant in a household with Dougie there. Maybe her father could help her? Yes that was something to be considered; after all, as a butler in a well known house, he must know influential people in other households.

Her spirits lifted, she came to a decision. She climbed up the bank and set off along the clifftop towards the market at Brookington. It was late in the day but there might still be some stalls. If she *were* to visit Karl Thorsen's house, what would she buy with ten guineas?

She skirted Brookington Wood, turning her head away from the trees and the contrasting memories of the murder and Daniel's tender care. She brushed away a tear. She had nearly arrived at the market when she saw Daniel cantering along on Fiddle towards her. He drew alongside and dismounted immediately.

"Why so tearful, Lucy?"

Lucy looked up at him, tall, strong, tanned and full of abundant life and looking at her with such concern that it brought the tears back again. Should she tell him?

"This is not a time for crying, Lucy. You are soon to receive some good news which will mean you no longer have to work all day, every day."

He might have said more had it not been for Lucy turning on him. "I've already been told, though how you would know about it is beyond me."

"You know? You know that you will be going, in a grand carriage, I believe…"

"Yes, I know, and I've been *told* to buy some new clothes." Lucy was now very angry. How could Daniel know that Thorsen had asked her to marry him and all he could say was that this was *good news*! Thorsen was right. Daniel had been toying with her. Just like his mother had warned her. Perhaps she should do more than just research what she might have bought if she'd had any intention of accepting the proposal. Ten guineas to spend. The chance was unlikely to come again unless she married Thorsen.

"Then why are you crying?"

"Because I have no choice. I know that if I stay here, I shall have nowhere to live and I shall lose the good company of Martha."

"Why would you want to stay in Wintergate when you have the opportunity of living in grand style?"

Lucy wanted to scream at him – because I don't love him. I love you. But she only said, "I suppose I am afraid of the unknown."

Daniel took her hand in his. "If you have any qualms at all, then don't go. Stay here in Wintergate and I will arrange for you to live in your old cottage."

"You will?" Lucy could not believe this. Another choice had opened up even if she'd have no furniture.

"Yes. I don't want to tell you too much at the moment because I would be stealing a fine man's thunder. Don't make any hasty decisions. Promise me?" He squeezed her hand then took a white cotton handkerchief from his pocket and dried her tears. "I have just come from what could be your new home – if you wish it to be so."

"You have?"

"I have. Now promise me, no hasty decisions. Leave that sort of thinking for another day and by Sunday you will have more information. Before you make important decisions, you must have all the facts."

One Dark Night

Very formally, Lucy said, "I promise I will make no decisions until Sunday."

"Sunday afternoon."

Lucy nodded. "No decisions until Sunday afternoon."

"I must say, I find you baffling but perhaps that is why you fascinate me." He mounted his horse, took hold of the reins, and said, "If you do not like your new situation, I am holding some money on your behalf which would enable you to live comfortably until you marry." Daniel hesitated, he looked as if he might say more on the subject, but thought better of it. Instead he turned his horse towards Jerusalem Farm, but before he cantered off he said, "Lucy, my father, and others, are to be hanged next week. I shall be there. And then it will be some time before I can see you again. Carry this word with you: wait."

Before she could ask what money, and how long should she wait and wait for what? Daniel had gone.

She did not visit the market.

One Dark Night

Chapter Thirty
"Were these two men in league?"

Early on Sunday morning, Lucy lit the fires in the kitchen and Thorsen's sitting room. She hoped he wouldn't come in while she was there; he had cornered her yesterday and pressed for a response. Confidently she had responded that she would let him have an answer by Sunday evening. She wasn't sure if he was angry or impatient. He definitely did not look pleased at this answer. Was there a connection to the letter delivered to him on Friday? Why did he suddenly ask his lowly housekeeper to marry him? Why was Daniel involved in this change of circumstances? Had he been to Whitchester Manor? Were these two men in league? Or had they come to an agreement?

Just as she finished and the fire was blazing, Thorsen strolled into his sitting room.

"I'm glad I've caught you, Lucy."

Caught was the right word, she thought.

"Please sit down. I have something to tell you which affects your future."

Lucy's heart thumped and she took a deep breath.

"Lucy, I received another letter on Friday afternoon, this time from Mr Douglas Harper's father, Sir William Harper."

Her hand flew to her mouth to stop the gasp.

"I visited him yesterday. He has much to discuss with you." Thorsen sat down on his favoured chair opposite Lucy. "Mr Douglas Harper will come this afternoon and take you back to Faefersham Court where good news awaits you. You must pack your belongings, you may take my small trunk, and say goodbye to Martha."

"Take my belongings? Am I to stay there?"

One Dark Night

"It is, of course, your choice, but I think you will want to."

Choice? Surely as all roads lead to London, so her choice must lead to this. Were they planning to employ her? Her thoughts went to Martha who had no choice whatsoever, yet was happy with her lot. "How will Martha manage?"

"She will be packing too. We shall all be departing for Whitchester later this week."

Timing. The timing! That was why he was hoping she would give an early answer to his proposal. And that was why Daniel had told her to wait. He had been to Faefersham Court – not Whitchester Manor.

Karl tried to sound agreeable when he said, "We shall be able to see one another on a regular basis so do not forget my proposal. It stands. But you have family affairs to attend to first." Even matters of the heart sounded like instructions.

It was all so confusing. Daniel had been to Faefersham Court. Why? He had brought back a letter saying that Mr Douglas Harper, her Dougie, would be taking her to speak with Sir William. Why? She was to take all her belongings because Thorsen would be leaving Wintergate and only taking Martha. This left her with his proposal still to consider because Thorsen thought he would continue to see her at Faefersham Court. Would her father be able to help her? As the butler, he would have many duties. Would he even be pleased to see her? How long would she be able to stay? Then what would she do? Thank the Lord God that Daniel had given her an escape route. An independent life in China Cottage might be the most acceptable choice.

One Dark Night

Chapter Thirty-One
Daniel
"While Wintergate slept"

Wednesday 10th October

Daniel held Fiddle to a trot. He wanted to think and Fiddle's preference for galloping could not be considered an aid to planning. Josh preferred Fiddle's trot too.

Uppermost in his mind was the money he had withheld from Annie Yorton, money meant for Lucy. Initially he'd hoped to give it to her so that she could become independent of Thorsen, but her circumstances had changed rapidly and she no longer needed money. Yet somehow he must return this money to her in a manner in which only she would benefit. If she did not like living at Faefersham Court he would give it to her immediately and she could, if she wished, return to Wintergate.

It had been four weeks since Lucy inadvertently indicated where that pirate's plunder was buried. How odd she'd never mentioned it to anyone. Perhaps she had no one she could trust. Surely she could have mentioned it to Parson Raffles? But finding it still there was proof enough that she had told no one. As soon as possible he'd taken the spout lantern down to the rocks on a dark night when the tide was out. Shifting the heavy chalk boulder marking the position of the buried treasure was easy with Fiddle pulling the rope. Josh had positioned himself in his favoured guard-stance ready to alert his master if necessary and Daniel had dug deep until his spade hit something hard. He'd strapped the small metal casket, wrapped in oilskins, to the top of Fiddle's saddle, shovelled sand back into the gaping hole leaving the tide to tidy up. His driving thought was to hurry back to Bethlehem farm and wrench it open.

One Dark Night

Yes, he'd been tempted to keep the contents: eight hundred gold sovereigns all minted in 1817, the first year sovereigns had been minted for well over a century. It was obvious to him that some corrupt official had been shipping them out of the country and they'd been intercepted by the pirates. If he had kept them, too many questions would have been asked and how could he build a new life on stolen money? Too much could go wrong. And he'd not be able to look Lucy in the eye, nor the parson, nor Sir William. Turning it in to Thorsen was not even to be considered – it was unlikely to have been revenue. He'd tossed many solutions around and thrown out all but one.

Then, one night, while Wintergate slept soundly, he'd tethered Fiddle to the church lych gate, quietly walked the few yards to the parson's doorstep, and left the casket of sovereigns in a sack with a note. He'd written, quite truthfully, that the money had belonged to someone who had died and it was to be used for the good of the local villages. He'd included a few suggestions too. He'd ridden back across the harvested fields to nearby Jerusalem Farm where he'd spent the rest of the night with his mother.

Daniel grinned as he remembered the parson's reaction the following morning. Always early to rise, he would inspect the world from his doorstep and, if the weather was fine he'd take three deep breaths. He told the tale of how he had found a baby, wrapped in rags on the step. Another time there was a half-starved donkey, too weak to bray. When he'd arrived to inspect God's world that morning he'd found another strange offering. A dirty sack which he'd dragged inside the hall, then after a quick look around he'd slammed the door shut.

Some weeks had gone by and Daniel now steered Fiddle towards the parsonage.

"Good morning, Daniel." The parson hurried to the gate. "Are you able to spend some time with me? I have some plans to discuss with you."

It was a relief that the parson was keen to confer. "I should be delighted to hear your plans; you have listened to mine so often." Daniel dismounted, tied Fiddle to the gatepost and ushered Josh through to the doorstep where Mrs Raffles was putting water and a bone ready

One Dark Night

for him. "You're a lucky dog, Josh. I think you should say thank you." Josh sat down, barked, wagged his tail and held up his paw.

"And a very good morning to you too." Mrs Raffles beamed and shook the dog's paw. "Were you on your way to visit your mother?" she said, turning to Daniel.

"There's no need for me to hurry. She'll still be there this afternoon."

With Josh contentedly gnawing his bone on the doorstep, Daniel and the parson made themselves comfortable at the table in the parlour.

"I could not resist calling you in to see my plans," said Parson Raffles, spreading several sheets of paper before Daniel. "Have you heard?" The parson took a deep breath. "Of course you have. You always know everything."

Daniel laughed. "Are you referring to last week when you fell through the floor of the pulpit?"

"No! Oh did you hear about that too? Oh I am so aggrieved. I seem to have trouble with pulpits. When I was in Torwell Bridge, the jolly thing was on wheels – a temporary one, you see – and it rolled down the aisle with me clutching it in sheer disbelief."

Daniel roared laughing. "I can just imagine that!"

"Well this time, I reminded my congregation that if you allow yourself to become angry with someone, that person controls you, and anger is one of the seven deadly sins. I stamped my foot to demonstrate anger and it went straight through." Daniel grinned widely until the parson added, "Woodworm, I suspect."

The parson's girth sprang to mind, but he said only, "Can it be repaired?"

"Undoubtedly, but I shall not feel safe up there again." He sighed loudly. "I also suspect God is encouraging me to fast."

"Fast?" Ah, gluttony had crossed the parson's mind too, it seemed. The idea of the rotund, jolly parson fasting seemed highly unlikely to Daniel. He wouldn't be the same man, so loved and respected by all.

"Indeed! It is written in the Gospel of St. Mark that the disciples of Jesus did not fast while Jesus was with them but they would fast when Jesus had left them." Leaning back on his wooden chair, which creaked

One Dark Night

loudly, the parson continued. "So, like the disciples, I shall follow the ways of the Old Testament and fast between six o'clock in the morning through until six o'clock in the evening, two days each week, Mondays and Thursdays. Many monks have done this for centuries before us."

At this point, Mrs Raffles bustled in with a tray of tea and seed cake. "Well it's Daniel's good fortune that today is a Wednesday," she said, chuckling.

"Mine too," said the parson quickly. "Let us get on with our discussions. The church has been left a considerable sum of money." The parson looked straight at Daniel. "There is no need to feign surprise. I am sure you know of this even though most of your informants are no longer with us." He cocked his head to one side and raised an eyebrow well above his spectacles. He made such a comical figure that Daniel let his guard down and laughed. "Yes, you may well laugh, for it would not surprise me if you knew exactly how much I have, and where this legacy was found!"

Admitting nothing he said, "Most kind of you to think so, Mr Raffles." Daniel took a large bite from a slice of seed cake and, mouth full, mumbled, "Mrs Raffles is a very good cook. Quite a treasure."

"Indeed, indeed. She works hard, too hard, perhaps."

"Then perhaps you have included in your plans a way to make the parsonage easier to manage?" Parson Raffles was given no time to answer. "I think it is important that Mrs Raffles' time is more available for the needs of the parish. She is, as you said, a treasure and her talents should be used for the benefit of your flock." Daniel's eyes took on a look that once had been reserved for errant smugglers. "Have you thought to appoint a cook and parlour maid as well as your maid-of-all-work?"

Parson Raffles looked affronted for no longer than a second or two. "How strange. That was the first suggestion made in the note left with the money." His suspicion confirmed, he added, "It seems you and I are the *only* ones who will know how this money came into the possession of the church."

A pact had been formed.

"Show me your plans, and let me see if I can help in any way."

One Dark Night

Parson Raffles shuffled the papers in front of him and brought forward the one at the back. "Priority now is to give employment to two of the widows in the village. My wife will train them. One will be a daily parlour maid who will also have parish duties and the other a cook. I shall set aside sufficient funds to pay their wages." Daniel merely nodded so Parson Raffles moved on to the next sheet of paper. "The school will recommence by Christmas and this time we shall be funded to ensure its continuance."

"Mrs Raffles is clearly an educated and well organized lady and perhaps she could be responsible for administration, maybe even a little teaching."

"A fine thought, Daniel. I shall prevail upon her to approach parents of the children in Wintergate and beyond. Classes will start as soon as Mrs Raffles employs the two servants here in the house and I have found a competent teacher!"

Daniel listened intently as the parson laid out his plans, interrupting only to show his approval. "Your plans will improve the villages hereabouts, Mr Raffles. I'm sure the money is better used in your hands than in anyone else's."

"*Together* we can rescue those in dire poverty and keep them out of that necessary institution, the workhouse." The parson stood up, stretched himself, and called for more tea, "But no cake, my dear, or I shall spoil my dinner tonight." He turned to Daniel. "And now I am anxious to hear of your own plans."

"For some years, as you know from our discussions recently, I have been transforming Bethlehem Farm. It has made good profits in the past and I have ploughed those into my new venture."

Parson Raffles looked over the top of his spectacles. "Your idea to build a village devoted entirely to those wishing to take their holidays hereabouts is far ahead of anything I have heard before. Be assured, I have mentioned it to no one."

"When you next visit you will find three large country style cottages almost completed. Inside there will be all the latest conveniences for the wealthy folk whom I hope to attract. They can bring their own servants, who will stay in separate, excellent accommodation themselves. I am

One Dark Night

hoping that their servants will see this as a benefit of being employed. Thus, wealthy families may find that Bethlehem Farm is a more attractive place to visit than the big hotels in Merrygate."

"Oh you will need more than that to compete with those…"

"Mr Raffles, there will be so many attractions on the farm that Merrygate folks will be coming to stay with us!"

"But won't you lose the income from the farm?"

Daniel did not disguise his satisfaction with his plans. "At first, until profits meet my requirements, we shall continue with farming but, in a year or two Jerusalem Farm will be more productive and Bethlehem farm will cease to grow a potato crop and much else besides. My mother has found it necessary to take on a farm manager, a local lad who lost his father recently." Daniel paused while both he and the parson reflected on the hanging of eighteen men with many more imprisoned. "I'll oversee him for a while, and when he's ready, we'll take on more hands and we can return to farming the land properly. My aunt and uncle will move there soon; they'll be company for my mother and, being such good farmers themselves, they can oversee the manager."

"And," said the parson enthusiastically, "slowly you will increase the number of cottages at Bethlehem and the number you employ?"

"Indeed. My plans are slowed only by a lack of available money. You may be able to help me there, Mr Raffles. I am applying for a loan from the bank in Merrygate next week. Would you be able to support my application? Never having had the need for banking services, I am unknown to them."

Parson Raffles lowered his head and clutched his many chins. Then thoughtfully he began, "So there you are, hoping to borrow money from the bank, for which they will charge you, and I have just deposited nearly eight hundred sovereigns with them. The interest you will pay on a loan from them will be more than the interest they give me. I think we can come to a better arrangement than that."

They had arrived at another pact.

One Dark Night

Chapter Thirty-Two
Lucy
"Finally penetrated Karl's armour"

May 1822

Seven months after Daniel's conference with the parson, Lucy sat on the bench under the big oak tree near the lake in Faefersham Court. She watched a mother duck leading her ducklings, seven of them, into the water. Swimming lessons. Her mind went back to the time she had hidden in the branches of this oak tree, watching her mother with Sir William. Nine years had passed since she'd seen that mother duck and her one remaining duckling. It was now early in the summer of 1822 and she had time on this beautiful evening to reflect on all that had happened to her.

She remembered the cold winters in Wintergate, the long, hard work at Jerusalem Farm, and the time Daniel had introduced her to his endearing dog, Josh. Seeing Daniel on rare occasions had lightened her spirits when she'd thought nothing ever could.

Thoughts of her mother battered around in her head. Would she ever find out where her mother had gone? To be in her cottage one day and gone the next – with all her belongings – was inexplicable. And nobody, *nobody* knew where she had gone. But then she was always unpredictable.

This led her thoughts to the day when Karl Thorsen had called at the cottage and her mother had been caught hitting her. He had ordered her to present herself at Watch House. She'd had no choice. Daniel's weasel-like father, the treacherous Sydney Tynton, had made it perfectly clear there was no job for her any longer. No job, no pay. Of

One Dark Night

course, had Daniel been at Jerusalem Farm all the time, things might have been different. She allowed her mind to wander and imagine Daniel holding her hand as they strolled along the beach but that led to darker thoughts.

The scene of the failed landing of smuggled goods caused her to put her head in her hands. So many died. And those left alive and caught had been hanged, gibbeted, or sent to Van Diemen's Land. But Daniel had not been caught because he had been injured – by Karl Thorsen! She smiled and whispered, "God moves in mysterious ways indeed."

She missed Martha and her peculiar words. It didn't matter to her that she didn't know the right words, she knew there ought to be something that would express her feelings, and she happily invented an approximation. Hadn't Shakespeare invented words? Yes, she was sure she'd been taught that. How fortunate that Martha had always respected the unrelenting Karl and his quest for revenge. Or, as Martha rightly put it, *justice*. That loyalty had earned her Karl's respect and she would always have a home now.

How strange it was that Douglas had become such good friends with Karl. She still addressed Karl as Lieutenant Thorsen, though he had often told her she should call him Karl despite the fact she still refused his offers of marriage. She had been surprised to find how likeable he could be and wholeheartedly agreed with Douglas: it was because he now channelled all his energy into something worthwhile, something positive, rather than letting revenge destroy his soul. That topic had been one of the parson's favourite sermons. She wondered if Raffles' sermons had finally penetrated Karl's armour? She smiled as she remembered the way Parson Raffles always examined his pulpit before mounting the step. The parson had been a great encourager when she had needed it most. She could almost hear his booming voice urging his congregation to seek the rainbow through the rain. Better days would come.

And come they did! To find that she was Sir William's daughter and that Douglas was her half-brother astounded her. She remembered the scene exactly. Soon after arriving at Faefersham Court, Douglas had taken her to see Sir William in the library. Sir William had sat with his

One Dark Night

back to the window and Douglas sat alongside Lucy on the couch opposite. It was a scene she replayed in her mind constantly for it was such a shock. Sir William explained that her mother, when with child, had been encouraged to marry his butler, who had always loved her, because it gave both her and Lucy respectability and kept them close. The recognition that Douglas was her half-brother was like the dawning of a summer's day, each moment brought more light. So many strange things fell into place.

It was even more strange that Daniel occasionally visited her father, for that is what Sir William now openly declared himself to be. They would sit in the library and talk for what seemed far too long before Lucy was invited to join them. Then Daniel would hasten away to return to Wintergate. Each time he'd said, "Wait, Lucy, wait. It will be all the better for your waiting." Just how long must she wait? And what was she waiting for? He had not declared his intentions as Karl had. Karl was open and constant and Daniel had not visited since March.

She had one regret: that she could not have seen the man she had known as her father all those years before he died. She'd had no opportunity to thank Mr Yorton, and this hurt, for he had clearly loved her as if she were his own. If only he knew how much she loved him. The beginnings of tears pricked her eyes.

She stood up, pulled her fine woollen shawl around her shoulders, and made her way back to the house which shone brightly in the day's last rays of sunlight. Once again she could call this "home".

One Dark Night

Chapter Thirty-Three
"The bold bringer of the rose"

"Good morning, Miss Lucy."

Lucy smiled as consciousness broke into her dreams. *Miss Lucy*, how good to be just that. She had not been born with the right to be Miss Harper but Miss Lucy suited her new life. Fleetingly, she wondered how and where her mother was. No one mentioned her at all.

"'Tis a lovely sunny morning," said Sarah, Lucy's maid, as she crossed the room to place the tray beside her bed. "Look, see?" She pulled the curtains and shafts of sunlight highlighted the dancing motes. She returned to plump up the pillows and placed the breakfast tray on Lucy's lap. As an unmarried lady of the house, she usually had breakfast with her father and brother but as Douglas was going to be away for a few days, her father had suggested they both take their breakfasts in bed. Such luxury! Now that Lucy had taken responsibility for being the lady of the house, meeting with the cook on Monday mornings, arranging dinner parties with the housekeeper, writing letters and so much more, she was usually up early. To have breakfast in her room was a real treat.

"Oh Sarah, what's this?"

"'Tis a rose, Miss Lucy," Sarah said barely able to smother her grin.

"From the garden – how thoughtful of you."

"No, 'tis from the doorstep."

"The doorstep? Sarah it's too early for jests."

"It's not, Miss Lucy, 'tis nine o' clock already and 'tis not a jest, though I must confess, 'tis a riddle to me. There's a note though. Shall I read it to you?"

One Dark Night

"No," said Lucy raising an eyebrow at Sarah, "I think I should have *some* secrets from you." She missed the banter with Martha, so enjoyed Sarah's cheeky chatter all the more.

Lucy broke the seal and read the note. "I am none the wiser, Sarah. You must help me here or I shall be puzzling all day."

Sarah puffed out her ample bosom and took the proffered note and, haltingly, read aloud, "A pure white rose for an angel."

"It must be from Mr Harper; it cannot be anyone else." Lucy looked puzzled. Who else but Douglas would have sent such a sweet token?

"You have forgotten, Miss Lucy, Mr Harper has gone away this morning."

"I haven't forgotten; it will certainly be from Mr Harper. It is his way of saying farewell."

"So Mr Harper has left a rose with a sealed note on the doorstep to give to his sister," Sarah said dismissively.

"Sarah!" Lucy snapped playfully. "The dogs would not let anyone else near the grounds and certainly not the doorsteps. Which doorstep was it found upon?"

"The kitchen doorstep, Miss Lucy. I was first out this morning. I saw it addressed to you and brought it in."

"Who else has seen it, Sarah?"

"No one, Miss Lucy. I promise you. You know I would not want to go back to being a maid-of-all-work again," she said as her fingers played with the burgundy frill, denoting her seniority, on her white apron.

"I must eat this lovely breakfast, Sarah," said Lucy, thinking it might be wise to deflect attention from who had left the rose. "Lay out something with flowers on for me to wear, please."

"The dress with the little *white rose* pattern, I'll put that out for you."

Lucy watched Sarah enjoying her little jest and wistfully running her hand along the many fine dresses hanging in the wardrobe. "What is it like to be the youngest of nine sisters, Sarah?"

"Always last, Miss Lucy."

~

One Dark Night

"It's happened again, Miss Lucy!" Sarah said as she burst through the bedroom door with her muslin cap askew and strands of long, dark hair falling over her eyes.

"Again?" Lucy sat up with her arms out ready to receive the breakfast tray. "Pull the curtains quickly."

"'tis sunny again."

Lucy ripped open the note hoping for a clue to the identity of the "bold bringer of the rose," as Sarah had been calling the unidentified admirer.

"Can't be Mr Harper. He's still away," Sarah said unable to conceal the smug look on her face.

"Sarah, I think you're right for the note says, 'A yellow rose, kissed by the sun for you'."

"Can you tell who's written it?"

"It's in a beautiful hand," Lucy said furrowing her brow.

"Got past the dogs again. Think we need to let the geese loose to protect us."

"Oh Sarah, are you alarmed? I shall have a word with Taylor. I'll ask him to ensure our security more carefully."

"But if you get Mr Taylor to set men to watch, then you may not get another rose."

"I think you would miss it more than I, Sarah," Lucy teased. "It's strange, neither this one nor yesterday's had any thorns on it. Put it in the same little vase as the white one and I will have a word with our butler later today."

She didn't.

~

The following morning, the first day of June, a red rose arrived on the breakfast tray with another note attached to it.

"I cannot read it Sarah, my heart is bomping," said Lucy feigning a fit of the vapours in an attempt to conceal her real excitement.

"Bomping? Never did I hear such a word, Miss Lucy. I'll read it for you so your heart is kept from bomping." She snatched at the note but Lucy clutched it tightly. "Thank you, Sarah, I will take courage as indeed the bold bringer of the rose has taken courage to pass the dogs."

One Dark Night

"But not the men and the geese," Sarah said batting her dark eyelashes at Lucy.

"Rather than tell Taylor, I thought I might take watch myself. You are sure it is not someone within the household who is acting on instruction?"

"I'm sure as eggs is eggs. 'Twas on the doorstep again. Mr Taylor locks all the doors at night and takes the keys to his room, holding them up for all to see."

"Does he do that every night?"

"Oh yes, Miss Lucy. Mr Taylor just rattles the keys to make sure we all know not to have *clandestine meetings*."

"Oh I see. Clandestine meetings. What fun." She thought for a moment. "Then how will I get the keys?"

Sarah wandered to the bottom of the bed, pushed out her best asset, and said, "He snores. Leave it to me."

Lucy laughed. She suspected there was much jollity in the servants' quarters and wondered, with little hope, if it had been so in her mother's time. She also noted that she must take charge of a *complete* set of keys as her own did not contain one for the kitchen.

"Will you be reading the note?"

As Lucy held up the deep red rose a dew drop fell onto her arm. She dipped her finger into the dew and pressed it to her lips. "Kissed by the sun," she whispered.

"That was yesterday's! What about today's note? Will you be reading it?"

"Yes, Sarah, but please go and fetch me some milk. You have forgotten the milk." Sarah's face fell from urgent expectation to mortification. "Then I shall have some privacy," said Lucy with triumph.

Lucy opened the somewhat crumpled note with a mixture of anticipation and curiosity. It read, "O, my luve's like a red, red rose... Till a' the seas gang dry."

She was still holding the rose in one hand and the note in the other when Sarah returned breathless, almost spilling the little jug of milk.

One Dark Night

"I am more puzzled than ever, Sarah. It seems to be a quotation but I do not know from what, or even how I can find out. Mr Harper might know but he is still away." Lucy ate some toasted bread and toyed with the plum cake before she put the tray to one side on the bed and said, "Quickly, Sarah, fetch me my dressing gown. I'm going to the library. A memory has just flitted past."

"Flitted past? Miss Lucy, do memories do that?"

"Oh you are so full of cheek, Sarah. Come quickly with me, I may need you to help me if it's up high," said Lucy as she teased her toes into her slippers.

Once in the library, lined from floor to ceiling with carved oak bookcases, Lucy scanned the books of poetry. "A Scottish poet, Sarah, I am looking for a Scottish poet."

"How do you know he's Scottish?

"I am not sure, but the spelling is not right; not right for English anyway. Mrs Raffles, the Wintergate parson's wife, once read something Scottish to me – strange words it had but it wasn't about a rose, it was about a mouse. It might be the same poet though."

"You miss the parson, don't you Miss Lucy?"

"Indeed, I do, but one cannot have everything. We must invite them to stay sometime soon though." A moment later Lucy stood back in triumph clutching a book of poems by Robert Burns. "It may be in here." She rushed over to the window seat and turned page after page until she exclaimed, "This is it!" She bent her knees up to put her slippered feet on the seat and began to read.

"A Red, Red Rose"

O, my luve's like a red, red rose,
That's newly sprung in June.
O, my luve's like the melodie,
That's sweetly play'd in tune.

One Dark Night

As fair art thou, my bonnie lass,
So deep in luve am I,
And I will luve thee still, my Dear,
Till a' the seas gang dry.

Till a' the seas gang dry, my Dear,
And the rocks melt wi' the sun!
O I will luve thee still, my Dear,
While the sands o' life shall run.

And fare thee weel, my only Luve,
And fare thee weel a while!
And I will come again, my Luve,
Tho' it were ten thousand mile!"

Till a' the seas gang dry. Was that a clue? Daniel loved the sea. But Karl Thorsen had been a naval officer. If only it could be from Daniel. Lucy sat silently reading the poem again. Karl could offer a life of ease: she didn't want a life of passive ease. She wanted to make a difference, not in the world of the rich but for those who really needed it.

~

That night, after all the servants should have been in bed, Sarah tapped on Lucy's bedroom door.

"'tis all ready, Miss Lucy. Come quickly, we don't want to miss him."

"I doubt that he comes until early morning, Sarah. There were dew drops on the roses."

"That doesn't mean we should tarry."

They extinguished their candles in the hall and cautiously felt their way into the dark kitchen. The outside door was built into the kitchen so that a small window overlooked the doorstep with a curtain drawn across it. Sarah had placed two chairs by the window.

One Dark Night

"Sarah, you should go back to your bed. You'll be so tired tomorrow."

"Miss Lucy, please. How could I not wait with you? It might be a dangerous man. He might see you. He might break the glass. You need me here to run and get help." A moment later, she thought of another reason which she delivered with a mischievous smile. "Besides, I must lock the door again and return the keys. You will not want to do that, will you, Miss Lucy?"

"Shush, Sarah, you must not make me laugh tonight. Very well, you may stay with me but you must not talk. I'll leave a note for Taylor to say that I've given you permission to sleep later tomorrow."

"Tomorrow is today now."

"Hmm…" mused Lucy, "summer nights are short, fortunately," she pulled her gown around her and cuddled a cushion, "he must come soon."

It was almost an hour later and still dark, when Sarah tapped Lucy's arm. "Forgive me, Miss Lucy," she whispered, "but look, quickly, 'tis a dog."

From the doorstep came a low, barely audible growl. The dog had heard them.

"The keys, Sarah, quick, we must let him in before our dogs get wind of him."

Sarah fumbled with the keys then Lucy opened the door just wide enough for a dog, but seeing that the dog had already gone, she tried to shout and whisper at the same time, "Come here, boy." She bent to pick up the note and the red rose he'd deposited on the step. She called for Sarah to bring a lighted candle but before this could be arranged, the dog bounded back and almost knocked Lucy over in his exuberance. "Josh, where is Daniel? Take me to Daniel."

"No, Miss Lucy," cautioned Sarah. "No, our dogs will surely make an almighty din and they'll go for this dog, him not being one of ours."

"Thank you, Sarah. I'm not thinking too well."

"I wouldn't be either if I were having roses brought to me by a dog! What's the matter with him, Miss Lucy? He's covered in some black stuff and it's coming off all over you."

One Dark Night

"It's soot," said Lucy. "He's really a black and white dog but I suppose he's less visible like this." Lucy thought of the smuggling runs – Josh had probably taken part. "Oh, do give the bold bringer of the rose a morsel of cake or something." Lucy smiled, not a gentle smile but the radiant smile of someone in love as she read her latest note, unmistakably from Daniel, and twirled the red rose. She looked at Josh panting, with his pink tongue lolling to one side, "And now I know why the thorns have been removed."

"What does it say, Miss Lucy?"

"Have we a quill nearby? I need to write an answer."

Sarah dashed to the kitchen cabinet and produced a quill and ink.

Lucy wrote just one word and gave Josh the note again. His tail was wagging to such an extent that she wondered if he was too excited to return to Daniel. She tried to calm him, and talked to him, and stroked his shaggy coat, muddied from crawling along the ground, and blackened with soot. "Daniel is so clever but, Josh, be careful. Mind those big, bad doggies out there."

Josh's eyes shone, eager to take his chances outside in the dark. So Lucy opened the door and Josh shot out – a sleek streak, invisible in a second. From too far a distance to worry Josh, the Faefersham Court dogs had caught the sound and the scent and raced around the corner and out into the dark night.

While Lucy stood in a trance, Sarah bustled round with a broom. "Now just how am I going to explain this soot everywhere and crumbs and doggy footprints?"

Lucy looked down to see that she was covered in soot, just as Sarah had warned her.

"Miss Lucy, do you want the washerwomen to know?" Sarah bustled around pulling Lucy's arms up to brush her down. "Here let me attend to you."

"Brush me down and then go to bed yourself. But first I need the quill again, and paper too now for that note to Taylor."

Chapter Thirty-Four
"Who was I to point the finger"

Sunday 2nd June

The following morning, Lucy slept later than usual. She had been dreaming of Daniel; could there be a nicer way to wake? The whole of today would be like a dream and this evening Daniel would be here. She chose a dress; "rose-red," she said aloud.

One hour later, she descended the stairs on her way to the morning room. Sarah, having slept late herself, looked flustered when she intercepted her.

"Miss Lucy, a phaeton is approaching. A phaeton!"

Lucy ran into the room which, facing east, caught the morning sun and provided a good light for her to work at her desk. Sarah followed closely and they both stared out of the window. "Douglas and… and Lieutenant Thorsen. Whatever is he doing here?"

"I don't know, but do you think the phaeton is his?" said Sarah, staring. "Will they take it round to the stables? I should so like to see it – unless you need me, of course."

"Thank you, Sarah. I'll call for you if I do." Any other day and Lucy might herself have been excited at the prospect of a ride out in the gleaming carriage pulled by two Prussian greys.

Douglas burst into the morning room and greeted Lucy by hugging her as if he had been gone for years. Polite bows and curtseys were reserved for when servants or guests were present and this told Lucy that Karl was far more than an ordinary guest. "Karl is coming to stay with us for a short while. We have some business to discuss. Ideas

One Dark Night

really. We can plan so much better here. Then later this week perhaps you would like to come with us to Whitchester Manor?"

Karl bowed to Lucy. Eager to converse he said, "You would like the Manor, Lucy, and the Manor would like you, especially in this charming rose-red dress."

Lucy acknowledged Karl with a short curtsey. The sparkle in his eyes was discomposing her and she lowered her own as she said, "I should very much like to see Martha again." To draw the attention away from herself, she asked what they would be discussing. She knew this was not how a young lady should behave but, as they were both so fond of saying, she was not like other ladies and Douglas would always take the opportunity to say she was his beloved sister.

"You will approve, I am sure, Lucy. There is much to be done to alleviate poverty for the deserving poor. The taxation system in this country is iniquitous and Karl knows it to be the root cause of all this smuggling."

Lucy felt he was stating the obvious and so merely nodded slowly, awaiting further exposition.

Karl took the opportunity. "I've recently met Mr William Wilberforce, a fine Member of Parliament. He's fighting for the abolition of slavery. He cautions me to be patient but says that bit by bit, with a constant drip, we can both win."

"Don't you think Karl is the right man to stand for Parliament, Lucy?"

"It will cost me a lot of money to become a Member. As much as ten thousand pounds."

Lucy's eyes betrayed her surprise. "Are you prepared to pay such a vast sum?"

Karl shrugged, preferring to launch into his plans. "If taxation were to be cut drastically on these luxury items, they would become available to many more people at a reasonable price and it would destroy the market in smuggled goods. The Exchequer currently operates on the basis of obtaining the highest tax possible on certain goods which become the most profitable to smuggle. If they were imported in greater

One Dark Night

numbers and the taxation reduced proportionately, the Exchequer would not lose."

"But then how would the local people make a living?" queried Lucy.

Karl looked at Lucy with respect for her grasp of the issues involved. Douglas's pride showed in his smile as he said, "Karl, you will find your match in Lucy." Douglas clasped Karl by the shoulder and said, "This fine, incorruptible, forthright Lieutenant Karl Thorsen is a man driven by an ambition to set things right, Lucy."

"I hope to do just that," responded Karl with a tilt of his head. "Britannia will gain much from having her population in gainful employment. This is a cause, like war, that we must win."

Lucy, for one short moment, wished she could stand by this man's side and support him in this fight. Karl, taking advantage of the brief silence began to set out his ideas on employment in minute detail.

He finished by saying, "Crucial to these plans is a lowering of taxes on the goods. Fewer will be forced into a lawless way of life to feed their families and, consequently, fewer will be transported to Van Diemen's Land for attempting to be good parents. Some of our most enterprising people have been transported, hanged even!"

Douglas chimed in enthusiastically, "And the most advantageous place for him to be is in Parliament. He is almost certain to be elected shortly." Douglas looked at Lucy for her approval and Lucy was close to giving it. She could respect Karl Thorsen now, but not love him.

~

Delayed by Karl's enthusiastic plans, it was with some haste that they drove to the nearby church in Karl's phaeton. The bells were still ringing but there was no time to spare.

"We have much to thank God for and much to present to Him for his approval," said Douglas with the authority of a man with the guiding hand.

Karl added, "That's the only reason for going, because your parson is the most boring speaker I have ever heard."

"Well, that in itself teaches us much. When you are in Parliament, Karl, you must model yourself on dear Parson Raffles," Douglas

One Dark Night

winked at Lucy, "though perhaps not in all ways," he said patting his stomach.

~

Lucy spent the afternoon with her father. He was clearly approaching the end of his days. He loved to spend time with his books, so sat in the library. He liked nothing more than to listen to Lucy reading and she would also remind him of the wonderful entertainments that Faefersham Court had provided. The Summer Ball was her favourite, and she would make him laugh with her descriptions of the ladies' haughty ways.

Early in the afternoon, Sir William called for afternoon tea to be served just for himself and Lucy in the drawing room.

"Lucy, I have asked for tea to be served earlier than usual because I must speak to you about your future." Sir William was clearly having difficulty breathing and his chest sounded wheezy. "Sit close to me so that you can hear me."

"Father, do not concern yourself…"

"The time has come to tell you of some arrangements being made for you."

Lucy stiffened; suppose he favoured Karl? But this was her dear father and she knew she could trust him. She nodded, "Thank you, Father."

Sir William did not speak while a pot of tea, tea cups and tiny cakes were brought in on a tray. When the footman had left, he resumed. "Lieutenant Karl Thorsen has asked for your hand in marriage and I did not refuse him."

Her worst fears were realized. "Father…"

Sir William held up his hand to silence her. "Hear all I have to say, Lucy, before you answer me. I did not give my blessing, for as Thorsen knows, you have another suitor." Sir William watched as Lucy's expression relaxed. "Mr Daniel Tynton and I have, as you are aware, been discussing business matters. We have not yet discussed your future but he has requested a meeting with me later this afternoon."

Lucy's heart was pounding, way past the bomping of the previous morning's. Should she tell him about the note? "Father…"

One Dark Night

Sir William continued, wheezing all the time. "I would not give my blessing to the son of a murderous…" Sir William coughed and choked and Lucy tried to attend to him but he waved her away. "…unless he could prove to me, not just by words alone, that he would give you a life worthy of your gentle soul. You know what he said?" He spluttered a little before continuing. "He said, and I remember this clearly, he said you had poise and charm, despite the ill-fitting and shabby clothes you'd been forced to wear and you were untouched by the hatred and corruption around you. He also said, most refreshingly, that you had a complete lack of guile and there was no other young lady like you in the world."

She felt a blush rising. Was this really what he'd said? She mentally made a note to find out what guile meant. "When did he…?"

"Ah! He visited me last September. At first I was not at all pleased to see this son of Tynton. But his charm, intelligence and manner persuaded me to listen. He said that it was obvious there was a history unknown to him or anyone else in Wintergate and that your mother… well, I don't have time to repeat it all. Suffice to say, I was impressed with this young man and all his plans to provide employment for those who could no longer continue with their free trading. And who was I to point the finger at him? I had been heavily involved myself." Waving his hands to stop Lucy interrupting, he indicated that now would be a good time to pour some tea, then he succumbed to another fit of coughing. Lucy drank her tea and ate a cake until he felt better. "While we are talking here, this fine young man is discussing with your brother and Lieutenant Karl Thorsen as to how to improve the lives of many. Douglas has all the connections in London society and Thorsen has the drive and authority to command the respect of the people and fellow Members of Parliament. His future lies there, rightly so for he is driven by an ambition to set things right and he is forthright and incorruptible unlike… ah well," he sighed, "I digress." He coughed a little before adding "Mr Tynton, your Daniel, will work to change the fortunes of many towns and villages along the coast – those whose livelihoods are in disarray currently."

Lucy had listened intently. "Father…"

One Dark Night

Sir William stopped her yet again. "Yes, I know you want to tell me that Daniel has sent you a note." He waited for Lucy's surprise to turn to agreement. "Lieutenant Karl Thorsen can offer you a fine house, of which you will be Mistress; many social engagements, just like the Summer Balls you remember so fondly; a carriage of your own, the phaeton is yours if you wish; the respect of society; security for your children; and so much more. He would make a fine Prime Minister and needs a lady like you by his side.

"Mr Daniel Tynton can offer you, and these are his words, a worthwhile life which you will find fulfilling; a life of interest, with the opportunity to help others; a life of challenge, but also of comfort and security.

"Now the question I have for you is this: which one of these two good gentlemen would you like to marry? Karl was born a gentleman and Daniel will soon merit that title by dint of all that he is accomplishing."

Was he hoping she would choose Karl? He had weighted the advantages of marriage very much in his favour. "My choice may not please you, Father."

"My child, I shall not be of this world for much longer, you must choose the man who will make *you* happy."

"You make no mention of love."

"Only you will know who truly loves you."

"How will I know, Father?"

"Oh, my dear, have they not told you?"

The words of the poem flooded through her.

One Dark Night

Chapter Thirty-Five
"If only time would stand still"

Not knowing of her impending assignation, Sarah had laid out a pale pink silk dress for Lucy to wear for dinner that evening. Lucy, however, chose to stay in the rose red dress and just added a black velvet spencer and her rose red bonnet with the black and white trim. When the long-case clock in the gallery chimed eight, she took three deep breaths to calm her pounding heart, picked up her reticule, adopted a nonchalant gait and skipped down the staircase where once she had stood with Dougie to watch the Summer Ball. In her reticule was Daniel's note which requested the pleasure of her company for dinner al fresco.

Daniel appeared, as if from nowhere, to greet her at the bottom. He held out his arm for her to catch hold of, and whispered, "Come with me; your father knows where we are going, but no one else." He led her to the main door where no lesser person than the butler, Taylor, held open the door for them, revealing a chaise pulled by Fiddle. "Fiddle's none too pleased to be in harness, Lucy, but he'll behave in front of a lady." All her apprehension disappeared: Daniel's warm charm and reassuring demeanour chased all her unease away. A footman was waiting by the carriage door and one of Faefersham Court's grooms was sitting atop, ready to drive them to she knew not where.

After half-an-hour Lucy saw white chalk cliffs rising from the shore, not her own Wintergate Bay cliffs but equally impressive.

"Tarenton," said Daniel. The driver had struggled to keep Fiddle at no more than a trot and Lucy and Daniel had shared many amused looks. He finally brought Fiddle to a commendable halt by a pathway leading through a gap in the cliffs. "I'll whistle like a blackbird when I need you," called Daniel as he leapt from the carriage and pulled down

One Dark Night

the step for Lucy to alight. He fetched a large willow basket from alongside the driver and, in silence, led her down to the beach.

The sun was low in the west, filling the sky with glowing red gold streaks and, as she marvelled at the sun's glory she saw something she would remember all her life. There in the protective hollow of a shallow cave was a small table with a pretty, blue cloth covering it. A single large shell was anchoring the cloth against the light breeze. Daniel drew her attention to the setting sun and deftly produced a bronze candelabrum with five white candles. He lit them and the shadow of the cave turned to a warm, flickering glow. From underneath the table, he produced two small stools and, taking hold of Lucy's hand, he led her to one. Then he put a little vase with three roses on the table. One was white, another yellow, and the largest was red. This was swiftly followed by two glasses and a flagon of wine, and several dishes of savoury delicacies. "Listen," he said with a smile as he sat down.

Floating down from the top of the cliffs was the faint sound of a flute. He leaned across the table, took both her hands in his and, in rhythm to the tune, he recited the words of the poem by Robert Burns:

"O, my luve's like a red, red rose,
That's newly sprung in June.
O, my luve's like the melodie,
That's sweetly play'd in tune.

As fair art thou, my bonnie lass,
So deep in luve am I,
And I will luve thee still, my Dear,
Till a' the seas gang dry."

The tune continued. It was magical: conjured from the wind it seemed and mixing with nature's symphony of the sea. Yes, this was the most special moment of her life and then Daniel crowned it with, "I love you, my cherished Lucy, and I shall be honoured if you will marry me."

One Dark Night

Every fibre of her body screamed in affirmation but she could not speak.

Daniel smiled, and said, "The answer in your eyes is all I need. The words can come when they will." He poured some wine for each of them, took a sip, then took hold of her hand and pulled her into his arms. As he did so, the flautist began to play a hauntingly beautiful tune and he danced her out onto the beach.

A paper-lace moon, the size of a dinner plate, hung in the pink-flecked eastern sky. As he spun her round she saw lilac and pink wispy clouds suspended against a turquoise sky blending into the liquid silver sea, so still, she felt she could walk on it. No one, not even those ladies who arrived in their fine gowns and fashionable carriages for the Summer Balls, could ever have felt as she did tonight.

If only she could capture this moment, this sight, if only time would stand still. She became aware that the music of the flute had stopped and only the constant rhythm of the rippling waves continued, as though confirming Daniel would be with her always. She now knew she could not face being without him. She would accept his proposal.

He led her by the hand back into the mouth of the cave where he took her in his arms and lightly kissed her cheek. Her knees felt as if they would not hold her, her whole body tingled as his warm lips enveloped her mouth. He stepped back, held both her hands in his, then letting one drop by her side, he took a parcel from under the table and gave it to her with another kiss. "For you."

Lucy unwrapped the parcel and inside was a light green shawl with pink tassels. There had been a time when such a gift would have been greeted with relief, relief that she'd have something to keep her warm. Now no gift would be as precious as this.

Daniel took the shawl, draped it gently over her shoulders, and pulled her closer. His fingers played with one of the curls escaping from her bonnet still tied tightly because of the open air ride in the carriage. He undid the ribbons and pushed the bonnet off, letting it fall to the ground. Then his finger traced the line from her forehead, past her lips, her chin and down to the warmth of her bosom, where he hooked his finger into the top of her dress. "As the sun goes down it will become chilly and I have much I want to talk to you about. This shawl will keep you warm."

Lucy smiled, a pale reflection of the feelings welling inside her. She had spent so many years when not a soul cared for her. To have someone put a shawl around her shoulders and touch her intimately, with love in his eyes, caused an explosion of emotions she'd never felt before.

"My body aches for you, Lucy, but I have promised myself, and your father, that I must first tell you what life would be like away from the luxury of Faefersham Court and the chances it would give you."

Lucy, her body tingling, cared not one whit at this moment for luxuries.

"Will you forgive me if I tell you of the plans I have had pounding through my mind for a long time now?" He looked serious and reluctantly unhooked his finger.

She stepped away and sat down. "I would love to hear them."

"I know that Thorsen has asked you to marry him and he has much to offer you. He is also a man of passion and I know that many a woman has sought to steer that passion in her direction." He laughed. "You haven't known that, have you?"

"He always seemed so cold and calculating. I think I have been the most naïve girl who ever existed."

"His passion was consumed by his mission to destroy but now he has something more positive to absorb that energy. And, as far as the ladies are concerned, he has been the gentleman at all times. I am merely indicating to you that he has pushed away chances of a good marriage because he is waiting for you to say that one word. He will make you a fine husband."

"But I don't love him!"

There was no doubt about it, Daniel, normally so calm and in control, looked now as if he'd just been granted ownership of the sun, the moon and the entire earth. "If you accept *my* offer of marriage, Lucy, your life will be very different from how it would be with him."

"I know that."

One Dark Night

Daniel sat down and pushed the little dishes of sweetmeats towards Lucy. "You would not be a working farmer's wife as I shall employ a farm manager for half of the acreage I own. My aunt and uncle have moved in with my mother at Jerusalem Farm which is more manageable for them all."

Lucy looked puzzled.

"The larger farm, Bethlehem, is now mine. I own it outright."

"But you say you will not continue…?" She paused.

"No. When I saw what happened to that poor customs' man on the horse, I knew I could no longer dismiss this way of life as inevitable. When, by the grace of God, I was injured and unable to take part in that last run, I felt sure that my tentative plans were approved by Him." His finger pointed to the sky and he laughed. "I conferred with the parson who confirmed my feeling on that matter."

Daniel offered Lucy some freshly cooked shrimps from another dish: there was much more to convey.

Lucy didn't mind. She could listen forever. It was wonderful just to be with him alone at last. She ate hardly anything.

"Bethlehem Farm will retain its name but it will now serve as a vacation residence for some of the many visitors who usually go to nearby Merrygate. It has become fashionable to 'take the waters' and visitors are entertained in a variety of ways: spas, reading rooms, clubs, the theatre and much more."

"I have been reading about the hotels in Merrygate. I cannot believe I lived so close and knew so little. When I lived at Watch House I used to see the hoys ferrying passengers from London to the coast and had made up my mind to buy some suitable clothes and walk into Merrygate and see if I could apply for a position in one of the hotels."

"As my mother would say, 'aye I'm that glad you didn't'." They both laughed and Daniel watched Lucy; his blue eyes shining. At this point, Daniel took a swig of wine, popped a sweetmeat into his mouth, and returned to his plans. "Bodger has little income now. His father was a successful craftsman, a wood-turner, and he has inherited his tools but not his skill. He fears he will one day be threatened with the workhouse because he won't be able to pay his rent."

One Dark Night

"Oh no, not dear Bodger."

"It's not only Bodger. There's too many families receiving too little relief from starvation. Remember, eighteen men were hanged. All had families. Even those men left in the village are finding life too difficult and talking of doing some free trading again, one way or another."

However far away she lived, there must surely be a way of helping. "I have an allowance now, Daniel, and I shall make time to help the villagers. Tell me, what is the best way to help?"

"By marrying me." His eyes sparkled. "The answer doesn't always lie in the rich emptying their pockets into the church Poor Box, though that is always welcome too. It lies in employment for the widows and many others who struggle to feed their families. The shawl you are wearing was made by Mrs Hendon. You will know that her son was killed by my father." He waited for a response. None came; her expression spoke for her.

He hurried on. "I cannot be responsible for the many sins of my father but I can, as Parson Raffles said, ameliorate the harm caused. My way of stopping her growing impoverishment was to loan her money to buy a small hand loom, a spinning wheel and some wool."

Lucy, her eyes blazing, questioned, "You have become a money lender?"

"Not one who charges extortionate interest, Lucy. No, don't think that of me. My intention is to lend the money long enough for her to repay as and when she can. And I was her first customer."

And Karl was probably her second, thought Lucy, as she inspected the shawl, so similar to the one Karl had given her. Lucy's expression reflected her changing thoughts: Daniel was not a rich man yet he had done what he could.

"The rich cannot be expected to continually provide for people they see doing nothing more than begging, stealing, free trading or breaking the law in other ways. But they do like to travel and then they need transport and accommodation. They also like to be entertained and perhaps buy a new shawl." He winked.

Lucy's eyes had changed from condemning to surprised and then to sheer elation. "You are right! You need a wife who will help you with

One Dark Night

this and I should love to use my time in such a way; ideas are already flooding my head. Children love animals – keep the animals. Ned and Nellie can give donkey rides and..."

Daniel lost all semblance of calm. In his haste to scoop Lucy up in his arms, he knocked over their stools and only narrowly avoided scooping up the tablecloth too. "You *will* marry me, won't you? You *must*. I shan't let you go until you agree."

Lucy, now being whirled around and around in his arms, yelled as if her life depended on it: "Yes."

One Dark Night

Chapter Thirty-Six
"My new son"

Tuesday 11th June

"In the midst of life we are in death."

Lucy had awoken with those words in her mind as if they were a banner on her bedroom wall. On that beautiful evening when Daniel had driven her back to Faefersham Court, she had arrived moments too late. Douglas had met her at the door, whispered something to Daniel, and hurried her upstairs to Sir William's chamber where he lay, having breathed his last. She had so wanted to share her joy with him.

"He knew," Douglas had said. "Daniel had asked his permission, and Father had given it and his blessing too. As you drove away together, he watched from his favourite seat in the library and he let out a long sigh, 'My new son,' he said lifting his arm in the direction of you both. He was tired and called for help to go to his bed. He also called for our parson and told him of his approval for your marriage. I shall always remember his last words. He addressed me as Sir Douglas Harper and said he was proud of my plans and of me, and proud of his daughter and her husband-to-be. I remember it all so clearly, he said, 'May God grant you all good health, the love of your children and good friends, and a life fulfilled within His will. For myself I ask His forgiveness.' I couldn't stop him, he insisted on speaking though his chest rattled. He said there was to be no long period of mourning. He said, 'I insist on you all forging ahead, for you have much to do. Use my money well.' He then handed me several pouches of gold coins. 'This is Lucy's money, stolen by her…' he could barely say the words,

One Dark Night

'*mother*. Retrieved for her by the man she loves, and returned to her by me.' He then smiled, breathed out deeply, and he was gone."

His last words, Lucy thought, and they were all about the future of his children. He had made provision for her, granting a generous dowry, and his blessing to marry Daniel. Dougie, the fun-loving companion of her childhood, was now a man of wealth and influence, and a baronet.

And now Sir William lay peacefully in his grave in the nearby churchyard leaving a legacy of which he could finally be proud.

One Dark Night

Chapter Thirty-Seven
"People are not presents"

Friday 21st June

Sarah bustled in to Lucy's room and broke her melancholy mood. "Miss Lucy, I've packed and packed, 'til I can pack no more, and you're only going for a week. Now what will you wear for the travelling?" Sarah searched Lucy's wardrobe and selected two suitable gowns for the journey to Wintergate. "Should you wrap in a black cloak, Miss Lucy?"

Lucy shook her head: her father hadn't wanted them to be in mourning.

"Miss Lucy, you're dreaming, aren't you?"

"When I marry, Sarah, I should like you to be my lady's maid. The house will not be so grand, but I would miss you. Besides, until Sir Douglas marries, you'll have no lady to attend."

"I thought you'd not require me! I've been that worried! And now I've met Martha, I think we'll get along very well."

Lucy laughed, remembering how Karl (she always called him that now) had said that his wedding gift to her would be *Martha*. She had been so cross with him. "People are not presents!" And Douglas had turned on him until he saw the jest in his eye. "Oh," Karl had said, "what about a fine pair of carriage horses? Can horses be presents?"

Lucy threw off her bed covers; today was to be special. She had not seen Daniel for ten days but Douglas was accompanying her to Bethlehem Farm in the barouche, and the groom would bring Sarah and the luggage in a following carriage. There was to be a celebration in the evening, and Lucy would stay for a whole week. A whole week with Daniel!

One Dark Night

~

Lucy could not believe her eyes. As their open carriage drew close to Bethlehem Farm she saw more than she had imagined. Yes, Daniel had told her how busy he was making it a perfect home and yes, he had shared his plans to build a village, but how had he achieved all this? Douglas called for the carriage to stop so that Lucy could see all that he had already seen some weeks before.

"Your future husband has been extraordinarily busy, Lucy. Do you think I have made a sound investment?"

"Investment?" queried Lucy.

"Father hinted to me that this would be one of the soundest investments I was ever likely to come across. It is not often one gets the chance to invest right from the start in a growing business. I took his advice." Douglas looked across to Lucy to see if she felt comfortable with this. "I have a ten per cent share in the profits from Bethlehem Farm in return for a non-returnable capital investment and," he said, tapping his nose, "sniffing out suitable guests."

The vision of a pig nosing out truffles set Lucy laughing. Of course, Sir Douglas Harper, baronet, would know plenty of people, not only in Kent but also in London, who would want to visit fashionable Merrygate or somewhere close. Oh well done, Daniel. What a clever man she was marrying and how good it was to have a brother, albeit just a half-brother, who had become friends with him and trusted him.

On her left was the sea; on her right were six cottages, with the added charm of thatched roofs, and roses around the doorways. Each faced the sea. They also had a view over a large sunken garden.

"Daniel says that the winds and the salty sea air make it difficult for plants to grow, so he has developed this garden with sheltered terraces leading down to the pond. By next year the plants will have grown more and you'll see the full effect. I am sure he will take you on a tour of his progress."

Lucy was already struck dumb with admiration until a doubt slithered into her mind, like the serpent in the Garden of Eden. "Will visitors come here in the winter?"

One Dark Night

"Ah! That is a problem we have considered." He ran his hand through his wind-blown hair. "Parson Raffles has been rather helpful in that respect. He has suggested to the Archbishop that the church could make use of Bethlehem Farm for their forthcoming conference. He even offered to be a speaker and gave his subject as 'Rebuilding Communities for Christ'. Rather apt, don't you think? And there are other opportunities which we shall develop."

Excitement replaced her doubts. "Look! He is building more."

"They are the foundations for another two cottages but work has stopped for the summer. He doesn't want visitors to be plagued by a lot of 'banging and crashing', he says." Douglas looked thoughtful for a moment. "You know, Lucy, you have chosen a remarkable man. I don't think I have ever known someone so in command and full of vigour. He is laying not only the foundations of cottages, but also a dynasty. Undoubtedly, you have chosen well."

Chosen? Was it not Daniel who had chosen her? Yes, it was clear to her now that he had chosen her a long time ago when she was in no position to make any choices whatsoever, and long before she had such a useful gift of a dowry. He had patiently waited until she would be free to *choose*. And she had made the right choice. "Douglas, the thought I have now," Lucy turned to him with a puzzled look on her face, "is that, if my mother had not left Faefersham Court and sent me to work at Jerusalem Farm, I would never have met Daniel."

"Hmm… sometimes we owe so much to those who hurt us."

Lucy dwelt on her brother's wise words before she said, "I wish I knew where she is."

"There are some people who do not want to celebrate another's good fortune and there is little we can do about it. The change must come from within."

She was quiet for a moment and Douglas allowed her just to sit and contemplate. "I must put my mother and her problems out of my mind." Then, with renewed delight, she said, "Hurry up, Douglas! Let's go and find my remarkable man."

The early eighteenth century farmhouse stood on the far side of the land and was shielded from the rest of the buildings by a trellis of

One Dark Night

yellow roses. Daniel was at the door to meet her. The groom leapt down from his seat next to the driver and opened the carriage door. Lucy's eyes were only on Daniel. She had never seen him look so… many words tumbled through her mind: happy, fit, healthy, successful, and downright handsome. The groom stood aside as Daniel lifted Lucy from the carriage and swung her around and kissed her.

"Welcome to Bethlehem Farm."

Josh was completely unable to contain his exuberance at seeing Lucy again and raced around her as if to claim her, barking non-stop. Daniel had to silence him before she could speak.

"Thank you, Daniel. I am so happy to be here at last."

"The luggage is following and will be here in good time for the evening celebration," said Douglas. With a nod to the groom, he jumped down and bowed to his host who returned his greeting.

"Celebration?" Lucy looked enquiringly at Daniel.

"Well, of course. We have an announcement to make, don't we?"

"Everyone already knows, Daniel."

"Nevertheless, we shall announce our forthcoming marriage in style."

Daniel led the way inside with his arm around Lucy's waist, then he led her behind the parlour door and kissed her again, much longer this time.

After some refreshment, Daniel asked Lucy if she would like to see the rest of the farm and she readily agreed.

Ignoring the long pergola leading from the house to the pond, Daniel, accompanied by the enthusiastic Josh, walked her around to where a blacksmith was working alongside the stables. He then introduced her to Hercules, the shire horse, pounding the ground in the stables. "Don't fret, my good fellow. I wouldn't leave you out; here she is." Hercules tossed his mane and thrust his muzzle down to Lucy to be stroked. Daniel explained how Hercules would still pull the plough when needed but also he would pull a decorated, comfortable open cart around the farm for the visitors to enjoy the country views, or take them down the pathway to the sandy beach below. "And bring them back up the steep hill," he said with a grin.

One Dark Night

"Can I see the cart?" asked Lucy, wandering into the stables.

"As soon as my uncle has finished the painting, you shall see it. Ten people can ride aboard at the same time." He leaned forward and twirled her curls in his hand. "*Our* children will love the ride too. We shall have lots, don't you think?"

"Well, not *too* many, I hope."

"They shall have a nursemaid and all the servants will adore them."

It was some time before they emerged whirling around each other like two courting butterflies. Josh had settled for a sleep – with one eye open.

Daniel showed her the animals. "We need to find a name for the little farm and names for all the animals too. Porkie has just had nine piglets. Nine! I hope you're good at naming ceremonies for we shall allow our visitors to name new-borns." Then he pointed out the sheep roaming the couple of acres set aside for them. "Sometimes I'll let them out and they can crop the grass around the village." Tethered on a long rope was a goat which looked affronted to be disturbed. "He needs taming," muttered Daniel, "Stay away from him."

"How can you call it a village with just six cottages, Daniel? Even with the new ones you are building, it will be small and it is missing the usual village amenities."

Daniel squeezed her hand and laughed. "With someone like you to prompt me, I'm sure I shan't leave anything out."

"Where are Ned and Nellie?" asked Lucy. "I thought they were going to give the children rides."

"There's room for them in the stables too and they are coming from Jerusalem tomorrow, a couple of days before our first visitors arrive."

"You'll have visitors arriving while I'm here? How thrilling!"

"Phew!" said Daniel. "I wondered what you'd think about that."

"Oh I want to be a part of all you do. You won't expect me to sit inside and do needlework, will you?"

"Only if you want to."

"Daniel, I shall be the happiest person alive. If I had been born a lady…"

"You were," interrupted Daniel.

One Dark Night

"Not completely and certainly not as my life continued in Wintergate." She began again. "If I had been born a lady, sitting in a beautiful house with nothing more to do than pull a bell to command a servant, or embroidering a cushion, I don't think I could be as happy as I shall be here."

Daniel took her in his arms and kissed her, long and slow before he said, "I have waited a long time to know that."

They walked on, arm in arm, past the pond and the barn that had been converted to servants' accommodation with stables attached for those visitors coming in their own carriages.

"Work – that is what all this is about, of course. I am employing six builders and two apprentices and there's enough work to keep them earning for a year or two yet. Then there's two men looking after our stables, plus Bodger."

"Oh! Dear old Bodger! Thank you for giving him something to do. Is he fit to work?"

"Probably not for long, but at least he'll end his life in the cottage he loves and earning a living wage. Some years ago he was nearly evicted. Poor old thing."

"Do you think the gentry will be interested in coming here?"

"Those who live in towns and visit their country estates in the summer won't give us a second look. But those who don't have country estates can use this village as a substitute; they can come on a regular basis, always assured of a welcome as if it were their very own with somewhere for their servants to be close at hand. It will also appeal to the growing middle classes, professional people and the merchant class with large families, they are the people I shall be hoping to attract and they are the doers…"

"Doers?"

"The ones that do a lot. They have businesses and I shall give them a rest from their usual routine and a chance to let ideas flourish."

"You amaze me, Daniel. I have so much to learn about you and I shall love you more each day."

One Dark Night

"More each day? I'm looking forward to that though I cannot say the same because I couldn't love you more than I do now. My heart would burst."

Lucy giggled. They walked on with their conversation becoming more and more playful until Daniel knelt down and patted the green, newly mown grass for her to sit on.

"And you'll need men to look after the little animal farm. Do you think that farmhand at Jerusalem, the one who liked to tell stories all the time," she thought for a moment, "do you think he could be dressed in a country smock and big hat and tell all sorts of animal tales?"

Daniel looked surprised. "What would I do without you? Yes, I'll get Ma to send him over and, if he reckons he can do it, we'll start him right away."

"He's quite old, isn't he? He'll probably like to be relieved of the heavy work."

Daniel agreed, put his legs across her legs and his arms around her waist and kissed her again. And again. And again, until they fell over.

Lucy wondered about work for the women who had lost their men – hanged, transported or imprisoned. But mucking out horses was best left to the men, she supposed. "What can I do, Daniel?"

"You can do whatever you choose. You've not had much chance to make choices before now, so…" he gave a broad smile and kissed her, surfacing from her warm lips only to say, "It is my pleasure to know that you will never have to work again if you don't want to. If you do, then I have just the job for you! Once we are married, you must arrange for a housekeeper. She will allow you time to welcome guests when they arrive."

"Oh but that is not a very big job!"

"But it is an important one. You will make them feel like welcome guests in our private village; you will add to their holiday something I could not. Besides, that will allow you to help in whatever way you wish." He kissed her again. "You will need to buy lots of things for the cottages and particularly our own house. And, most important, you must spend much time with me."

One Dark Night

Lucy hugged him. He wasn't cool like the moon, as she had once said, nor commanding with her. "It is fortunate that no one can see us, Daniel." They laughed and she wondered if she could ever be this happy again.

"Our house will be much bigger by spring time, because I am employing some very experienced builders to enlarge it. Will you take a look at the plans, Lucy? It must be an impressive sight to compete with Merrygate's big hotels."

It was his verve that attracted everyone who came in contact with him, yes, she could see that now. The way he comported himself spoke of innate style yet did not suppress his spirit. And he was hers. What treasure.

One Dark Night

Chapter Thirty-Eight
"An empty seat"

Lucy's mind was still reeling from all that she had seen and she was grateful for a short sleep before getting ready for the celebration. It was still warm in the early evening sunshine so she chose a pale pink silk dress with deep red ribbons trailing from a bow at the front. A little cap of pink feathers pinned securely in place by Sarah, complemented her costume. She paused and stared at herself in the looking glass. Who could have known two years ago, when she was working nearly every day in the fields planting potatoes, cutting cabbages, and pulling up those mangel wurzels, that she would soon have many silk dresses? If only her mother could see her now! Would she be proud? Or still jealous and angry that her cheating had been found out?

From the increasing chatter that floated up the stairs, there seemed to be many people arriving, so she hurried down to the parlour. One day there would be a drawing room and the parlour could be the morning room, and… oh so many things to do! So exciting. She pushed open the door and could not believe her eyes. There was Parson Raffles, tall as ever but somewhat slimmer, with Emmeline standing proudly by his side. Douglas was there, of course. Martha was holding a tray of sweetmeats and looked overwhelmed, yet delighted to be in such esteemed company. Daniel's mother and his aunt and uncle were also there. All curtseyed or bowed as Daniel welcomed her as "my future wife". He was so calm, it was as if he was not at all surprised at what he had achieved. Yes, he was as cool as the moon, and that is how she liked him. Today, though, he had revealed an eager passion and fire in those sparkling blue eyes.

One Dark Night

She became aware that everyone was staring at her and she had to halt her dreams.

A man in handsome red livery entered and announced, "Dinner is served."

Daniel took her arm and led her to the head of a long dining table stretching from the beginning of the pergola. He took his place at the head of the table and she was seated at his right hand. He clicked his fingers for Josh to lie down at the base of the pergola. "Whatever else changes, where I go, Josh follows. Except if you walk out on your own, perhaps to the sands, then Josh must go with *you*."

The butler showed the guests to their places while Lucy watched in awe.

"Daniel, do you now have a butler?"

"Just for tonight. But if he plays his cards right, I'll consider his long-term service."

He sounded in command, just like he always had, but now he had something worthwhile to command. She looked along the table and noted the white cotton tablecloths, the wine glasses and the cutlery, all laid correctly. "He is a competent man, Daniel."

"He should be. He comes with Karl's recommendation."

Lucy saw Douglas at the head of the other end of the table. Next to him was an empty seat which Daniel told her was for someone who might or might not arrive.

"Is it someone I know?"

Daniel hesitated before he said, "Karl is presenting a study of what can be done when an old smuggling community tries something different. He has obviously been delayed in London." He grinned and pointed to the wine which was being expertly poured. "Not smuggled French! English – my mother's home-made fruit wine."

Lucy took a sip. "It's good! Very good." Daniel's hesitation and that empty seat weren't quite right and she wondered if it was really for Karl. Somehow it unnerved her, but she didn't want to spoil the evening and so she smiled.

In between courses, she took time to appreciate the romantic scene. Never before had she seen anything like this, not even at Faefersham

Court. She looked along the length of the pergola, adorned by rambling red and yellow roses swaying in the breeze and saw lanterns of all colours hanging from the sides and strung along the top. In between the posts of the pergola, set back, were small, wooden booths. Each booth displayed the wares of a craftsman working at a chosen occupation.

"After dinner, I'll take you on a tour of the booths and you can see if there are any more skills we could incorporate." Daniel squeezed her hand and Lucy felt a rush of warmth, thankfully not a blush, but a feeling of sheer bliss.

At the end of the dinner, the butler took a tray of wine around to each booth and when he had done so, he called for silence from the dinner guests. Daniel stood and, after thanking everyone for coming, he announced that Lucy and he would be married in September. Everyone but Lucy stood as they toasted Daniel's bride-to-be and then there was loud cheering and clapping from all those in the booths. Daniel took her hand. "Come, it's time to show you what else has been prepared for your approval."

He led her to the far end of the pergola where, in the first booth Mrs Hendon had a fine display of woven shawls of all colours and patterns. She had also woven reticules, and fine woollen curtains "to keep the draughts out". In other booths were women who had recently lost their husbands. Some were showing clay pots filled with flowers for sale, others were making lace, jewellery, and knitted clothes and toys.

"And here we have all the Bethlehem Farm estate hands gathered together," Daniel said rather unnecessarily for there was Bodger holding his glass of wine high to Lucy, and several other men she'd seen earlier in the day. None spoke until Daniel encouraged them to explain what their role was in the holiday village.

"So, Lucy, what should we have in this booth?" Daniel asked as he moved to a vacant booth.

"Oh, your mother's wine," Lucy said immediately. "She'll have to show someone how to make it." She furrowed her brow. "Also, you must have a baker bring his loaves, so that the visitors can buy what they need from here and not have to send into Merrygate."

One Dark Night

"You're right! They might enjoy the lovely smell of warm bread too and choosing what their servants will serve! Do you think the visitors will like the opportunity to dine under the stars and the roses, Lucy? I thought we could have special dinners, perhaps even the occasional ball, if the weather's fine of course."

Lucy looked along the length of the pergola, with its lanterns glowing brighter now the sun had set. "It's a wonderful idea. I think this must be the best day of my life." She'd thought that nearly all the day. And then she thought of the evening on the beach when Daniel had proposed and her heart skipped a beat. "Well, certainly one of the best."

As they walked back, Daniel showed her a carpenter busy making a cradle, and a stonemason making statues.

"How is the statue of Diana coming along, Tom?"

"Aw, jes' fine, she'll be ready for next year when yer'll be gettin' the crowds."

Daniel slapped him on the back and explained to Lucy that Diana would be six feet tall and stand in the centre of the pond. "One dark night, Tom was shot in the leg and it had to be removed, so he could no longer work in Merrygate's hotels. His father, a stonemason and sculptor of some talent, has taught him the skill. Now Tom's going to make smaller versions of Diana for the visitors to buy and take home."

"I'll pay m' rent, don't you worry, squire. I ain't takin' no charity."

"Rent?" queried Lucy.

Daniel hurried her away. "The men in particular don't want to be seen as taking charity. They have pride in their work and that is good. So I paid the carpenter to construct these booths, and then they are available for rent at tuppence a week and I shall maintain the booths."

"Then how will you make money?" Lucy had been without money for long enough for it still to ride high in her mind.

"The tuppence is enough for this year as there will be fewer visitors. Next year they know they will have to pay a little more. Does that sound fair to you?"

Lucy nodded. She need have no worries, Daniel was an idealist: he helped others to become prosperous but knew he must do that from a position of strength. How interesting that he was already being regarded as the local squire.

In another booth, someone was making fishing rods. "In case the visitors don't bring a proper one but fancy doing a little fishin'," said the man seated on a broad, high-backed chair lest he topple over. He had no legs but he had a fine smile.

Lucy could feel tears welling in her eyes and flung her arms around Daniel and hugged him. "I don't care who sees me, or who hears. I love you more than I ever imagined it was possible to love anyone. And it hurts."

He held her face in his hands and with his thumbs he wiped away her tears. Looking down into her eyes he said, "I loved you from the moment you first came to our farm. You were just a girl and I wasn't much older. I went to bed dreaming of you, ragged, outgrown clothes and all. You shone like warm sunshine, making everywhere you went a little better. Everyone who met you, except perhaps my father," he paused, "was made to feel they were special. I knew I had to make you mine. To capture your sunshine consumed my every waking thought." He laughed, and pulled her closer again, whispering, "I wish it were September tonight for my nights are filled with the dream of making you mine."

One Dark Night

Chapter Thirty-Nine
"You're warning me, aren't you Josh?"

Saturday 22nd June
The following morning, after breakfast, Lucy wanted to see the beach. The guests at the dinner had all returned to their homes, and Martha was still awaiting the arrival of Karl. Lucy knew that Sarah had her duties and so she suggested to Martha that they take a walk on the beach together while Daniel and Douglas visited Merrygate on business.

"Daniel says we are to take Josh as our protector, Martha."

"Aw, fuddlepumps, whatever do we need a protector for? We've both growed up getting ourselves about the place and now we have to take a dog!"

"Martha, Josh is no ordinary dog. He is a friend." Josh, hearing his name, padded towards Lucy and sat beside her. "He's feeling dejected because he wasn't allowed to run alongside the horses into Merrygate."

"Jejected are you? Well, then 'tis only right you come with us, Josh, and make sure we're kept safe from dragons."

Josh wagged his tail as Martha spoke and eagerly followed them to the door; he'd been given an assignment.

Smaller than Wintergate Bay but with finer sand and very few rocks, the beach would be one of the main attractions of the village. While Martha chattered on, Lucy imagined the bathing machines drawn down to the water's edge by the very same ponies that had hauled carts for the smugglers. An old woman sat in a boat, facing the receding tide and mending a fishing net. This is such an attractive scene, we must have an artist in one of the booths, Lucy thought.

One Dark Night

"Aw 'tis cold, Lucy. That wind's restless and getting up a fair big breeze. Shall I go and get our shawls? Josh can stay here with you and I won't be more than a minute or two."

"Yes please, Martha, I won't go far."

While Martha plodded up the steep slope, Lucy strolled over to the woman in the boat. Wrapped all in black, with a thick woollen shawl over her hair, Lucy supposed she must be one of the many widows hereabouts. Josh did not approve and growled low.

"Good morning," said Lucy. "It's fine and sunny but a little chilly, isn't it?"

The woman climbed out of the boat, wrapped her shawl across her face, and picked up an oar using it as a crutch to hobble towards Lucy. Then with one swift upward sweep of the oar, she caught Lucy with a tremendous blow, sending her unconscious to the sand. Too late, Josh rushed at the woman, but she sent him tumbling back with a mighty whack under his belly. Barking furiously he bounded back and came at her again, tugging frantically at her dress until it ripped. All the time the woman was lugging Lucy into the boat but as soon as she could, she turned on Josh again, wielding the oar. Fearlessly, Josh dodged her blows and clenched her ankle. The oar being too unwieldy at close range, she punched him. Toppling her over, Josh jumped in the boat and licked Lucy's face in a futile attempt to wake her. The woman shoved the boat into the sea with Josh nipping at any part of her he could reach. As the boat drifted out, Josh set up a mighty howling.

When Martha returned to the beach there was no one there, the boat had drifted out of sight and the woman had escaped with only a slight trail of blood to show that anything untoward had happened.

Bodger, on watch from the top of the cliffs, had never before so regretted the loss of his tongue.

~

Lucy, still stunned, began to realize that the constant rough, wet thing slapping her face was Josh's tongue and to put a stop to it, she'd have to stir. Josh, in frenzied delight, leapt on the wooden thwart and, despite looking very insecure, resumed his howling. Lucy sat up and looked around. The rowing boat was no more than eight feet long and being

One Dark Night

swept eastward by the tide. She checked the position of the sun, yes, the boat was drifting towards France and how could she navigate past those treacherous sandbanks? On her left she could see only sea, but on her right, by her reckoning, the town on the shore must be Merrygate. Surely someone would hear Josh soon. Perhaps Daniel would. Oh please, Daniel, don't let me lose you now.

One glance around the boat told her there were no oars. Her head pounded and Josh's attempts to call for aid weren't helping. Oh how she wished she could swim but, however small, this tiny craft offered a measure of safety. Lying in the bow was a coil of rope used for hauling in the boat. Josh could likely swim. She propped herself up and edged close to Josh still howling from his precarious position on the oarsman's seat.

"Can you swim, Josh?"

If Josh could have spoken he would have said "Delighted to be of service." Pleased to feel Lucy's hand patting him, he stopped howling.

Lucy pointed at the shore. They had now lost the reassurance of the town and drifted around the headland. She could see only a deserted beach backed by tall chalk cliffs in the distance. She knotted the unsecured end of the rope and offered it to Josh. As if reading her thoughts, he took it in his mouth, leapt into the sea and began swimming towards the shore. Hope. There was now indisputable hope.

Josh began to tire and the reason became clear: the boat was taking in water, making his work so much harder. There was nothing to bail out with. She took off her petticoat and soaked up what she could and wrung it out over the side, then tried again and again, but the bottom of the boat was filling up rapidly. Looking around she noticed a small hole, no bigger than a farthing. "That's it!" Ripping off a piece of her petticoat, she plugged the hole. It wasn't watertight but it slowed the intake sufficiently for Lucy to mop up the sloshing water in the boat. She clung to her disappearing hope.

"Keep going, Josh."

She would have liked to add, *we're nearly there,* but they weren't. Though her head still hurt, she leaned over the side and paddled with her hand. The boat became unsteady and nearly tipped Lucy into the sea. She clambered back to the middle. Josh, tired, paddled on. Hauling Josh in to give him a rest would just cause the boat to capsize.

"Keep going, Josh. Keep going."

She returned to the one safe aid she could give – mopping up the seeping water. Whoever had put her in here intended her to drown and, but for Josh and his insistent rough licking, she would have. Someone didn't want her to marry Daniel. Dear God, please save us.

Imperceptibly, the tide changed. Lucy became aware that the boat was drifting in to the beach and with Josh paddling non-stop they would reach the shore. She chanced looking over the side. If it was shallow, she would jump over and wade in. Sea shells, a few chalky rocks, sand – she could see the bottom! Josh sensing the boat being off balance again turned and, if a dog could glare, he glared. He had swum such a long way and perhaps she should not rob him of his victory. She looked over the side once more; she could no longer see the bottom, what she had seen before had been a rocky ridge. Oh, well done, Josh, that had been a warning look, not one of offence.

She watched him struggling on only to see him react to something in the water and disappear. The rope slackened. Lucy rushed to the bow and tugged the rope.

"Josh, Josh!"

There was no sign of him. Any giveaway bubbles were lost in the waves crashing on another ledge. The boat slowly drifted to rest on a rock. She hauled the rope in: Josh was not attached. She'd never forgive herself. She had distracted him. Had he drowned? She clambered over the side and waded in the shallows. Then to her horror a shoal of jellyfish floated by and she was standing in the midst of them. Urgh! She wrapped her dress around her ankles as tightly as possible and stepped on to the wide rock which had impeded the boat. There, on the other side was Josh lying in ankle deep water, his nose propped up enough for him to breathe. Seeing Lucy, he struggled to stand. A scraping sound alerted her to the boat, now lighter, shifting off the rock. Ignoring the danger of the jellyfish, she grabbed hold of the bow, grasped the rope and tied it round her waist.

One Dark Night

She then made her way back to Josh who was standing on three legs, blood dripping from his fourth, held high. Although he was heavy, she lifted him over the side into the boat, and laid him on the thwart. He'd been stung! His belly had a nasty rash and the shock had probably caused him to smash into the rocks.

She looked at the shore – tantalisingly close. Going to the bow, she heaved the boat off the rock and, still standing on the rocks, she plugged the hole as much as possible, soaked up the water lying at the bottom, then dragged the boat away from the shallow water. She felt it tugging away from her. Somehow she would have to tow it into shore. With no one to bail out the water seeping in, it was getting heavier by the minute. She tucked up her dress and using her hands to steady her, she crawled along the edge of the ridge, dragging the rope and boat slowly behind her.

Then a wave took the boat and washed it in towards the shore. The rope around her waist dragged her against the side of the boat until, thank God, her feet touched the sand. Another wave pushed the boat on to the beach and Lucy staggered and fell beside it.

After a moment to catch her breath, she lifted the bedraggled Josh out of the boat and laid him on dry sand. He quickly stood on three legs, his right front paw still held up, panting, yet not beaten. Lucy hauled the boat in until she was sure it could not float away and for good measure, tied the bow rope around a rock.

To give herself time to catch her breath, she sat beside Josh. "You're a hero and when we get home, you shall have a dragon-sized bone." Breathing heavily, she was quiet for a moment before saying, "Martha shall be in charge of finding one; she's the only one who knows about dragons."

She dared not sit for too long and so retrieved the ragged bit of petticoat from the hole, and the rest lying in the boat, and wrung them out – they might be useful later. Clutching her wet dress and torn petticoat, she stumbled up the beach towards the cliff. The two of them sat down again and looked at each other. Josh's tongue was lolling from his mouth, long and red. Lucy hugged him. He'd hardly had the energy

One Dark Night

to shake off the salty water from his coat. She sat with her arms around him, both of them shivering, but his eyes were bright with triumph.

They were trapped on this beach with no way out now that the tide had rolled in. The restless wind turned cold and cruel; could they shelter in that cave? Dragging herself up, she encouraged Josh to follow; he didn't seem keen. At the mouth of the cave he dropped his head and growled low.

"You're warning me, aren't you Josh? You stay there, and I'll carefully take a look inside." Once her eyes had adjusted to the comparative darkness, she could see that what looked like the end of the cave was actually a rock fall.

Oozing from the chalky rock high up, fresh water trickled down. The retrieved bits of petticoat were indeed useful, she soaked them in the water and returned to Josh. There was little she could do about his sore belly but she could bathe his bleeding paw. She looked closely and felt the bones. He didn't object.

"You'll be all better by tomorrow, Josh."

She wrung the water from the length of petticoat, cleansed his wound then wrapped it around his paw and tied it tight enough to keep the sand out.

She returned to the trickle of water and tried to drink some. Josh limped forward and did the same until his tongue looked much better and he began to lick his belly.

Lucy looked around. This had likely been a smugglers' cave in the past, so there might be a way out. She started to climb the rocks with Josh growling from below. He scrambled up to Lucy and tugged at her skirt. When this didn't work, he seized her ankle gently. Lucy had to stop. "Let go, Josh. Please." Josh hung on, looking very apologetic. "Let me just go and see." She put her hand down to Josh's snout and stroked it and he let go very reluctantly only to sit and howl. "Josh, you're undoubtedly right, there's some sort of danger in there and we must find another way out." Josh's eyes were no longer condemning her and she carefully edged her way back to the sandy floor of the cave and out into the daylight.

One Dark Night

Daniel had trained Josh well and twice today she had ignored his warnings. So she hauled the boat up to the base of the cliff as far away from the mouth of the cave as possible. "Curl up here with me in the shelter of the boat, Josh, and we might even take a nap together and get our strength back." Josh understood and immediately settled down between the boat and the cliff and Lucy sat down beside him drawing her knees up and hugging them. She was tired, but she'd not sleep, not until they were safely in the next bay. All her thoughts gathered around Daniel, imagining him being just in the next bay, searching and soon they would find each other.

An unwelcome thought slunk into her mind: what should she do about whatever was buried in the sand near her sanctuary? Perhaps it was the cold wind, or the clear air that helped her come to a quick conclusion: she would *not* tell Daniel. How could she tell him that his father had sworn an oath on his life? She could tell him and not mention the oath perhaps? No. It might be some terrible secret which would cause uproar in the village. She'd decided, once and for all: one day, she'd borrow a spade and dig. If anything was still there, then she'd tell him. Most likely, it would be gone, and best forgotten.

Some hours later, and dark, Lucy judged that the tide had receded sufficiently to allow them to wade around to the next bay. Josh shook himself awake and followed Lucy somewhat reluctantly. "I know you're tired, Josh, but this time I'll be right, you'll see. Take a quick drink then we must go." Josh needed no telling. He lapped up all he could and now he had chalk all over his tongue.

The light of the new moon was of little help, but the white cliffs were like a beacon guiding them to safety. "It's a pity we can't go back around the headland to Merrygate but at least we have escaped being trapped against the cliffs, Josh." Josh clearly thought so too and plodded on with his tail low. Nevertheless, he employed what energy he could muster in looking for a way out. He limped along the edge of the cliffs. Then, glory be, he barked until Lucy trudged towards him. He had found an opening in the cliff, hidden behind overhanging scrubby plants. Josh's nose twitched then he turned to look at Lucy. He already

One Dark Night

had his injured paw on the first step and Lucy needed no more encouragement to follow him.

Inside the chalk cliff, steps led upwards but were difficult to negotiate in the dark. Josh scampered ahead while Lucy tried out each step before trusting her weight to it. One by one, all seventy-seven of them were behind her and they were safely on top of the cliff. Josh, ears pricked, suddenly dashed away, leaping over the tussocks, leaving Lucy wondering how he could recover so quickly. She gingerly attempted to follow. Then Josh howled.

She wasn't the only one to hear Josh. Douglas's carriage drew up and out jumped Daniel. Josh greeted his master enthusiastically, leaping up and bounding around him. Daniel rushed towards Lucy who flung her arms around his neck. He scooped her up and kissed her – oh how he kissed her. Warm, tender, strong, all of this and more and Lucy returned his kisses with irrepressible joy.

Snuggling into her neck, he said, "I have not been able to think of anything but you, Lucy. If I looked, I saw only you; if I heard a noise, I yearned for it to be you; and all the time I could smell the perfume of you, the sea in your hair and the warm scent of your skin."

"I knew you'd come. I couldn't contemplate any other outcome."

Douglas, who had been driving while Daniel peered into the darkness looking and calling for Lucy, stood aside while the two lovers were totally absorbed with each other. He finally managed to persuade Daniel to put Lucy down and allow him to hug her with warm, brotherly love, but it was only a moment later that, with tender care, Daniel scooped her up again and placed her on the carriage seat.

"We have brought you some warm clothes, Lucy. Perhaps you should take those wet ones off. Douglas and I will attend to Josh." He turned around. "My good friend, thank you for your part in bringing Lucy back to me." Daniel dropped to his knees to receive more of Josh's chalky-tongued welcome. "Your tongue, Josh. It's hard, white, curled and not at all pleasant. You need some water." From the back of the carriage he brought out a flagon of water, grabbed a dish from a basket, poured some water into it and Josh gratefully lapped it up, then presented Daniel with his paw wrapped in Lucy's torn petticoat. "My injured hero. I shall take a closer look when we reach home."

Meanwhile, Douglas opened the basket filled with milk, bread and honey and, once Lucy was in warm, dry clothes and wrapped in a blanket, he encouraged her to drink and eat before the journey back to Bethlehem Farm. Josh wasn't normally allowed bread and honey but he ate great chunks of honeyed bread before curling up on a blanket on the floor and probably deservedly dreaming of a bone the size of a dragon.

Chapter Forty
Daniel
"Lucy must never know"

Daniel, Lucy, and Douglas did not stir before noon that Sunday morning and enjoyed a late breakfast with Karl who had also joined the search the night before. He departed on Midnight soon after, with Martha getting ready to follow in the carriage.

"Won't be long, Lucy, before I live here myself," she'd said with unabashed glee.

Lucy, knowing that she would miss her hero, smiled broadly. "We'll be inviting Lieutenant Thorsen to visit, Martha. He has proved to be such a good friend."

"Aw… I'm that pinkled. He's a good man, Lucy. If you only knew what he saves this country from. We are all much honoured to have him living in the county and doing so much caring." She paused to think of more ways to bolster his achievements when Parson Raffles arrived and took over.

"Yes, indeed. A born warrior, using his Viking blood to fight for justice and the good of all."

Lucy was not yet able to join in with this hero worship in any overt form so merely waved goodbye to Martha and curtseyed to the parson and his wife, Emmeline.

Daniel, hearing the strong, clear voice of the parson, came to the door and bowed.

"We heard, Mr Tynton. The news was brought to us by Martha this morning. I was able to conduct the morning service with a good heart, thanking the Lord God for answered prayers."

One Dark Night

"Come in and take some refreshment with us in the parlour, Mr Raffles."

Lucy had covered the bruise on her forehead by tugging her curls down from her close-fitting bonnet and was otherwise none the worse for what she called "her adventure". She was delighted to see the parson and his wife, and she and Emmeline, together with Douglas, decided to take a stroll around the sunken garden. Emmeline was entranced with the many different flowers growing.

"I have brought you Echinacea for Josh," she said confidently.

"For Josh?"

"Yes, Lucy. I am learning about herbs and healing. I think it will be useful. Josh shall be my first patient."

Lucy laughed.

"Sir Douglas knows about Echinacea, is that not so?" Emmeline looked hopefully at Douglas.

He raised his eyebrows. "I know a little. It's like a big daisy!" He laughed at the thought. "And it grows in America."

"Ah but it has healing properties and if you will allow me, I shall treat Josh's wound with some."

Lucy smiled. "I am sure Josh will be most grateful for even more attention. He has been dining on chicken this morning and for the parson's wife to nurse him will be yet another treat."

Douglas encouraged them to sit on one of the benches and enjoy the sunshine and they twirled their pretty parasols like young girls.

"I hope the weather stays fine for the first visitors. I'm so looking forward to meeting them. With all that's happened, I haven't had time to think about my duties."

"You have duties already, Lucy?" Emmeline looked surprised.

"Not really. I shall find some and that will make the occasion much more memorable."

Meanwhile, Bodger, who had been invited to rest at the farm for the night, was nursing his badly bruised and bloodied leg on a couch.

"My good fellow, whatever has happened to you?"

One Dark Night

Daniel replied for Bodger. "Mr Raffles, I am sure I can tell you the whole story but please be aware that Lucy must never know all that I tell you."

"My lips will be sealed, and the truth will stop me wildly speculating." Parson Raffles made himself comfortable and Daniel sat so that he faced both the parson and Bodger.

"Lucy and Martha went to the beach with Josh. Martha returned for shawls. What neither of them knew was that I had asked Bodger," he gestured to Bodger who confirmed what was being said with a nod, "to watch over them from the cliff top."

"Did you have a reason for that request?"

Bodger, his eyes following the lips of the parson, looked uncomfortable.

Daniel gave Bodger a reassuring smile. He would never reveal Bodger's involvement in the disappearance of Annie Yorton, not even to the parson. "I had been able to invite Lucy's mother to come to the celebration to see her daughter."

The parson gave Daniel a tight smile. "Even her mysterious vanishing and her whereabouts are not unfathomable to you. You are a remarkable man."

Daniel could hardly say that the whereabouts of Annie Yorton was planned by him and certainly no mystery. It had been easy to send Annie Yorton's invitation to his old free-trading connections in France. He hurried on. "She chose not to attend. I believe her hatred of Lucy has embittered her, so I thought it best to provide Lucy with someone to watch over her. I regret disclosing where Lucy is."

"Ah… I see." The parson turned to Bodger and carefully enunciated. "Like one of God's guardian angels."

Bodger, his weatherbeaten face shining, nodded enthusiastically. Daniel considered the concept: Bodger – an angel! He continued. "Having sighted a seemingly innocuous woman on the beach, he saw her knock Lucy so hard that she dropped to the ground. He saw the boat pushed out to sea with Lucy and Josh in it. His suspicions as to the woman's identity were aroused, particularly when she tried desperately to knock Josh out of the boat. Bodger watched her hide the oars then

One Dark Night

followed her as she tramped along the beach into Merrygate and beyond. She was watching the boat and appeared to become more angry as time went on. Eventually, he caught up with her in a deserted bay and she was clearly annoyed. She could see Josh towing the boat back to the next bay but she could not reach that bay without first returning to Merrygate. Bodger made use of a fisherman's net, and captured the woman. The woman was Annie Yorton."

"No! That cannot be! Her own mother. Oh poor Lucy."

"We must never tell Lucy that the woman, heavily disguised, was her mother."

"You are right! No one should have to live with the knowledge that her mother has been so cruel."

"I likened it to seeing a man consorting with a woman not his wife, the wife being a good friend of mine. Would I tell the wife? No. I would confront the man. I can no longer confront Annie Yorton but I am relieved I did what I could when I could."

The parson furrowed his brow. "Does she not ask who the woman was?"

"I have answered that we have not found her."

"Does she worry that 'the woman' will return?"

"Bodger, in his own way, tells her she was a lunatic and has been taken away." Daniel shrugged his shoulders. "It's not what I should have liked him to say, but I suppose it will set her mind at rest."

The parson nodded. "My only consolation for my lack of earlier action is this eventual happy outcome."

Daniel returned to relating the events of the previous day. "Annie Yorton, stronger than anyone might imagine, and still under the net, knocked Bodger to the ground and stamped on his leg and then hit him on the head with a rock."

"A rock!" The parson was astounded.

Daniel raised his eyebrows in agreement. "Fortunately, the net did not allow her to hit out too hard and he wrapped it and the attached ropes around her, tied her up and gagged her. Despite being injured, he made his way back to Merrygate where he managed to get a message to me."

One Dark Night

"And you set off to look for Lucy?"

"Yes, Sir Douglas and I were on horseback and we raced back and forth but could see no boat. We sent another message for Sir Douglas's carriage to be brought to us. We insisted that Bodger return to the farm but he didn't.

"While Sir Douglas and I searched for Lucy, Bodger, in one of our small boats, rowed to where he had left Annie Yorton. By this time it was past midnight. He manhandled her into his rowing boat but found it difficult to row against the tide and back to Wintergate. The boat was drifting into the next bay and he just managed to row there and beach it. Annie Yorton had managed to free one of her hands and, despite still being in the net, was causing old Bodger considerable difficulty. He thought it would not be long before she freed herself. Then he saw a dark shape on the beach. It was Lucy's boat. He searched for Lucy and Josh without any success. He dragged that boat back to the water's edge and despite her furious struggles, Annie Yorton was pushed into the boat and he hauled it into the sea. He explained…"

"How can Bodger *explain*?" The parson was looking very puzzled. "I know you have developed…"

Daniel saved the parson some words. "Yes, we understand each other. In this case, Bodger drew maps for me." Standing up in a casual manner, Daniel wandered to the window, then moved behind the parson where Bodger could not lip read. Into the parson's ear he whispered, "What *Bodger* does not know, and must never find out, is that there was a small hole in that boat – Lucy told me. Bodger had thought Annie would have a chance of rescue after enduring a few terrifying hours. However, being tied up and with a hole in the boat, it is almost certain she has drowned. Just in case she has survived, I have sent two of the men along the coast now that it is daylight."

The parson's eyes were out like organ stops. Turning away from Bodger, he said, "So Bodger, inadvertently, has done to Lucy's mother what she had done to Lucy!"

"And you and I, once again, have more secrets to keep."

"God have mercy on her soul."

One Dark Night

"It seems there are some people that even you, a representative of God's love, cannot help. I have told you so that should she survive, you will know that Bodger intended her no certain death, only the fear of it."

The parson hung his head. "Our Lord himself could not help some people. Free will and the wily devil saw to that." Despite losing many pounds in weight, he still had more than one chin and now he shook those chins. "To stand before your maker and know that he already knows what you did and why is a very sobering thought."

Daniel sat down so that Bodger could be part of the conversation again. Bodger joined in immediately by tapping his head and pointing vaguely towards the beach.

"Perhaps this man is right, Daniel. The wretched woman may have been disturbed in the head. Though the evil of jealousy can drive one to desperate measures."

Daniel nodded in affirmation and then, turning to Bodger and with much explanatory waving of his arms, he said, "Bodger, how would you like to stay here on the farm? You'd have to give up your cottage but we could fix one of the storage outhouses at the back of the stables, near the well. What do you think?"

Bodger's eyes misted as if he were thinking of all the events leading up to this happy news: the time when as a deaf young man, not hearing the Revenue Officer behind him, he'd let slip the name of the bay for the landing; Sydney Tynton ordering his tongue to be cut out; the dark night when Tynton had thrashed him for not being quick enough on the sands; the boy, Dan, who'd stepped in and saved him and been beaten for his trouble; the young girl who'd brought him firewood when she had far too much to do…

Daniel leaned forward. "Bodger, what do you think?"

Bodger, never having known the feeling of a tear in his life before, struggled to hold back streams of them. Unaffected by this, his smile, wide as the English Channel, gave his answer.

One Dark Night

Chapter Forty-One
"More of this very soon"

September 1822

Parson Raffles, tall, imposing, and wearing a white surplice over his usual black cassock, radiated goodwill. He held up the palms of his hands and by lowering them, asked the congregation to sit.

"We have just witnessed the marriage of Miss Lucy Yorton to Mr Daniel Tynton. We have heard that it is the bond that holds two people together in the journey of life and it exists for the procreation and benefit of children and to give comfort and a shelter in stormy weather, offering warmth and a resting place in times of trouble."

The parson, always embellishing any service or ceremony with his own thoughts, did at least, for once, stand still. His feet were firmly planted in front of the young married couple and his arms stretched towards his God. His stance gave emphasis to his words, though his booming voice alone captured the attention of the congregation.

"Our choices are not sealed in the blood we inherit." He lowered his hands and held them towards Lucy and Daniel. "The sins of our fathers," and in a low mutter he added, "and mothers," then loudly held forth again, "hold sway over us until we call upon the strength of the Lord to fight evil *wherever* we find it. Standing before me today are a man and a woman who are not constrained by the blood they have inherited. They have each chosen to fight the battle we are all called to fight." He raised his fist as he said, "To fight against that tendency to evil inherent in us all and known as original sin. They have proved that our destiny does not lie within our blood." He lowered his fist, clasped his hands in front of him and said quietly, "The blood of *Christ* triumphs over all." He looked straight into the eyes of Lucy and Daniel.

One Dark Night

"Your past has affected your present but you have not allowed it to control your future. In your past, you had little or no choice. Now you are making your own choices and will be held accountable to God for what you choose to do and," he paused to give emphasis, "what you choose *not* to do." An accomplished speaker, he allowed time for those who listened to absorb the truths he sought to bring them.

The time had come to send Mr and Mrs Tynton out into the world together. "As the psalmist says, 'Go in the strength of the Lord'."

He took a few steps back and bowed low to Lucy, Daniel and the congregation. A few introductory notes from the recently purchased organ drifted into the consciousness of Daniel who took Lucy aside to allow the parson to walk down the aisle to the doors of the church. Then the organist played like he'd never played before, though this was mostly due to the fact that there had never been an organ in Wintergate before. Loud chords brought the congregation to their feet as Daniel, reaching out for Lucy's hand, raised it to his lips, kissed it, then whispered in her ear, "More of this very soon."

Lucy melted.

THE END

One Dark Night

If you enjoyed One Dark Night and can find the time, I should be so pleased if you would leave a review on Amazon.

If you 'Follow' Anna Faversham on Amazon you will be kept up-to-date with new releases. The 'Follow' button is near the author biography/author picture.

Other books by Anna Faversham:

Book Two in The Dark Moon Series is called **Under a Dark Star**.

On an island off the south coast of England, there are activities worse than smuggling and all the conflict points to one cruel and ruthless man. The women on the island call him the Dark Star.

Book Three in The Dark Moon Series is called **One Dark Soul**.

Journey into a dark heart. Lucy has survived hard times but by 1825 she finally has it all. Why does she throw it all away?

Another book by Anna Faversham is **Hide in Time**.

Hide in Time *is described by one reviewer as "part time travel, part historical romance, part mystery".*

One Dark Night

Twenty Questions for Book Clubs

1. What did you like best about this book?

2. What did you like least about this book?

3. Which characters did you like best?

4. Which characters did you like least?

5. If you were making a movie of this book who would you cast?

6. Share a favourite quote from this book and why did it stand out?

7. What other books have you read by this author? How did they compare to this book?

8. Would you read more of the author's books?

9. What feelings did this book evoke for you?

10. Which songs does this book make you think of?

11. Which character in the book would you most like to meet?

12. Which places in the book would you most like to visit?

13. What do you think of the title? How does it relate to the book's contents? What other title might you choose?

14. What do you think of the book's cover? Does it convey what the book is about?

15. How original was this book?

16. How realistic was this book?

17. Did any of the characters remind you of anyone?

18. Was the pace too fast/too slow/just right?

19. What message will you take away with you from this book?

20. If you had the chance to ask the author one question, what would it be?

My thanks to my writing friends for their patience and advice

Lexi Revellian
Alan Hutcheson
N.J. Benson

Printed in Great Britain
by Amazon

49904020R00145